D0517997

# THE IMPACT ZONE

RYDER BAY #2

JORDAN FORD

© Copyright 2019 Jordan Ford
www.jordanfordbooks.com

All rights reserved. This book or any portion thereof may not be reproduced or used in any manner whatsoever without the express written permission of the author.

This is a work of fiction. Names, places, businesses, characters and incidents are either the product of the author's imagination or are used in a fictitious manner. Any resemblance to actual persons, living or dead, actual events or locales is purely coincidental.

Cover art (copyright) by Emily Wittig Designs & Photography
https://www.facebook.com/emilywittigdesignsandphotography/

978-0-473-46847-7

*For Kristin…*
*The proofreader every author needs.*
*Thank you for being so amazing.*

# AUTHOR'S NOTE

When I first started writing this book, I wasn't even sure if I'd like it. I know that sounds weird, but I was still hung up on Harley and Aidan. I wasn't sure I could shift my focus to this new couple. I wasn't sure if I could fall in love with Savannah and Griffin.

Man, was I *wrong*! I have ended up falling hard for these two characters, and I just might like this book even more than the first. Or maybe it's a tie ;)

All I know for sure is that I wish Ryder Bay was a real place. I'd love to go there, hang out with these cool characters, surf some waves and just soak in the vibes of this small beach town.

I hope as you read this story that you find yourself in Ryder Bay. May you fall just as hard as I did.

I'd like to thank some key people for helping me put this book together:

Lenore, Beth, Rachael, Kristin & my proofreading team. I love working with you all so much. You're so generous with your time and support. I'm the luckiest author on the planet.

My readers who continue to support me and cheer me on. Thank you for all the emails, comments and amazing reviewers. You make this job brilliant.

My family whose laughter, noise and constant sense of fun pull me back into the real world. I love you all so much.

And to my Lord and Savior. Thank you for loving me just the way I am. I don't have to hide or pretend with you. You see me and you adore me no matter what. There's a huge comfort and strength in knowing that.

Enjoy your journey to Ryder Bay!

xx
Jordan

# 1

## LOST

### SAVANNAH

My best friend is in a coma.

And I'm lost without her.

Ever since Mom died, Skylar has been my buoy. I've clung to her through every storm, and she's pulled me up, led me, showed me how to survive. But now it's my turn to be strong, and I don't know how.

What happened to her last night?

The question keeps swirling around and around in my brain like a tornado.

Why was Skylar at the pier? The pier! The gross, creepy, dark pier.

Was she alone?

I bite my lip and try not to think badly of my friend, but she's a notorious troublemaker. Stirring shit thrills her, and the older she gets, the more dangerous her antics have become. She's no longer happy with pranking her dad by swapping out the salt for sugar in his coffee or hiding his car keys when he's late for an appointment. We'd hide under her parents' bed and stifle our giggles while he hunted around, getting more and more agitated.

That was when we were eleven and just starting out as besties.

As we worked our way up through middle school, the antics changed to sneaking out our bedroom windows and stealing down to the beach for late-night snacks. Skylar stole a bottle of rum from the liquor cabinet, and we tasted it for the first time on the rocks at the bottom of the stairs. I hated it and spat it into the sand. Skylar hated it too, but she wanted to like it, so she forced herself to drink some more before I finally convinced her to "quit it already."

Cigarettes were next on her agenda. We tried those on her thirteenth birthday...and I coughed so hard my eyes streamed for about five minutes. We were both hiding in my backyard, behind Scarlett's playhouse, and ended up dropping the cigarettes and starting a fire. We screamed and stamped it out, then got the giggles and laughed so hard and loud we were busted by my dad, who read us the riot act about how unhealthy smoking was.

At the end of his spiel, Skylar saluted him and yelled, "Yes, sir, Dr. Green, sir!"

I exploded with another round of giggles while Dad

snatched the cigarettes off us, rolled his eyes and sent Skylar home for the day.

Jeff's phone buzzes and I flinch at the sound.

"Work," he murmurs to Marlo before shooting me a weak smile and answering the call.

Marlo takes my hand, squeezing tight, the way she did when my mom got sick. Skylar's parents have become like my own. They treat me like a daughter, and I love them for it, but right now I want to cry.

I don't want Marlo holding my hand so tight, because it might mean that Skylar won't make it. Just the way Mom didn't. She was my mom's best friend, so I guess it's kind of fitting that I became best friends with her daughter.

The De Beers carried us through Mom's year of cancer, her death, the funeral, the numbing aftermath. I still feel like they carry us, but it's been nearly three years now, and apparently I'm supposed to be over the fact that I'm mother-less. I don't think I ever will be. I miss her every day. And even though life carries on, there's a huge hole in our family that no one seems able to fill.

"Everything okay?" Marlo asks as her husband takes a seat beside her.

"Yeah." He scrubs a hand down his face. "I've canceled the open home for tomorrow and Raylene is going to show the Pritchards through the four-bedroom on Palomino Lane."

"Great." Marlo's voice is weak, and Jeff gives her a pained smile.

I glance away from them and notice my dad hovering near the nurses' station. I unlatch myself from Marlo and walk over to him, resting my head on his shoulder while he finishes his conversation.

As soon as he's done, he turns to me with a tired smile. He popped home sometime in the early hours of the morning to check in with my brother and sister, then have a shower and a quick nap. But he was back bright and early. I stayed and managed a fitful doze on a couch in the waiting room. We're both wiped out, but neither of us can leave either.

I try to match his smile, but I can only grimace.

I'm silently terrified, and he knows it.

"How you holding up?"

"Okay, I guess."

He rubs my shoulders and glances at Skylar's parents. "Thanks for being there for Marlo," he whispers. "She really needs your support right now."

I glance over my shoulder, watching Jeff pull his wife against his shoulder, whispering something I can't lip read.

"So, I spoke to Dr. Whitfield in San Diego." Dad clears his throat, obviously more comfortable in doctor mode. It's his safe place. Information over emotion. That's how he survived Mom's rapid deterioration. "He took a look at Skylar's MRI and CT scans for me."

"And?" My breath hitches.

"He's agreed with me. We just have to wait for the swelling to go down. Skylar should wake from the coma soon."

I close my eyes. "Oh, man, I hope so."

"Honey, it's going to be okay." Dad's voice breaks and I glance up, trying to read his expression. But all I get is an affectionate smile. "You sound exhausted. You need to go home and rest."

I pull my shoulders back and sniff. "I'm fine."

Dad doesn't need the stress of worrying about me. He has enough on his plate. Trying to raise three kids alone is not an easy task. I help out as much as I can, but I've caught Dad sobbing at the dining room table at one o'clock in the morning before.

That was only five months ago.

He's still not over losing his wife. Neither am I.

Skylar's accident is cutting too close to the bone, unearthing all the nasties from that depressing time in our lives. I don't want to go back to the numb. Not when I don't have Skylar to pull me out of it. She's been my strength.

What am I going to do while we wait for her to wake up?

"Dr. Green?" A nurse approaches with a chart in her hand. She taps her pen on the top of it and softly asks, "Can I have a minute?"

"Sure thing, Theresa."

Kissing the side of my head, he pats my shoulder. "I'm sorry, bean. I gotta go. Can you call Mrs. O'Neill for me? Check on Lettie and Lou? I said they could have the day off school. I just couldn't face getting them ready this morning, and Mrs. O'Neill didn't seem to mind watching them for me."

He's such a softie.

"Yep." I bob my head, already pulling out my phone before he turns to walk after the nurse.

I glance behind me and notice another nurse approaching Marlo and Jeff. "You can go sit with her again, if you like."

"Thank you," they murmur in unison before searching for me.

"I'll be there in a minute." I lift my phone and they nod before taking off down the corridor.

With a thick swallow, I call my neighbor to check in on my siblings.

"Hello?" She sounds slightly flustered and I'm instantly alert.

"Hi, Mrs. O, it's Savannah. Is everything okay?"

"Oh, hello, sweetie. Yes, everything's just fine here."

"Are you sure?" I narrow my eyes.

She sighs and confesses, "Lettie and Lou are fighting over the TV."

I snicker and shake my head. "It's Lettie's turn on the laptop if that helps at all. She got the big screen yesterday."

Mrs. O'Neill lets out a soft chuckle. "What would we do without you, Savannah Green?"

I grin at her sweet words but can't think of a witty reply, so I just settle for a polite goodbye. "Thanks again for watching them. It's really nice of you considering they should be at school."

"Oh, they were upset and tired. When your poor dad asked me, I just couldn't say no. I'm more than happy to help."

"You're an angel, Mrs. O." I mean it. She's like the grandma who lives next door. The one who always says yes, no matter what. "I'm just going to check on Skylar again, and then I'll head home."

"Take your time."

"Thanks," I murmur before hanging up.

Pulling in a breath, I try to think positively as I head to Skylar's room, but it's hard going. All I want to do is bury my head in my hands and weep.

I always get tearful when I'm tired, but as I step into Skylar's room, I know that's not the reason my insides are trembling. She looks so small in the bed, dwarfed by tubes, drowning in the noise of monitors and equipment.

I sniff, wrapping my arms around myself and hovering in the doorway.

Jeff glances over his shoulder, spotting me and putting on a brave smile.

My lips try to curl in response, but they're too heavy to lift.

Dad says we just have to wait, but we all know how painful that can be.

We all waited for Mom to get better. We hit that cancer threat with the full armory. It wasn't going to beat Wendy Green—no sir. So we banded together, and we waited.

Waited and watched as each treatment battered and weakened her body. As each treatment failed.

We waited and watched her die. Twelve months of wasting away until finally, she passed. It was this weird sense of relief and devastation. She was no longer in pain. She was no longer with us.

"Savvy, sweets, come sit down." Marlo pats the chair beside her, putting on a brave smile to match her husband's.

She looks very un-Marlo today. Her lipstick has worn off, and she has smudges under her eyes from all the crying. Her normally olive skin is so pale and wan.

"I'm okay," she whispers, and I force my eyes away from her.

She's not okay.

None of us are.

Skylar, the strongest chick I know, is in a coma.

She was at the pier and she fell into the water, smashed her head, and then nearly drowned.

Why? Why was she at the pier?

And how did she fall? Did her wild, impulsive side take over? Was she being an idiot on the railing?

She wasn't drunk. Blood tests showed no signs of alcohol or drugs in her body.

So, what does that mean?

What if she was with someone at the pier?

What if they pushed her?

Swallowing becomes impossible as I play with that idea. Skylar's antics have led her to hang out with some shady people. I think of that guy at her party last weekend and shudder.

I tried to warn her away from him, but she got bitchy with me, so I hid in the shadows and sulked. But I should have gotten over myself, realizing how snarky drunk Skylar can be.

I shouldn't have let her insults eat at me.

I should have muscled my way onto that dance floor and made sure she didn't do anything stupid. But instead, I sat on a rock feeling bitter and sorry for myself, then jumped at the chance to ask my ex-boyfriend to walk me home.

What a waste of time that had been.

I gave him every chance to kiss me, and he didn't.

I never should have broken up with him, but Skylar told me to. And then when I regretted it, she started to work her magic and get us back together again.

Closing my eyes, I turn my head away so Marlo and Jeff won't see the sheen in my eyes.

Skylar has to wake up. She has to come back to me.

She let me down that night at the party, but I let her down too. I backed away for a few days, wanting to silently punish her for talking to me that way, telling me I needed to get my own life and stop being so clingy. She was just saying that because she knew I was right. The crew-cut guy was bad news, but she wanted to go for it anyway.

But now look what's happened.

I might lose her forever, and I can't stand that thought.

I'm not sure how I'll survive without her meddling. Her troublemaking. Her ability to pull me out of whatever funk I might be moping in.

A weak smile draws my lips north. Damn, I love her so much. Even when she drives me crazy, I need her.

*Please, Sky. Please come back to me.*

## 2

# THE TRUTH, BUT NOT THE WHOLE TRUTH

## GRIFFIN

The ocean breeze kisses my face and I inhale the salty scent. I'm right down at the end of the pier, gazing out across the water. No one else is around, the sun is shining above me, and I'm overcome by that sense of peace I can't stop chasing. It never stays with me for long, but when I do get my hands around it, I like to hold on and feel it course through my entire body.

I've always loved the ocean. The endless blue. An unreachable horizon. No matter what's happening in my life, this vast body of water gives me a sense of hope. Like maybe anything is possible.

As a kid I used to imagine it taking me away from the pain. If I walked straight into those waves, they could wash me clean and every bad thing around me would be wiped away. But life doesn't work like that, and childish dreams only make reality hit that much harder.

I close my eyes and shake the dark thoughts loose. It's my day off; I don't want to cloud out the sunshine or kill the peace with shit from my past.

It's my past.

And I never have to go back to it.

Vallejo is a lifetime ago.

I'm not that person anymore. I never have to be him again.

Guilt niggles as I think about Marshall, my new boss. I lied on my application form. He has no idea that my driver's license and social security number are fake. If I was fully transparent, he'd learn that I've never even taken a driving test. I kind of taught myself and then bought the ID...along with a social security number that hides who I really am.

My first name's still the same, but everything else is just a cover.

I've been living this lie since I skipped out two and a half years ago. The fake documents cost a pretty penny, but I've been Griffin Ayala for nearly two years now and I've managed to make it work. As far as anyone knows, I *am* that guy, and I always have been.

I scan the beach of Ryder Bay and wistfully hope I can stay here, but it's a pipe dream. I'll be lucky if I make it through to the end of the summer. Staying in one place too long is never a good idea, but damn I wish I could. Something about this beach speaks to my soul.

Yeah, I may have seen prettier. The two resorts I worked at in Mexico were amazing. The beach where I learned to surf—white sand, clear water...a freaking utopia.

But this place. I don't even know what it is.

It's like my soul has some connection with Ryder Bay, because the second I drove into this small town, I felt like I'd come home.

It's a dangerous feeling. I should have ignored it and just kept driving.

But I pulled into the parking lot. I got out of my truck. I fell in love and applied for the first job I could find—renting out surfboards and boogie boards on the beach.

I get to spend my days on the sand, watching people have fun in the water.

It's a pretty sweet deal.

My new boss, Captain Marshall Swinton, is a lifeguard, but he owns Ryder Rentals as a side business. Suits me just fine. I like that he's around to chat with. I've never worked for a nicer guy.

Things just keep falling into place for me here. That should be a freaking siren warning, but I keep ignoring it. I'll stay for as long as life will let me.

I just hope it's more than—

A noise over my shoulder makes me tense. I glance behind me and notice a cop ambling down the pier. My muscles knot a little tighter. Cops always have that effect on me. He doesn't say anything as he stops beside me, his feet spread apart. He rests his hands on the cruddy railing and lets out a heavy sigh before looking at me and slowly removing his shades.

The right side of my mouth twitches with a nervous smile. "Afternoon, Officer. Can I help you with something?" I can't help swallowing, and pray he doesn't notice.

The man studies me for a second longer, then sticks out his hand. "Officer Malloy."

I glance at his hand for a beat before forcing myself to take it and then mirror his smile.

"I'm just trying to figure out what happened to a member of our community last night. She was down here and..." His voice trails off with a sad sigh.

"The girl," I murmur. "I heard about that."

"Oh yeah?" He looks back at me, his gaze sharp. "What'd you hear?"

Instant caution makes me hesitate. Cops don't always care about the truth. They just like to catch a bad guy.

I scratch the side of my mouth and glance out to the ocean. "Not much. Marshall said she fell and hurt herself. Aidan De Beer dragged her out of the water. Did CPR. She's at the hospital now, right?"

"In a coma." Officer Malloy nods and looks at the railing again, obviously troubled.

I step back and point. "Was it here?" Crouching

down, I study the railing for weaknesses, cracks, broken bits of board. I can't see anything. The railing looks solid. Old, but solid.

"I did the same thing this morning. Structure seems solid, and as far as I can tell, no one was around to see her. We've got to get this damn light fixed." He flicks his hand at the broken bulb above us. The lamp has been broken ever since I've been here, but that's only been a month.

Damn, this cop seems gutted. He obviously cares about this place.

I give him a pained look and ask the question that's no doubt running through his brain. "You think she jumped?"

The man clenches his jaw, then mutters, "Or she was pushed."

My insides jerk with surprise. Marshall had only mentioned it to me this morning. We didn't discuss it at length because the conversation shifted to talking about Aidan De Beer and what a great job he did, saving his cousin's life. He murmured something about Aidan making a great lifeguard and I agreed with him, then ended the conversation so I didn't have to make up another excuse for why *I'm* not considering lifeguard training. Marshall tells me I'd be great, but he doesn't know me as well as he thinks he does.

Shit. What if that girl was pushed?

That's a whole new ball game.

Jumping or falling by accident is bad enough, but

pushing brings in an element of sinister that makes me nervous. The feeling only grows when Officer Malloy pulls out his notebook and pen.

I swallow, trying not to shuffle my feet. "Well, I hope that's not the case. I hope neither option is true."

"Agreed." Officer Malloy opens up his book. "So where were you last night?"

*Is he for real?*

I study his face and, with a sinking sense of dread, realize that he is. He's questioning *me*. Wanting to know where *I* was.

Shit!

*Go for as much truth as you can, man.*

I scratch my short beard and tell him what I can. "Uh...I got off work at six, then headed home. Vegged out in front of TV."

"Can anyone verify that?"

I hate that question.

I hate that I have to shake my head and admit, "I live alone."

Malloy's mustache twitches. "Just to keep track of my investigation, do you mind if I jot down some details? I recognize your face but can't remember your name."

The air in my lungs is getting icy.

A cop wants to know my name.

I have to remind myself that my ID is secure. It was super expensive. I got it from a top guy. He even helped me set up a mailing address so the IRS has a place to send my tax stuff. No matter where I end up living and working, I'm covered on all sides. He assured me that as long as I keep my nose clean, there'll be no red flags.

My ID is solid.

It'll hold.

My tongue brushes the edge of my mouth and I pray to God my voice doesn't shake. "Griffin Ayala. I'm—"

"You're working for Marshall. I remember." Malloy seems to relax, which helps the muscles in my shoulders do the same. His smile helps too. "He can't stop bragging about how great you are."

My lips curl at the corners. "He's a good guy. I'm grateful for the opportunity to work for him."

"So where are you living?"

Shit, I can't answer that.

I'm scrambling for a decent reply, my heart rate accelerating, my palms starting to sweat.

The radio on Malloy's belt squawks and I actually flinch at the sound.

Thankfully he doesn't notice. He's too busy unclipping it and talking into the device.

"Yeah, what's up, Cadence?"

"We've got some trouble at Danny's liquor store. Some kid trying to shoplift a bottle of vodka."

Malloy lets out a short laugh and shakes his head. "Oh boy. Okay. I'll head over there right away, although I'm sure the kid will be terrified if Danny was the one who caught him."

The woman at the other end of the line chuckles. "Roger that."

Malloy clips the radio back onto his belt and flips his notebook closed. "Thanks for your help today."

Relief is flooding through me so thick and fast I almost can't speak. It takes my brain a second to remind myself to smile and nod, then actually talk. "I didn't really do anything."

Malloy laughs and points at me. "Keep up that good work for Marshall. I'll see you on the beach."

"Yes, sir." I watch Malloy walk away and sag back against the railing.

As far as policemen go, he's not bad.

Thank God I didn't have to tell him my address.

The last thing I need is a house call from the cops. As soon as they knock on the door, they'll know the truth.

I wait until Malloy's squad car is out of sight before strolling back down the pier. I work my way to the sand, toying with the idea of a sunset surf when I spot something out of the corner of my eye.

Blonde surfer girl is jumping into Axel's truck.

That can't be good.

My gut clenches with unrest.

Axel and his crew give me bad vibes. It's the same feeling that used to roil through me whenever my brother pulled up in his car and ordered, "Get in."

## 3

# ANOTHER GIRL

## SAVANNAH

This has been the longest day of my life.

Well, nearly. I try not to think about the day Mom died. She waited until 11:42pm before finally slipping away. We all knew it was coming, but Dad still broke down and cried when the nurse announced it.

"No pulse," she whispered. "I'm so sorry, Kevin."

She then touched my shoulder and gave me a sad smile while Dad lay down on the bed beside Mom and wept.

Lettie and Lou were thankfully asleep on the couch in the nurses' lounge. I didn't have the heart to wake them. They stayed awake for as long as they could. They said their goodbyes. Lettie cried herself to sleep, and Lou just went really quiet.

I wonder what they're doing now. Knowing my

sister, she's scrolling through Instagram. The girl is kind of obsessed with bookstagramming. I love that she's into reading and not other stuff. Some of her book photos are freaking amazing, but I can't help wondering if she does it to hide.

Lou will be out front playing basketball with Charlie. Neighbors and best friends. I'm happy for the kid. The last few years have been hard work. Louis is only ten. I want his life to be filled with everything fun and good. No kid should have to lose their mother.

I sniff and wash my hands under the faucet. My complexion looks pale and ghostly in the hospital mirror. Ugh. I look hideous. My makeup from the day before has worn off, and my hair is a mess. I'm sleep-deprived and pasty. I should have gone home the way I said I would, but when Dad said he'd pop home at lunchtime to check on Lettie and Lou, I just decided to stay.

But now...

I should seriously go home and shower. Sleep.

At least try to sleep.

I step out of the bathroom door, and my resolve to be sensible disintegrates when I spot something that wakes me up. Like a lightning flash through my body, I'm suddenly alert again.

Aidan—my ex, the guy I kissed last night—is running out of the hospital.

"Where are you going?" I murmur under my breath and instinctively follow him.

He rushes out the double doors and hauls ass to his car.

Why is he splitting?

I feel like he only just got here.

I was sitting by Skylar when he walked into her room. He smiled at me across the bed, but it didn't hold the kind of warmth I'd been hoping for.

We kissed last night.

He held me like he cared about me.

Shit, I never should have broken up with him.

I should have ignored Skylar's advice and just stuck it out. So the fireworks feeling had died; that isn't the crux of a relationship. I miss having a boyfriend. I miss holding Aidan's hand and talking to him about... anything...everything.

I miss having someone to call my own.

Aidan tears out of the parking lot and before I think better of it, I head to my car.

I text Dad and Marlo, letting them know I need a little space. I outright lie and type the words *home* and *rest*.

As I slip into my car, I get two reply texts.

They both believe me. Marlo has sent emoji hearts, and Dad told me I'm a wise girl.

If he knew I was chasing after my ex-boyfriend, he may not think so.

When Skylar noticed how restless I was after dumping Aidan, she finally told me to stop being an idiot and just get him back. She was working her magic behind the scenes. She never actually said it, but I'm pretty sure she had a word in Aidan's ear and told him to get his act together.

The night of the beach party was supposed to be our big reunion, but after Aidan walked me home, he didn't go for it. I was sending all the right signals, and he just stood there *not* making a move.

He's definitely been pulling away, moving on after the breakup...just when I want to get back together. Perfect timing—not!

But we kissed last night. We comforted each other and it felt so incredibly familiar.

I want that again.

So I'm following Aidan to wherever the hell he's going and I'm telling him exactly what I need. He's too nice a guy to turn me down. He'll be there for me, because that's what Aidan De Beer does.

That's half the reason I fell for him.

Aidan's convertible swerves into the parking lot at the south end of the beach. What the hell is he doing down at this end?

I find a parking spot and rip my key from the ignition.

He's standing at the top of the stairs, looking really stressed.

What is going on?

"Aidan?" I call as I slam my door closed and weave around his car to join him.

He spins, sees it's me, then lets out a heavy sigh like he's really disappointed to see me.

Okay, ouch.

"What are you doing here?" He says the words quietly, but they still feel like a slap in the face. I was kind of hoping for a relieved smile, some form of pleasure, but instead he looks like I'm just another burden.

When he looks to the ground, I'm not sure what to say at first.

The silence is a little painful, so I figure I'll just answer his stupid question. "I needed a break. I've been at the hospital for nearly twenty-four hours. When I saw you take off into the parking lot, I followed you to make sure you were all right. You were running pretty fast. Is everything okay?"

He shoves his hands in his pockets. He's still in his uniform from school. Personally, I hate our school uniform, but it's always looked good on Aidan. He's got the perfect body to look good in anything, really. His broad shoulders and triangular torso really suit the Walton Academy blazer and shirt. He's not wearing the blazer or tie right now. He's rolled up the sleeves of his shirt and is unfairly looking super-hot and sexy in the ensemble.

He glances up from the pavement and lets out another sigh before admitting, "I'm looking for someone."

"Who?" My heart is already sinking. I can feel it melting into my stomach.

Glancing out at the water, he scans the waves, not looking at me.

"Is it a girl?" I ask, hating that my voice is shaking, but I know now. I know why Aidan's been pulling away. He's fallen for someone else.

So quickly?

It hurts.

His nod is a puncture wound to my already fragile heart, but I still ask, "Who is she?"

"My surf instructor. We've...grown close."

Double ouch. He's over me.

Why did I follow him to this stupid parking lot?

*Don't cry, Savvy. Don't you dare cry.*

"I really care about her. A lot. I mean, I'm falling for her."

*Thanks, Aidan. You're really* not *helping!*

I manage a small "Oh."

"I'm sorry." He brushes his finger lightly down my arm. "I shouldn't have kissed you yesterday. That was wrong of me. I just wanted you to feel better, but it probably did more damage than good."

It's hard to speak, but I force the lump from my throat with a thick swallow. "I thought we were maybe getting back together."

"That's what I wanted for so long." He blinks and casts his eyes out to the ocean again. "But then I met Harley, and things started to change. She..."

Harley.

I kind of like that name.

I want to hate it.

But what right do I have?

I dumped him. I stupidly broke it off and dug my own frickin' grave. I can't be mad at Aidan for that. Just because I've had a change of heart. Just because I desperately need him right now.

"Savvy, I—"

A tear slips from my eye and I slash it off my face, turning my body away when someone appears at the top of the stairs.

It's bad enough that Aidan's gonna see me cry. I don't want this stranger in on it as well.

I hope he walks past quickly, but he stops.

Dammit.

"Aidan, right?"

I glance over my shoulder to look at the guy. He's a beach bum. Baggy board shorts, a pale green T-shirt with a surfing logo on it, short beard and dreads. Shoulder-length dreads that I shouldn't think look cool.

But they totally do.

"Griffin?" Aidan points at him.

"Yeah." He nods, glances at me, then back to Aidan. He looks kind of worried. "You still friends with the blonde surfer girl?"

My insides ping tight at the mention of her.

He must be talking about Harley.

So she's blonde. Huh. I thought Aidan always fell for brunettes. Turns out I was wrong.

My bitterness is just forming a shoot when Griffin says something that quickly stunts the growth.

"I think she might be in trouble."

The look on his face tells me he's serious.

Aidan's face drains of color, his voice pinched tight with fear. "What?"

"I saw her drinking with that guy Axel, and then she jumped into his truck, with all his friends, and they took off." Griffin hisses and shakes his head. "I don't know. Maybe I'm reading it wrong, but I just got a bad feeling in my gut. If I'd been able to get to my truck fast enough, I would have followed them. But..." He sighs. "I don't suppose you have any idea where they might have taken her?"

"Shit." Aidan whispers the word, looking panicked as he jolts away from us and runs to his car.

"Where are you going?" I chase after him.

"I think I know where they might have taken her. At least I hope I do." He jumps into his car, and before I think better of it, I pull open the passenger door.

"What are you doing?" he snaps.

"I'm coming with you."

"What? No, you're not. It could be dangerous."

"Then you're going to need all the help you can get," I retort.

I still think it's really sweet that Aidan wants to protect me. But screw him. I may not be his girlfriend anymore, but I still care about him, and he looks really worried right now. I want to know who this Harley chick is. I want to know what kind of trouble she's gotten into. And I want to help Aidan.

"I agree." Griffin leans down to speak through the car window, then turns to smile at me. Damn, it's a really nice smile. I look down, not wanting to be affected by it. "I'll jump in the back."

"Okay." I can't help a small grin. This feels like an adventure, and after the shitty day I've had, I could really do with the distraction.

Aidan lets out an irritated groan, but I ignore it, slamming my door shut and saying, "Let's go."

After another scoff, he reverses out of the parking space and punches the accelerator.

I don't know where we're going, but I say bring it on.

I'm not usually the type to ruffle feathers or upset anyone, but tonight, I don't give a shit if Aidan's annoyed with me. I need this adventure. I need to find out what's so great about this Harley girl and how she managed to steal Aidan's heart so quickly.

## 4

## A RARE SOUL

## GRIFFIN

Aidan is stressing big-time.

He must have encountered these guys before. I haven't had much to do with them. The first day I spotted them in the water, I stood back and watched for a while. Resting my surfboard in the sand, I chose to take my time getting in, and I'm glad I did.

Axel and his crew don't share waves. They dominate out there, and they don't like new people invading their turf.

I know that mentality, have lived around it, and so I've kept my distance.

But not tonight.

Tonight, we're heading straight into the fray, because Aidan's girl is in trouble. I can feel it in my core.

There hasn't been much chatter on the way to wherever we're going. I do know that the girl sitting next to Aidan is named Savannah, and I'm guessing these two are (or used to be) more than just friends. The tension between them is intense.

I'd love to know the story behind it all, but that's not my business.

Aidan turns right, heading off the main road onto a gravel, trail-like road.

We must be heading to some kind of private cove. And I'm right. After a bumpy ride in the back, Aidan jerks to a stop beside Axel's truck.

"Stay in the car," he barks at Savannah.

I don't like the tone he's using with her. She's only trying to help. I would normally get pissed, but I can see how tense he is, and I'm guessing he's just trying to keep her safe.

Aidan shoulders his door open and storms toward the guys.

Shit, they're drunk. I can almost smell the liquor from here.

Throwing Aidan's seat forward, I jump out of the car just as Aidan starts an argument with one of Axel's guys.

He shoves him and the guy topples over into the sand, drunken laughter spurting out of him.

"Axel!" Aidan roars, but is stopped by a tall guy with a crew cut.

I run forward as his fist bunches into a cannon ball.

Aidan ducks, but I catch the guy's knuckles before they can deliver a blow. Squeezing hard, I stare him down. The light is fading, and he can't really see me, but I keep my expression steely.

This is too familiar for my liking. I've dealt with guys like this in the past, and all you can do is put on the toughest damn show you're capable of.

He snarls at me, ripping his fist from my hand and coming after me.

Thankfully he's drunk and wobbly. When he tries to tackle me, it's easy enough to flick him off. He hits the ground and rolls, struggling to regain his feet.

His friend is staggering up as well, a dopey smile stretching across his face. "Hel-lo, sweetheart."

I spin and notice Savannah standing by the car.

Shit. Why didn't she stay inside?

She's staring out at the ocean, looking worried.

I glance behind me and spot Aidan running into the surf. Instinct wants to chase after him, to back him up, but there's no way in hell I'm leaving Savannah to deal with these two idiots.

Crew Cut has regained his footing and is already heading across to Aidan's car. His long, sloppy strides eat up the ground and he's soon looming over her.

She shrinks away from him, obviously disgusted, but that doesn't put the guy off. I'm trying to understand the look on her face. I think she's seen this guy before. Her upper lip is curled, and again, I want to know this story. Has he tried to talk to her before, flirt with her, touch her?

My blood boils at the idea.

I lurch back, running around the vehicle and batting his hand away before he can touch her. Stepping between them, I turn myself into a human shield.

"Back off," I warn him, lightly pushing him back.

"What's the matter?" he slurs. "I just wanna talk to her."

She lets out a little scoff behind me.

"You know this guy?" I mutter over my shoulder.

"He was pawing my best friend at a party last weekend." Her voice trembles for a second, and I wonder just how much 'pawing' went down.

Crew Cut takes a step closer.

"Back. Off," I warn him, hating how much he reminds me of my brother.

Nerves course through me as I pull my shoulders back and try to look bigger.

He's taller than me. Bigger. Bulkier. But I could take him down. I just don't want to have to.

"Just one little kiss," he mumbles.

I roll my eyes, and as he takes a step closer, I meet him with another hard shove.

"Hey," his friend complains, then starts giggling as Crew Cut hits the dirt.

"Back off!" someone shouts.

I glance to the water. Aidan is carrying his blonde surfer girl up the beach.

Shit. Is she okay? Is she injured? I'm about to run across and check on her, but then her head pops up before leaning back against Aidan's shoulder. Good. She's breathing.

Thank God.

Aidan is fuming as he walks up the beach. I read his expression quickly and usher Savannah into the back seat of the car.

It's kind of squished, and there's no way I can avoid our knees touching, but she doesn't seem to notice. She's too busy watching Aidan gently place his girl in the passenger seat and then buckle her up.

"I can do it," she mumbles.

Damn, her lips have a blue tinge to them. She must have gotten pretty close to the edge of not breathing. No wonder Aidan's hands are shaking.

"You can't do it," Aidan snaps, pushing her hands away from the seat buckle. "Let me help you." The desperation on his face belies the tone of his voice. She just scared the living crap out of him. Having already had to rescue his cousin last night, this is probably hitting way too close to the core. It's obvious how much he cares about his surfer girl.

I wish I could remember her name.

It's kind of an inappropriate time to ask, so I keep my mouth shut, glancing at Savannah as Aidan tears away from the cove.

"You all right?" I murmur as softly as I can.

She glances at me, obviously surprised by my question, then gives me a weak smile and nod.

She's not all right.

She looks like she's on the verge of tears.

Was it Crew Cut? Did he scare her?

Or is it the fact that Aidan is so obviously into someone else?

I don't say anything. What can I say?

Love has always been a complication I've tried to avoid. Sure, I hooked up with a couple of girls when I was working in Mexico, but they were just short-lived flings. Working in resorts can be a transient lifestyle, and no one stays around for long.

I've never been in love before. Hell, I would even say I haven't had a girlfriend. That's not my style. Girlfriend has a certain sense of permanency to it, and I can't be a permanent guy.

Savannah stares out the window as we drive back to Ryder Bay.

I'd love to know what she's thinking. What I could say to make her feel better.

It's a painful trip, and I'm grateful when Aidan pulls into the southern suburbs and a few minutes later is turning into a driveway. He clicks off the engine and rushes around to the passenger side. His girl is struggling to open her door.

"Come on," Aidan murmurs as he helps her out of the car.

She groans and leans against him. "I feel sick."

I can't hear his reply as he starts helping her to the front door, but I get out of the car in case they need me. Her small body jerks and she falls to the side, heaving all over the house and grass. Aidan holds her steady, scooping the hair off her shoulder.

"It'll make her feel better," I call out, trying to wipe that look of worry off his face.

He glances at me with a quick scowl before turning back to her. I shut up and slip back into the car.

As I take a seat, Savannah lets out a little clicking noise like she's disappointed, then looks down at her lap. Her long hair creates a curtain over her face, and I really wish I could pull it back and see her.

She has a pretty face. It's not hard and defined like Aidan's new girl. There's a soft roundness to it that I liked the moment I first saw her.

"He really cares about her," she whispers.

My heart squeezes with sympathy as Savannah clears up the picture a little more.

"Did you guys..." I run a finger over my bottom lip. "You and Aidan..."

"We used to be together, until I dumped him. And now he's moved on and I'm too late to get him back."

I wince, wishing I knew exactly the right thing to say.

She lets out a shaky breath.

Aidan is carrying Surfer Girl into the house now, cradling her against him like she's precious.

It must hurt to watch.

Savannah blinks and sniffs.

"I know it must suck." I clear my throat. "But uh… you must have broken up with him for a reason."

She shrugs. "Yeah, I guess."

"Well…maybe he moved on so fast because you two aren't meant to be."

She looks up at me. I can't see her face clearly in the dim light, but her eyes are glassy. I can tell that much. She sniffs again and then gives me a sad smile.

Kind of like a 'thanks for trying.'

I'm wrestling to find more words, to improve what I've already started. I'd love to transform that smile into something bright and happy.

I glimpse a flash of dimples and feel my insides stir. How cute are they?

"Thank you," she murmurs and leans forward to release the passenger seat. "I'll just go in and see if he needs a hand."

"Are you sure?" I give her a dubious frown.

"She's soaking wet. Aidan can't put her into bed like that, and I doubt he'll be comfortable undressing her. He's too much of a gentleman."

Her dimples flash for a second and my opinion of her skyrockets.

She's going in to help her ex-boyfriend's new squeeze.

That takes courage. Grace. A soul full of nothing but sweetness.

I try to tell her everything I'm thinking with my

smile, but I'm not sure my message is truly clear enough in this terrible lighting.

And so she gets out of the car without knowing.

And I stay where I am, leaning my head back against the headrest and marveling at her selflessness.

She's a rare soul.

How many teenage girls would go and help someone they probably have every right to despise?

## 5

## THE STRENGTH OF COOKED SPAGHETTI

## SAVANNAH

I'm going to do the right thing if it kills me.

It's not Harley's fault I want Aidan back. And it's not Aidan's fault either.

I'm bigger than the spite roiling through my chest. Nicer than the nasty jealousy eating my guts.

I can do this.

Walking through the door, I cast my eyes around the tiny, old kitchen and into the cluttered living space. This house is a shoebox. It doesn't help that every available surface is cramped with everything from balled-up chocolate bar wrappers to empty cigarette packets, knickknacks and stacks of books.

Two words—Housekeeper Required.

It makes me grateful for ours. Rosalie has been with us since before Mom died, coming over twice a week to help keep the house clean and functioning, to stock the freezer with meals, and to fill the pantry with home baking.

I should send her here for a day. She'd have this place shipshape in no time.

Clearing my throat, I try to push my judgments of Harley's home aside and step into the hallway.

I spot Aidan immediately. He's crouching beside Harley, who seems to have passed out on the floor. And he's looking totally lost.

"I'll clean her up." I make the offer before I can change my mind. Forcing my legs to move, I approach Aidan and tip my head, silently ordering him out of the bathroom. "Can you find her some dry clothes?"

"Sure." His grateful smile makes my heart bleed.

I'm such an idiot.

Why?

Why'd I dump him?

"Because the magic was gone," I murmur, trying to comfort myself with all the reasons Skylar and I discussed.

I just wasn't feeling the spark anymore. Being around Aidan didn't excite me the way it used to. He seemed to be withdrawing into himself as Craig and Simon started to charge ahead in their swimming, and I don't know. I guess I was getting bored with the relationship.

But damn, I miss having him around.

In times like these, I miss having someone who cares specifically about me.

I need a bae.

Harley groans, drawing my attention back to her and what I'm supposed to be doing.

Searching for a washcloth, I dampen it and start with clearing the sick from around her mouth. I then go a step further and wash down her arms and legs. She'll be covered in salt water, and I always hate the feel of that on my skin.

It might be different for her.

A surf instructor?

She's probably half mermaid.

A light knock on the door makes me turn, and I take the boxer shorts and T-shirt from Aidan.

"Thanks," I murmur.

"I'll just wait outside. Call me when you're done."

I nod and give him a sad smile before pushing the door closed with my foot.

The sound jolts Harley. She jerks and her eyelids flutter open.

"You need to help me." I talk softly, crouching back down beside her.

She frowns at me, then looks around her. "Where's Aidan?"

"He's waiting outside. I'm gonna get you changed, and then you need to sleep this off."

She goes still, her eyes glassing with tears. I don't understand the small smile on her face, but it soon melts away, her lips wobbling as she admits, "I feel… like shit."

The way she slurs the words almost makes me snicker, but I bite back my smile and help her sit up. "That's what happens when you down bottles of straight liquor."

"He said it would kill the pain," she grumbles.

I don't know what that means, and I'm not sure I want to ask.

What pain?

"Lift your arms," I instruct.

She tries, but her body is acting liked cooked spaghetti.

I grunt and struggle to get her shirt off. As soon as she's free, she slumps back against the wall.

"I know why he loves you," she whispers.

I go still.

"You're kind. You're the kind one."

My hands are shaking as I unclip her bra, then quickly dry her off with a towel.

She swallows, a tear slipping free down her cheek. "I love him too, but don't tell him. Love hurts. I don't want to love him."

My breath goes on hold as I reach for her shirt. "Come on." I help her lean forward so I can slip the soft cotton over her body.

Harley whimpers. "He's so good. And you're good. So you should be together."

I pull back to look at her face. She just stares at me

for a second; then her eyes kind of roll back and she slumps to the floor. I only just manage to catch her head from hitting the hard surface.

With a little gasp, I lean over her to make sure she's okay, but then a light snore whistles out of her nose.

Slumping back with a relieved sigh, I gaze down at her and shake my head.

She doesn't know.

She doesn't know how Aidan feels about her. Maybe that's why she got wasted and tried to drown herself.

Sucking in a shaky breath, I strip her wet shorts off and wrestle her boxers on. She's petite like Skylar, so it's not too hard.

I can't stop thinking about her words. They swim around in my mind: *You should be together.* But those words crash straight into Griffin's: *You two aren't meant to be.*

With a thick swallow, I turn for the door. My head is pounding, and I just want to get away from all of this. I want my soft bed and oblivion.

Aidan spins as soon as I open the door, his face etched with worry.

I try to calm his fears. "She's asleep." I point over my shoulder. "You want to carry her to bed?"

He nods and slips past me, crouching down to cradle Harley against him. I can't take my eyes off his face as he gazes down at her. She scared the pants off him tonight. He really cares about her. The way he's holding her, his tender gaze.

I shouldn't be with him. She should.

Turning to get away from the ugly feelings in my chest, I find Harley's room and quickly straighten her covers, then step back so Aidan can lay her down. I stand by the door, torturing myself by watching as he brushes his lips across her forehead, then tucks a tendril of hair back off her face.

And there's that loved-up look again.

I clear my throat, unable to stand it, and he turns to look at me. "Thank you," he rasps.

"You're welcome." I can barely choke out the words as I point over my shoulder. "Can you take me back to my car, please?"

"Sure."

I make a beeline out of the house and slip into the passenger seat, slamming the door behind me.

"You okay?" Griffin's voice is soft and soothing.

I give him a stiff nod. "She's fine. All tucked up in bed."

He lets out a soft snicker. "I asked if *you* were okay."

Glancing over my shoulder, I take in the kind sadness in his eyes and want to weep. Swallowing hard, I turn back to stare out the windshield and whisper, "I have to be."

## 6

# A GIRL LIKE SAVANNAH

## GRIFFIN

I reach forward and give Savannah's shoulder a light squeeze.

I'm not sure what else to do.

Poor thing.

Watching the guy she likes—maybe even loves—caring for another girl must suck.

I can only imagine how much courage it must have taken her to clean Surfer Girl up, when all she probably wants to do is spit in her face.

Aidan gets into the car and stares at the house for another beat before reversing out the drive.

I keep my mouth shut, only half listening as Savannah replies to a text on Aidan's behalf.

Savannah obviously knows Aidan's cousin as well. I'm not sure how, and I want to ask.

I want to know if it's another burden on poor Savannah's shoulders.

Shit, this must be turning into a total suck-fest of a day for her.

If only I could make it better. Savannah seems like a sweetheart—a good soul. It doesn't seem fair when people like that get hit with hard times.

Gazing out the window, I focus on the contours of Ryder Bay as Aidan drives us back to the beach. My truck is parked up by the lifeguard office. It'll only take me a few minutes to walk to it from the south lot.

Aidan steers his lush car into the same parking space he left from and turns to smile at me. Holding out his hand, he acts like the gentleman Savannah said he is. "Thanks for your help tonight."

"I didn't do much, man." I take his hand and give it a shake, feeling like a full-blown adult. "You were the one who rescued her."

He lets out an embarrassed scoff and shakes his head before getting out of the car and flipping his seat forward so I can climb out.

As soon as I'm standing, I drive my point home. "Two rescues in two days." I grin. "You ever considered a career in lifeguarding?" I chuckle and lightly smack his chest with the back of my hand. "Think about it, man. I'm pretty sure Marshall would be all over that."

And that's the truth.

Aidan would make an amazing lifeguard.

Like Savannah, he has an inherent goodness about

him. I can sense it. I've been around enough bad to be able to detect the gold within the silt.

I'd like to hang out with the guy some more.

After the shit I've lived through, all I want to do is surround myself with solid gold goodness.

Glancing to my left, I spot Savannah on the other side of the car and smile at her. "'Night, Savannah." I hope my voice rings with the admiration I'm feeling.

"Good night." She swallows and looks down, picking at some invisible spot on the car roof.

Maybe not.

If I see her again, I'll have to make sure she understands how awesome she is. How even though Aidan's moved on, there's gonna be another guy out there who will flat-out adore her, because she's adorable.

The thought kind of throws me off guard a little, so I give Aidan a quick nod and take my leave.

As I jog back to my truck, I can't stop thinking about Savannah and what she did for Surfer Girl tonight. I can't stop thinking about this other future guy who will someday win her heart. It can't be me. I'm too nomadic. It'd only hurt us both to go falling for someone. Those resort flings were different. Those girls were there on vacation and had no expectation of seeing me again once they'd left. Every make-out session, every kiss, every date had a timestamp.

But a girl like Savannah, you couldn't do that with her.

So I can't be that guy.

Not that she'd want me to be.

"Not that *you* want to be," I snap at myself, annoyed at the way my head just went on up to those clouds and started drifting.

I'm in Ryder Bay to earn me some summer cash, surf some summer waves, and then move the hell on. I can't stay.

As I reach my beat-up truck and grab the key out of my pocket, I have to physically remind myself of that fact.

"You can't stay." I slam the door shut behind me and grip the wheel. "Don't even go there, man. Just do the job and move on out."

## 7

# CAN'T STOP THINKING ABOUT HIM

## SAVANNAH

It's Sunday morning, and I can't stop thinking about Friday night.

Not because of the drama at Hatchet Cove. And not because Aidan made it official—we are over.

No, what I can't stop thinking about is Griffin. He keeps popping into my head without warning. It doesn't matter if I'm taking a shower, brushing my teeth, trying to eat a meal, or sitting in Skylar's hospital room. He's there, his dreadlocks and kind smile swirling through my brain.

The way he squeezed my shoulder in sympathy. His soft voice as he tried to make me feel better.

My lips curl into an unexpected smile, which I quickly try to squash.

What am I doing?

Dreaming about some mystery guy?

I don't have time for that kind of thing right now!

I have the last week of school to cope with, siblings to look after, a BFF in the hospital. I can't be wasting my brainpower dreaming about Griffin. I have enough on my plate as it is.

I let out a little groan as I scrape my fingers through my hair and head downstairs to the kitchen. To my surprise, the sounds and smells of sizzling bacon and frying eggs hit me before I even reach the bottom of the stairs.

I walk into the kitchen and smile at my dad who is standing over the frying pan, brandishing a spatula with a dishtowel draped over his shoulder.

"Good morning." I give him a confused smile.

Breakfast is usually my department. I've been making it for everyone since Mom got sick.

Dad grins. "I thought you could use a break."

"Thank you." I walk around the island and give him a kiss on the cheek.

He lightly rubs my back, winking at me before turning back to the bacon.

"Smells good," I murmur, grabbing a glass from the cupboard and filling it up with orange juice. That's the best start to the day in the world—fresh, cold orange juice.

I down half the glass before pulling the toast from the toaster and starting to lightly butter it. "Are you heading to the hospital today?"

"No." Dad glances over his shoulder at me. "And I don't think you should either."

"What?" I stop buttering the toast and frown at him.

"Come on, Sav. You were up there all day yesterday. You need a breather. The staff at Aviemore are amazing. Donna has promised to call me if anything changes. We both need to switch off, even if it's just for half the day."

I shake my head and resume buttering with a little more fervor. "I'm going, Dad. You can't keep me from seeing her."

"I'm not—" He sighs and grabs the frying pan off the stove. His spatula cuts through one of the eggs, breaking the yolk.

"I'll take it," I murmur, knowing how much Louis hates a broken yolk. Scarlett would eat it, but she'd complain first.

He sighs and is a little more careful with the next two eggs. "I'm not trying to keep you from her. I just worry that it's all too much for you. You already help me run this house and look after Lettie and Lou. I just don't want you burning out."

I flash him a grateful smile and snatch a piece of bacon off my plate. "She's my best friend. I want to see her every day. They say coma patients can hear people talking to them. If she can hear me, I want her to know that I came by each day."

"Okay, fine." Dad dumps the pan into the sink. It

sizzles and hisses against the cold water already in there. "I'll make you a deal." Flicking the dishtowel off his shoulder, he wipes his hands and says, "You go up to the hospital after breakfast. I'll take Lettie and Lou to the beach, and you can meet me there in an hour or so. I'd like to go for a run. Would you be happy to watch them while I do that?"

Giving him a greasy bacon kiss on the cheek, I flash him a triumphant grin and agree. "Of course I'd be happy to."

He gives me one of those smiles that tells me he loves me, and my heart tingles with warm fuzzies. Although losing Mom was the worst thing ever, being left with a dad who really cares about us is a huge blessing. He's a good dad. He tries so hard, and I'm grateful for him.

Grabbing two plates, I head into the dining room. "Scarlett! Louis! Breakfast is up. Pause whatever you're watching or playing and come eat."

I hear Louis groan, and I bet a million bucks my sister is rolling her eyes. They hate it when I act like a mother, but it's not like I have much of a choice. I was forced into the role before Mom even passed away. It's not like I asked for it. But Dad needs me. Until my siblings are old enough to look after themselves, I have to play daughter and mother. It's kind of exhausting, but it's what I have to do.

I head to the hospital as soon as I'm done eating.

Lettie got all snotty when Dad told her the plan about the beach. She'd rather stay inside reading all day.

"I have a bunch of photos I want to take for Instagram!"

"And you'll have all afternoon to take them." Dad gave her his stern look, his voice deepening just a touch.

It's hard not to smirk when that happens. Dad hardly ever tells me off, and I know he's just putting on a show to make a point when he gets all gruff with my siblings.

Lettie glared at me across the table and I moved my feet out of kicking range, tucking them under the chair and eating just a little faster.

When I left the table, Lettie started up with a new barrel of complaints about how I always get special treatment, and it's not fair that I get to go to the hospital while she has to go to the beach. Dad's scoffing laughter followed me up the stairs, and I shook my head as I listened to him trying to explain that my friend is in a coma and Lettie was being a selfish little shit.

Which she totally was!

He didn't say those words, of course, but his meaning was adamantly clear.

I made sure I was in my car and out of the driveway before Lettie could barge into my room and try to bitch at me. She's gotten feisty in the last year or so. Puberty is bringing out her inner dragon. The mood swings are something else.

I try to be sympathetic. She lost her mom at the age of ten. We all fell apart that first year and were held together by Marlo and Jeff, Rosalie—the housekeeper— and our neighbors. It took me months to find enough strength to be the person Louis and Scarlett needed. I'm doing the best I can, but some days I just want to slap my little sister.

Pulling in a calming breath, I try to shake off my stress as I walk into the hospital. Marlo and Jeff need me to be upbeat and positive. Skylar needs me to be the girl I was before she fell...or whatever happened to her.

I swallow, hating that sick pill that seems to release in my stomach whenever I try to figure out what happened to her that night.

It doesn't matter. All that matters is that she recovers. We can deal with the rest later.

My hands form two fists in spite of myself, and they clench a little tighter when I round the corner into Skylar's room and spot some black guy in there talking to her.

He's leaning against his broom, staring down at her and talking softly. Quiet music is oozing from the phone in his pocket.

"What are you doing?" I snap.

He jerks like I've just electrocuted him, his dark eyes bugging out. "Uh..."

I glare at his round face, then cross my arms and try to channel a little Skylar sass. "Well?"

"I'm just cleaning." He swallows, looking guilty as hell.

"Cleaning?" I spit out the word.

He lifts up the badge attached to his scrubs pocket. "I work here."

I'm too far away to read the small print, but it's obvious it's an official badge. This steals a little of my thunder, but I still manage to snap, "I doubt you're supposed to be talking to patients."

I glance at Skylar, my protective instincts kicking in.

What the hell was he saying to her?

My precious best friend, small and bruised with tubes coming out of what feels like every orifice. They only make her look smaller and more broken.

Tears burn my eyes and I blink fast to stop them from forming.

"Sorry, I just..." The guy's voice draws my attention back to him.

He looks young to be working in a hospital. My eyebrows flicker with a frown and I glance over my shoulder. "Where are Skylar's parents?"

"I think they left about ten minutes ago. They said they'd be back after breakfast."

Great, so Marlo and Jeff know about Mr. Cleaner. Do they know he talks to their daughter when they're not around though?

I rub my temples, trying to ward off the looming headache. "Can you…get out, please?"

"Yeah, sure." He jumps toward the door and has to turn sideways to get past me. He's a big unit.

I give him a sharp frown before turning my back on him.

I've got enough on my plate right now. I don't need some creeper talking to my best friend while she lies in a coma. That's *my* job.

Taking a seat beside her, I reach for her hand and give it a gentle squeeze.

"Hey, Sky." My voice wobbles. "It's me, Savvy." Sucking in a breath, I try to think of the right thing to say. It's so awkward when I know she won't respond to anything.

I hold my next breath, then let it whistle out of my mouth before going with the news I know Sky will want to hear. She's all about the drama, and even though my life isn't hugely dramatic right now, I can keep going with my story about Friday night and Mr. Dreadlocks.

Leaning against the edge of the bed, I get comfy and put on a smile. "So, I can't stop thinking about him."

## 8

# SUNNY SUNDAY GETS A LITTLE BRIGHTER

## GRIFFIN

It's not really my job to look out for people.

I work at Ryder Rentals, renting boards out to people who want to have some fun on the water. Even so, when I'm not busy dealing directly with a customer, I find myself perched outside the shed, watching the people around me.

Keeping an eye on those in the water and making sure no one's in danger.

Marshall's in the lifeguard chair today. He doesn't need me to quietly back him up, but I do it anyway. It's just natural instinct.

I sometimes wonder if I was born that way. Even as a kid I was always looking out for my older brother. Sure, he pulled me into trouble a lot, but I was there to

57

protect him from himself. At least that's what I was trying to do. I can't help feeling like I failed big time.

I never should have taken the fall for the robbery. Maybe if I hadn't, he would have learned a lesson and turned his life around.

A scoffing snicker shoots between my lips and I adjust my shades, keeping my eyes on the water. It's a beautiful, sunny Sunday, so the beach is full, buzzing with activity as people start to shift into summer mode. We're on the cusp of the vacation season, and the locals are starting early.

I smile as a young dad chases his toddler down to the water's edge, catching him just before he face-plants into the wet sand. A few kids are digging a moat just to the right of them, and beyond that a couple of tweens are boogie boarding.

I soak it all in, scanning from one happy beachgoer to the next. Enjoying this peaceful oasis. It's so far removed from the life I grew up in. There was no dad to stop me from face-planting. No sand castles. No laughing with my friends. No boogie boarding on the weekends.

Brent Anderson taught me how to swim. I'll always be grateful for that. Without those basics as a kid, I never could have learned to surf in Mexico.

Shit, I would have loved to have stayed with the Andersons. They were good people who probably would have adopted us if they could have. But life is never fair. After only eleven months, they had to suddenly up and move when her dad got sick. So, we were shifted to another foster home. A crappy one with people who didn't give a rat's ass about me and my bro.

In spite of not wanting to think about my shitty childhood, my mind shoots back to the night that changed my life forever. I try not to dwell on it, but sometimes the memories fire back like a shotgun bullet, exploding in my mind and burning holes through my happy.

I should be grateful I got busted and thrown into juvie.

It probably saved my life.

But it killed the only real relationship I had.

It turned me into a runaway…a drifter. From the heart of gang life to flying solo. It's been a bumpy ride. When I first ran, I was haunted by fear and isolation, but I forced myself to keep going. Too much was at stake. If I went home, I'd be dead.

Now the isolation and solitude are a comfort.

Although I'm surrounded by beachgoers, I can feel that bubble of protection around me. I'm safe here in this crowd. Anonymous little me, just doing my job and not getting caught.

I pull in a contented breath, but it kind of rattles in my chest when I expel it. I can't quite shake the guilt of lying to Marshall in order to get this job. I haven't told anyone who I really am since the night I split Vallejo. It's like that person doesn't even exist anymore.

That's probably a good thing.

The real me was an orphan loser who let his brother pull him into nothing but trouble.

I try not to think too hard about Phoenix. About the fact that he'd probably kill me if he ever saw me again. I'm not his brother anymore, I'm just the guy who took off with the money. Money he still thinks I have. Money he still wants.

Forget the fact that I paid for his crime.

I don't think the guy ever really loved me. I was just someone useful.

The bitter thoughts are turning my mood black, so I force my focus back to the beach, studying the people in the water first before letting my eyes drift to the couple walking hand and hand away from me.

A small grin twitches my lips.

Looks like Harley (yeah, I found out her name) and Aidan worked things out.

Marshall told me this morning when I got to work that Aidan will be joining the Ryder Rentals crew. I'm stoked. Within the next three weeks, once school is well and truly over and families are heading away for their summer vacations, this place will be bursting at the seams. It'll be great to have the extra support, and hanging out with Aidan will be fun.

"Vacation," I murmur, thinking about how busy the beach might get. Marshall warned me that it's like a different place during the height of the summer.

A niggle of worry skitters through me, but I push it aside for another day. It's not here yet. I just have to live each day, trust my identity and do my damn job.

I shuffle in the sand, blinking to regain focus. I hate it when my mind wanders like this. Ever since meeting my surf instructor in Mexico, I've made a real effort to be in the moment. That's what Pedro taught me. The guy was big on mindfulness and presence. He taught me how to read the water, love the water, find salvation in it. He taught me how to focus and be present, to not let the past cloud me out or to let worry over things I can't control (like the future) consume me.

So that's what I've got to do. Switch off to everything else and just be.

With a determined sniff, I stretch my arms above my head and take a few paces away from my spot, swinging my arms to wake up my body. Harley and Aidan are walking toward the pier. She's laughing at something and now her head is leaning against his arm. I'm glad they're together. They seem like a cool couple.

Too bad for Savannah though.

I wonder how she's feeling today.

I'm glad she's not around to see Harley and Aidan all loved up together.

Turning north, I amble away from the shed. Not too far, just enough to stretch my legs. Marshall is down from his perch, walking along the beach. He smiles and greets the kids who say hi to him, dishing out a couple of high fives and checking in with families.

He stops by a blanket and bends down to talk to a

family of lily-white kids who will turn into red lobsters if they're not careful. I bet he's telling the mom to get sunblock on them or make sure they cover up.

While he's doing that, I scan the water, checking the surfers, counting them to keep track of the numbers. There are only three out today. Harley and Aidan will probably be in there soon enough. The main one I'm looking for is a black guy with no hair and an intimidating glare.

Thankfully Axel and his buddies aren't around.

Being a sunny Sunday, they've probably looked for a quieter spot where no one will invade their waves. I'm glad. I don't like those guys dominating out there. They ruin it for everyone else. I've actually watched a surfer approach the water before, see Axel, and then change his mind about going in. That's not cool.

A kid with a boogie board skips past me and I smile at her. "Having fun?"

"Yep!" She giggles and runs into the water.

I watch her go, then scan the beach for a parent. I see a mother eyeing her carefully and am relieved she's doing her job. It makes the lifeguard's job a hell of a lot easier when caregivers help out by watching too.

My gaze travels past the woman and up the beach.

And that's when my breath hitches.

Damn, I wish it wouldn't do that.

But...there she is.

Savannah. Looking gorgeous in a chocolate-brown bikini with white trim. I try to turn away as she wiggles out of her shorts, but I can't seem to. She's talking to her dad, capturing locks of wayward hair blowing in the breeze. She tucks them behind her ear and smiles.

As her dimples pop into place, my lips curl at the edges and I force my eyes back to the water.

Man, she has one of the most beautiful smiles I've ever seen.

# 9

# BRIDGE REPAIRS: INCOMPLETE

## SAVANNAH

I stretch and look out across the beach. It's busy today.

My eyes graze the lifeguard tower, then cross over to the Ryder Rentals shed. I'm disappointed not to see a guy with dreads, but I'd have to walk farther forward to see the front of the shed. I wonder if he's working today.

I try not to think about it. I've just spent the last couple of hours dissecting it with Skylar, and although she couldn't give me any advice, it was good for me to think it through. I stopped talking when Marlo and Jeff returned, but my mind kept going on it.

Crushing on Griffin is probably a bad idea.

I have too much on my plate right now. With

summer just around the corner, Skylar in the hospital, my dad needing me to help with Lettie and Lou...I just can't be falling for some random guy I don't even know.

It's ridiculous. So he's hot. So what? He could be a complete dick.

*He's not.*

I think about the way he talked to me on Friday night, tried to make me feel better. The way he protected me from creepy crew cut guy.

Griffin is a good person.

But—

"Your brother's in the water." Dad pulls me into the present, resting his hand on my shoulder and pointing down to the waves. "On the inflatable surfboard thing. Just watch him. That kid is overconfident."

"Got it." I shade my eyes and spot Louis. He's having a blast, laughing and oblivious to the fact that he's splashing everyone around him with his big kicks.

I grin and shake my head. Little Lou. Although he's ten, he still acts like a five-year-old most of the time. I figure he'll grow up eventually. At least I hope he does. The constant niggle about the impact Mom's death has had on him eats away at me. I try not to let it consume me, waving to Dad as he heads off for his run.

I glance down to my left and check on Lettie. She's on her stomach, engrossed in a paperback.

"Do you have sunscreen on?"

"Yes," she snaps.

I try to ignore her tone.

"Just checking." I force a friendly smile, but my insides are simmering. It's getting harder and harder to look after Scarlett. She hates being mothered, but who the hell else is going to do it?

I thought as she got older I could mother her less and we'd become friends, but we just can't seem to work out our relationship, so instead there's this big wedge between us.

I don't know what to do about it.

Glancing back to the water, I check on my brother. That's an easier job.

He's doing fine, and I smile at his playfulness.

Then my gaze drifts to the right and I spot those dark ginger dreads I can't stop thinking about. I take a moment to admire Griffin in the daylight. Man, he's so much hotter than I realized.

I scan his body and even from this distance, I can see how muscly and strong he is. I love the shape of his legs. I love the way the wind ruffles his white tank top, making it cling to different parts of his torso. He has nice shoulders and a broad chest.

I wonder if the freckles on his face pepper his whole body. I'd like to see that.

The thought makes my face hot and I clear my throat, looking away from him and crossing my arms like I haven't been undressing the guy in my head.

"Hey, Sav." I turn to see Craig approaching with Jonah.

My stomach curdles just a touch. I used to like Craig, until he started dating my best friend. I can't help feeling like Craig brings out the worst in Skylar. I don't even know what she sees in him.

Actually, yes, I do. She sees a hot guy with a great bod and an excellent status at school.

I so don't get my best friend sometimes. She could do so much better, if she'd only let herself believe it. Or get over the fact that she has to be with the hottest guy, rather than the nicest.

Forcing a smile, I bury the thoughts and put on my polite face as Craig and Jonah stop beside me. They don't usually venture down to the middle part of the beach. They tend to stick to the north. I'm about to ask them what they're doing when I spot Craig's face and, for the first time in my life, actually feel sorry for the guy.

He looks miserable.

"How's she doing?" he murmurs.

"Same." I bob my head. "I was with her this morning. Are you going to go see her?"

"Yeah." He nods and swallows, but I can't help feeling like that's bullshit.

He showed up the night Skylar fell, and it was obvious how uncomfortable he was. I can't imagine Craig spending too much time by her bedside. He'll no doubt pop in just enough for people to be like "Yeah, Craig was definitely around."

"Do they know what happened yet?" Jonah's drawing circles in the sand with his big toe.

I glance at him and cross my arms, hating the question.

"No." My voice is small and shallow.

"Dad's asking around. He'll find something." Craig stands tall, pulling his shoulders back.

Craig's dad is our favorite cop in town. Officer Malloy. He's nice, friendly, and goes easy on us over the little things. Skylar's fall has really rattled him though. It's rattled all of us.

"Apparently Wyatt was down at the pier with her. I'd like to get my hands on that little creeper and knock the truth out of him," he mutters darkly.

I roll my eyes behind my shades. All I'd heard was that Wyatt was a crying mess on the beach after Skylar fell. I don't know why he was down at the south end. He likes to follow Skylar, but he seems as harmless as a fly. Annoying, but harmless.

Worry curls my stomach into a tight knot.

Did his true colors finally show that night? Is there another side to the guy that none of us really knows about?

I make a face, shaking my head and murmuring, "I don't know. I can't imagine him hurting anyone, especially Skylar. He practically worships the ground she walks on."

"Maybe he thought Sky and Craig were broken up after their big fight. Decided to take an opening," Jonah suggests.

I frown at him, then glance at Craig. His hands are curling into fists.

These macho assholes.

"You better leave him alone," I warn. "No one knows anything yet. It's all speculation." I'm loath to say it, but a small part of me is trying to protect Wyatt. Craig's the kind of guy who will punch first, ask questions later. What if Wyatt did absolutely nothing wrong? "For all we know she was down there crying over her fight with Craig. Maybe she jumped."

"She wouldn't jump," Craig bites back. "She's your best friend, you know that much."

I look to the sand, agreeing with him but not wanting to say it. Instead, I shrug and leave my idea hanging out there.

Craig scoffs and whips off his shades. "Look, I know we had a fight, but we didn't break up. I still care about her, and I was going to apologize and make things right. But then this happened, and I haven't had my chance yet. As soon as she wakes up, I'm gonna be back by her side, you got that?"

"I heard she told you that you were never to touch her again." My insides tremble as I engage. I'm terrible with arguments, I always back down, but Craig's pissing me off and I'm ignoring my instincts to shut up.

"Why would she say that, Craig? What were you trying to do to her?"

He looks like he wants to slap me, his face mottling red as he shoves his shades back on and mutters, "She cheated on me. You saw her. Everyone frickin' saw her! I was just trying to make up with her again. Make things right between us."

I let out a scoff, knowing exactly how Craig was expecting to make things right.

He and Skylar have had make-up sex at school before.

It makes me want to throw up.

I'm still a virgin, and I just don't understand Skylar's ease at spreading eagle. Especially for a guy like Craig.

I nearly gave it up to Aidan once, but just couldn't go through with it. Thankfully he was sweet enough not to push it. He just held me and kissed me, told me it was okay. He may have been disappointed, but he never made me feel bad. He understood that sex is a big deal.

I wish Skylar thought the same way. I hate how much she lets guys paw her, and I wish I'd had the chance to tell her how proud I was of the fact that she finally put Craig in his place. But I was still sulking over the party. Whenever Skylar plays mean (which isn't too often with me) I'll back off for a few days. Usually she comes crawling back with an apology and we're all good again. It didn't happen like that this time.

She spewed nasties, I retreated, leaving her to go crazy at this party...and then she was never the same. She didn't text or call me on that Sunday. I figured maybe she was mad with *me*, which was royally unfair, so I stayed in my cave and let too much time pass. We still hung out at school, but our conversations were quiet, shallow murmurs. We were stuck in limbo, waiting for the other to bend, to start repairs on our broken bridge.

But it never happened.

And now she's in a coma.

Clenching my jaw, I wonder how much I'm to blame. I accuse Craig of making her cry so hard she jumped, but what if I made her so upset she jumped?

*She wouldn't jump!*

I cling to the reminder, but don't love the alternatives. If she didn't jump, she either slipped...or was pushed.

But who would have pushed her?

Craig's muttering under his breath, obviously annoyed, and I have that flashing thought—was it him? Did he follow her—or lure her—to the pier to try to make amends and when she wouldn't relent, he got pissy and shoved her?

Maybe that's why he was so uncomfortable at the hospital.

Maybe that's why he doesn't want to go visit her.

My lips part, ready to ask the question, but courage fails me. What if I'm wrong? He'll go ballistic if I start accusing him in front of Jonah. If I start accusing him at all!

The thought scares me and instead of being brave, I look away from him, gazing out to the ocean to check on my brother.

I don't see him.

My heart lurches into my throat and I step side-ways, hunting for the inflatable surfboard he was playing on.

I spot it floating by itself in the deeper water.

With no sign of my brother on top.

Fear clutches me, its sharp talons digging right into my center.

"Louis!" I whisper and start sprinting toward the water, frantically searching the people splashing in the waves. Louis is still little and short for his age. Brown hair. Short, spiky brown hair.

"Shit." The word wobbles out of my mouth, panic setting in as I start scanning the beach, wondering if he's gotten out of the water and is walking back up to Scarlett.

I spin and see she's still reading on the beach towel, all by herself.

Craig and Jonah are standing nearby, staring at me in confusion.

"Louis!" I shout, not caring if I look like an idiot.

He's my responsibility right now. Dad is trusting me to look out for him.

"Louis!" I scream, running back to the water, and that's when I spot Griffin.

He's sprinting into the waves, his legs kicking up high as he gains some depth, then dives into the water. I track the direction he's swimming and that's when I finally spot my brother, arms flailing as he struggles to keep his head above water.

# 10

# WHO KNEW DIMPLES COULD BE SO BEAUTIFUL?

## GRIFFIN

Not that I'm a lifeguard, but as far as rescues go, this is going to be an easy one.

The kid in the water is way out of his depth, but not mine. I wouldn't have even noticed him if I hadn't heard Savannah's scream. She was sprinting down the sand, and my eyes instantly swung to the water and started hunting. Marshall was down at the other end of the beach. He hadn't heard anything yet, and I didn't care that it wasn't my job; I acted on instinct and started sprinting the second I spotted those little flailing arms.

The kid had swum out too far and then started to drift outside of the monitored area. He was a lone buoy. A lone, sinking buoy.

I crawl the last two feet and grab his thrashing arm.

"It's okay, buddy. You're gonna be all right." He whimpers and wraps his arms around my neck, clinging so hard he nearly chokes me. "Calm down, buddy. You're safe now."

Securing him against my chest, I tread water for a minute and spin around to face the shore and get my bearings. Marshall is running into the water and I head his direction.

Tucking the boy against my shoulder, I start to scissor kick and crawl back to shore. I'll be able to touch the bottom soon enough, and then I can just carry the kid.

The inflatable he was chasing is still floating out to sea, but I spot a man grabbing it and am grateful he will pull it back to shore so I don't have to try and get it later.

My primary focus is this scared kid, who no doubt thought he was gonna die today.

He's letting out these panicked little sobs.

"We'll be able to touch the bottom in just a sec. We're nearly there." A couple more pulls and I'm able to start walking. Swinging the kid in front of me, I hoist him into my arms like I'm carrying a toddler. He wraps his arms and legs around me so tight I could let go and he'd probably stay exactly where he is.

"He okay?" Marshall stopped running when he saw I had things under control and is now waiting in waist-deep water for me.

"Yeah, he's fine."

"Thanks, man." Marshall's voice wavers. "You did a good job." He pats my shoulder as soon as I'm within reach, then starts talking to the kid. "How you doing, Lou? You all right, little man?"

"Uh-huh." He nods, his chin bumping against my shoulder.

The people around us have all stopped swimming. They're now openly staring at us, curiosity killing any sense of subtlety.

"Louis!"

I glance up as Savannah comes hurtling into the shallow waves. As soon as he hears her voice, the kid in my arms wrestles free of my hold and hits the sand. He spins to find her, but his jelly legs give out and I have to catch him.

I guide his sagging body straight into her arms.

"Are you okay?" Her voice quakes as she leans down to kiss the top of his salty head.

He doesn't say anything, just wraps his arms around her waist and starts crying.

"I'm so sorry," she blubbers. "I should have been watching more closely. I'm sorry."

She keeps apologizing as she hugs him, then glances up at me.

Her tear-streaked face is beautiful, in a heart-breaking kind of way. I smile at her and rest my hand on Louis's back. "Hey, he's fine. It's all right."

She sniffles and nods, then glances at Marshall. She obviously knows the guy and I wonder how.

"He's gonna be just fine, Sav. Don't worry about it. I'm sorry I didn't see him sooner. By the time I heard your scream, Griffin was already in the water." He flashes me a proud smile and I'm not sure what to do with it. Not many people have ever smiled at me that way before.

I swallow and focus back on Savannah, who is still clinging to her brother and crying. I wish I had the right words to bring her a little more comfort. Her reaction is pretty full-on, considering her brother didn't really come that close to drowning. Sure, he was getting tired out there, but I ran in and got him with time to spare. If I hadn't been around, Marshall would have noticed and grabbed him in time. Sure, it may have been a little closer to the wire, but... heck, Savannah probably could have run in and made it.

Her pale complexion and shaking limbs tell me that she thought her brother was a goner.

I glance past her shoulder and notice a younger girl with some of Savannah's features. I have to assume she's a sister. She's hovering a couple of yards away, clutching a book to her chest and looking on the verge of tears.

I remember seeing a man jogging away from them about twenty minutes ago. It's easy to make assumptions. Father with three kids who left Savannah in charge while he went for a run.

So where's their mother?

Savannah sucks in a shaky breath, obviously ready to pull herself together.

I'm glad, because people are still staring, and I want them to get the hell on with their day now and leave this little family alone.

I catch Savannah's eye. "You okay?"

She sniffs and nods, biting her lips together. "Yeah, I just... he's my responsibility and if anything ever..." She lets out a shuddering breath, kissing her brother on the head before giving me a wonky smile. "Thank you."

I grin. "It's no problem, really."

"I'll make a lifeguard out of him yet." Marshall slaps my back with a chuckle, then checks on Louis one more time before turning away to continue his lifeguarding duties.

Savannah lets out a watery laugh as he walks away.

I give her a quizzical look, trying to figure out what she's thinking.

She shakes her head. "I swear if I have to see another person dragged out of the ocean... That's two in like one week. I don't know how much more I can take."

I keep my smile in place as I study her. She seems stressed and burdened. I know she's linked to the girl in the coma somehow, plus I now know she has siblings to look after. Damn, I want her story. I want to pull her into a hug and tell her that everything is going to be okay.

"Sav, I wanna go." Louis is shaking, his skinny body twitching beside hers.

"Yeah, in a minute, bud." She squeezes his shoulder. "I've just gotta find Dad. He never takes his phone running with him," she murmurs under her breath, obviously irritated by this.

She starts searching the beach, rising to her tiptoes.

"Hey, why don't you head home?" I brush my hand down her arm to get her attention. Her skin is smooth and soft. My fingers tingle with delight, and I have to swallow to keep my voice steady. "I can keep an eye out for your dad and let him know you've gone."

"Are you sure?" Her perfectly shaped eyebrows wrinkle.

I smile, loving how sweet she is. "Yeah. Absolutely."

"Okay, well, thanks." A small smile makes her dimples appear, and I'm pretty sure I adore them way more than I should.

Who knew dimples could be so damn beautiful?

I turn to check on the shed and notice Marshall lingering near it while he scans the beach.

"Hey, Marsh, I'll just be a minute!" I call to him.

He raises his hand to acknowledge me and I follow Savannah up the beach. She hands me her father's keys, wallet and phone, thanking me again for my help.

She really needs to stop doing that.

"It's not a problem," I remind her.

She just flashes her dimples again and makes it really hard to turn back to my job.

But I force my body away from her, not even waiting to watch her walk away with her brother and sister.

Tucking her father's belongings safely under the counter, I let Marshall know what I've done.

"Good idea. I'll keep an eye out for Kevin as well."

"So you know the family?" I grab a towel off the chair inside the shed and dry off my face. The tank I'm wearing has already started to dry in the sun. The spandex and nylon material is quick to dry, and I tend to leave the shirt on most of the day. It saves me having to slather sunscreen all over myself. This way, I only have to cover my arms, neck and face.

I pull out the sunscreen tube and reapply a little more to my cheeks, nose and forehead while Marshall tells me about his connection with Kevin Green.

"It's a tight-knit community. Kevin's daughter was dating Aidan for a while, and Aidan's dad is a really good friend of mine. You end up seeing each other at parties and cookouts."

I nod and glance down the beach. Savannah's father will return soon, and we'll have to flag him down and explain what happened.

I wonder if I should let Marshall handle this one.

He knows the guy, and it's probably better than having a stranger tell him his son nearly drowned.

## 11

## SLACK, LOOSE EDGES

## SAVANNAH

No one says anything on the ride home, which is kind of painful. As soon as we walk in the door, Scarlett mutters something about reading in her room before disappearing up the stairs.

She looks kind of pale, and I make a mental note to go check on her later.

She likes space before confrontation. Not that I want to confront her, I just want to make sure she's okay. But the way she's been acting lately, even that kind of conversation will no doubt feel like an attack from me.

She's so prickly these days. I don't really know how to handle her.

The thought makes my eyes burn and I have to force

a smile, putting on my best bright voice as I tell Louis to go take a quick shower.

"I'll get some milk and cookies ready for when you get out."

He sniffs and shows me his smile. "Rosalie made oatmeal raisin on Thursday."

"Perfect. I'll get you two of those."

With a little nod, he heads for the stairwell, then pauses and turns back with his best "wounded" face ever. "Can the milk be chocolate?"

How the hell am I supposed to resist that?

I give him a half smile and nod. "Sure, kiddo."

He grins and trots up the stairs.

As soon as he's out of sight, I wobble into the kitchen and sag against the island counter. He could have died today.

The thought is an iceberg floating through my brain.

I can't steer clear of it.

That mammoth 'what if' is tearing right through me, taking out any sense of logic and calm. Tears burn the back of my throat and sting my eyes as my imagination plays out the scenario. Louis's dead body floating in the water, his lips blue, his skinny limbs limp. Dad would never recover. He's barely survived Mom's death, but to lose a son as well?

The front door slams and I jerk straight, quickly wiping my face and pulling it together before Dad sees me.

"Louis!" Dad's voice is loud and panicked.

I hear his keys hit the bowl on the side table and catch him just before he races up the stairs. "He's in the shower."

Dad spins to face me, his ashen features making me sick to my stomach. He's been playing 'what if' too.

I blink and force the tears back. I don't want him to see me cry.

"Where's Lettie?"

"In her room. Reading." I shrug.

Dad sighs and nods. "I'll go check on her in a minute."

I can't help noticing the slight tremble in Dad's arm when he runs a hand through his sweaty hair and kind of deflates on the spot.

"I'm sorry," I squeak before spinning away from him and getting busy with milk and cookies.

He doesn't say anything, but I hear his sneakers on the shiny floor as he slowly walks into the kitchen.

"I spoke to Marshall. He told me what happened. Thank God for Griffin, right?"

I pull a glass out of the pantry, but can't look at my dad. "He saved Louis's life."

"He wasn't there when I collected my stuff, so I didn't get a chance to thank him, but I've got the inflatable in my car."

"Oh yeah, the surfboard thingy." I wince and spare a quick glance at my father. His hands are on the counter, spread apart like stabilizers. If his elbows give out, he'll smack his head on the shiny black marble.

I know exactly how he's feeling.

"I'm sorry," I murmur again, unable to fight my tears as I wrestle with the baking tin lid. "I should have been watching more closely. I was talking to Craig and Jonah, and I got distracted and I shouldn't have. I'm sorry, Dad. I'm so sorry."

Tears are blinding me, and I can't get the freaking lid off this stupid tin!

I drop it on the counter with a huff.

"Hey." Dad's soft voice finds me, and I sniff, pressing my knuckles into my eyes and trying to pull myself together. "It's okay." Two strong arms encircle me, and I rest my chin on Dad's shoulder, clinging to the back of his sweaty shirt.

"I'm sorry," I mumble.

"You can stop saying that now." He cups the back of my head. "Honey, it's okay. Everything is fine."

"But it could have gone so badly! We could have lost Lou."

"I know." His voice trembles. "But we didn't." Pulling away from me, he holds me at arm's length and forces a smile. His eyes are a little glassy. He never used to cry before Mom died, but ever since she got sick, he's been a lot more fragile.

That's partly why I feel so bad. I hate that I put him through this today. I can only imagine how rough it must have been to arrive back from his run, his family gone, and then he has to hear how his son nearly drowned. Thankfully Marshall was there, although I'm kind of sad Dad didn't get to meet Griffin and thank him personally.

I expel a shaky breath and can't hold back my next set of tears. They trail silently down my cheeks.

Dad notices and swipes them away with his hand. "If you don't stop crying, I'm gonna start."

I snicker and cross my arms, trying to pull myself together.

"We both got a fright today, but it's okay." He swallows. "Everything is okay."

I nod but can't speak.

"I'm sorry that I put you in that position. You already have so much on your plate right now."

"So do you," I counter.

"But you're my kid. You're *my* responsibility, and I'm so aware of how much you already do around here. You're supposed to be a free-spirited teenager, one week away from a fun summer vacation."

I scoff and shake my head. "I can't see this summer being that great. My best friend is in a coma, Aidan and I are definitely over, and I just…" My shoulder hitches. "What else am I going to do but be here to look after Lettie and Lou, or hang out at the hospital with Sky?"

"No." Dad shakes his head. "That's not acceptable. You are not spending your summer doing that." He grabs the cookie tin and pulls off the lid.

I snatch two out and put them on a plate before heading to the fridge.

"You need a hobby." Dad leans his hip against the counter, watching me pour Louis's milk.

"A hobby?"

"Yes, something you can do to fill the space while Skylar's not around."

"But I should be there for her," I argue, slamming the milk back into the fridge door.

"And you will be" Dad counters. "But you're not spending every day of your summer by her bedside or looking after your siblings. Your brother will be away with your grandparents soon, and your sister is old enough to look after herself...sort of. We both know she'll probably spend most of the summer either in her room reading or in the backyard taking photos of books."

We grin at each other. Dad's probably so relieved that he's got a bookworm for a daughter. There's a certain safety in that. It must be a hell of a lot easier than a thirteen-year-old who's out dating some guy he doesn't like or sneaking out to parties with her friends.

"You need to do something for you." Dad points at me. "Something *you* want to do."

I sigh and shake my head. "I don't know what that is."

"Well, it's about time you figure it out." Brushing past me, Dad grabs the grocery list off the fridge and starts jotting a few extra items down. "Now, I am going upstairs to check on Lou and Lettie. Can you go to the store and grab a few things for us?"

"Sure." I take the list and scan it. "Mind if I walk?"

"I was hoping you would. It'll give you time to decide what kind of hobby you want to pursue."

"Dad," I complain. He chuckles, then gives me a serious look. "I know your teen years haven't been like most. You've had to carry a lot for this family, and you've lost—" Dad's voice cuts out and he has to swallow before he can keep talking. "It's your time, Sav. You deserve all the happiness you can find."

I give him a watery smile and kiss his cheek. "So do you."

His eyes glass over, and I slip out of the kitchen, not wanting to see him cry. Running up to my room, I quickly change into dry clothes before grabbing the Visa card out of Dad's wallet and slipping it in the back of my skirt pocket. The heavy door shuts behind me, and I slide on my shades and start walking down the path.

A hobby.

I shake my head and almost laugh.

I don't even know where to begin. Since moving to Ryder Bay and becoming friends with Skylar, my hobby has been hanging out with her. I don't even know what I like doing without her. When Mom got sick, my world shrank. All that mattered was my family and Sky. When she was away last summer and Aidan and I got together, my world expanded enough to fit him into it.

But being Skylar's cousin, it wasn't exactly a huge stretch.

Now the edges of my tight little world are slack and loose. The things that usually fill it aren't around and it makes me feel unsteady. I want to shove the familiar into that space—looking after Lettie and Lou. Being the person Dad needs me to be, to take the pressure off him.

But I guess he made a fair point. I am a teenager one week away from summer freedom.

I've never had freedom like this before, and I seriously do not know what to do with it.

Reaching the end of my street, I turn right and decide to go to the big store in town rather than the smaller one just outside of Cliffton Terrace. That way I can stroll along the beach and think a little longer.

A hobby.

What kinds of hobbies do teenagers even have?

Reading. That's Lettie's domain, and although I do like a good book, I'm not obsessed with living in other worlds the way she is.

Arts and crafts?

My nose wrinkles. Not really my thing.

Music?

I like music, but it's not like I play anything, and my singing voice is only just passable.

Glancing out at the ocean, I spot a couple of surfers in the water. I strain to see if it's Aidan and Harley. I don't know why. It's not like I actually want to see them together, having fun and being all boyfriend and girlfriend.

I slow to a stop, staring as one surfer paddles hard, catching a wave and jumping to his feet. His board flies across the water, his body bending and twisting to make the board go up and then snap back down onto the wave.

It does look pretty cool.

Exciting.

I've always loved the water.

Maybe surfing is something I could do.

I think about Aidan and how much he's changed since Harley taught him to surf. He seems happier, more relaxed and carefree. It's like she's opened his eyes to a whole new world.

Maybe surfing would open my eyes too.

My brain starts formulating a plan before I can stop it. I wonder if Harley would be willing to teach me a thing or two.

Would that be weird?

Asking my ex's new girlfriend for surf lessons.

*Hell yeah, it would be weird!*

The voice is Skylar's. I can hear it so clearly in my head. She'd scoff at my lame idea of getting a hobby.

But you know what? She's not around right now to scoff at me or make me feel bad for wanting something she doesn't agree with.

I love her, but she can be pretty damn dominating when she wants to be.

As much as I'm desperate for her to come out of her coma, to come back to us, maybe I need to take this small opportunity to start something without her.

Maybe when she wakes up and has recovered, she'll want to follow *me* into something for a change.

My lips twitch with a small smile as a thrill races through me.

I wonder if I'll have the courage to actually pursue this idea. What's the bet that I won't be able to stop thinking about it until I do?

## 12

## BLACK HOLES

### GRIFFIN

I can't stop thinking about Savannah.

It's driving me nuts, but even my irritation can't fester, because the second her sweet smile filters into my brain, I feel a warmth I can't even understand.

Girls don't tend to have this effect on me, and it feels dangerous. I've lusted after them before, relived some pretty awesome experiences with hot holiday bunnies after a good time, but Savannah's different. She's young and sweet, not some rich wild child on vacation wanting a quick hookup.

I roll over in my sleeping bag, punching the pillow under my head and willing sleep to take me. But I can't switch off tonight. Today was a busy one. Things are heating up at work and I imagine I'll have a steady stream of customers for the next few months. Marshall will be happy. His side business is really taking off and he deserves the success.

I think about the lifeguard and find myself yearning for his life.

He's happily married to an absolute sweetheart, living in a beach town, spending his days patrolling the sand and keeping the community safe.

I snort and punch my pillow again. As if I could ever become a lifeguard. I don't even have a high school diploma. No, what I have is a past that's constantly lurking in the back of my brain, reminding me that I don't have the luxury of thinking ahead...or imagining a future where I get the pretty girlfriend and a steady job.

A creak from the living room makes me flinch.

My body pings tight, instantly alert as I stop breathing and listen for noises within the house. I count to ten without hearing anything but am too unsettled to stay put. Sliding out of my sleeping bag in stealth mode, I gather my stuff and creep into the darkest corner of the room. Standing against the wall, I keep my eyes on the black hole of the doorway, my heart thundering as I wait for someone to walk through it.

Shit, staying in this place is a really bad idea.

Phoenix could be around any corner.

My original plan was to head east, not north up the coast, but the thought of leaving the ocean behind kind of killed me.

I could have stayed in Mexico. Hell, I probably *should* have, but when Pedro suddenly died of a heart attack, I just had to get out of there. It hurt too much to walk the same sand he taught me on. I was a scared, clueless wreck when I first snuck across the border to Tijuana, but he found me. Took me in. Taught me to surf. Hooked me up with those jobs at the resorts.

The guy freaking saved my life.

He became my family.

I couldn't stay in a place that he no longer existed.

But man, returning stateside only heightens the risk of Phoenix finding me. We're in the same state right now. If he's stayed with the gang in Vallejo, which he probably has, he's a seven-hour drive away.

Seven hours.

That's nothing.

Shit, I dread the day when I turn to find my older brother behind me, demanding to know where the money is.

When it's the middle of the day and I'm thinking logically, the chances of him finding me are pretty slim. But nighttime darkness weakens the mind, letting ugly scenarios play out. Reminding me of the one time he did nearly catch me.

It was about a month after I split Vallejo. I hadn't moved far enough away. I'd made the mistake of going to a friend's. I hadn't seen him in about five years, but still, it was someone we both knew. I heard Phoenix's voice in the other room, so I scrambled out the window and ran. Who knows what he did to the guy I was staying with? I hate to think, and I'll carry that guilt forever. I should have revealed myself and just taken the fall.

But I can't tell Phoenix what I did with that money he stole.

I won't.

He'll kill me.

It wasn't enough that I took the fall for him, kept my mouth shut when the cops were trying to offer me a deal to rat on my brother. I was loyal back then. I was loyal all the way through my stint in juvie. I was loyal until the day I got out.

Thanks to my counselor, they released me early on good behavior and I was put back into the foster system. The only thing I had to keep doing was my counseling sessions and a weekly stint of community service for six months.

It was my chance. I was going to be the good boy and turn my life around. But then Phoenix showed up, trying to pull me back in, demanding the money.

I couldn't tell him where it was, even when he tried to beat the truth out of me.

In the end, he left me no choice.

I had to break the rules.

I had to run.

And I haven't stopped running since.

Two and a half years and I still feel like a fugitive. I should have graduated from high school this year, but instead I'm living this false life. Pretending to be the adult that I'm not.

The house seems to be quiet again.

My fingers ease their grip on my bag, and I sag against the wall.

I'm safe for another night.

Safe for now.

I just wish I knew how to make this feeling last.

## 13

# THE TIE REBELLION

## SAVANNAH

It's the last day of school.

I'm now free for the summer.

But that exciting thrill of freedom is nowhere to be found as I walk through the sliding doors and into Aviemore Hospital.

I was supposed to be here an hour ago, but I had to drop Louis at his friend's place, and Lettie was going to a sleepover but forgot her overnight bag, so I had to run home and grab that, then travel all the way back up past Walton Academy to drop it off to her.

I'm hot, sweaty and irritated.

Lettie didn't even say thank you. The little cow.

With a sigh, I walk past the nurses' station, smiling at Dr. Donna Meads who gives me a distracted wave. She's having an in-depth conversation with one of the nurses, and my ears start burning when I'm past the station and realize they're talking about my bestie.

Pausing against the wall, I eavesdrop out of sight.

"I spoke to Kevin about it at length this morning. It's been a week since the incident. She technically should be awake by now."

"So, what's stopping that?" the nurse asks.

"We're not sure. The scans she had this morning all show that the swelling has reduced. The brain is healing at a normal rate." I hear a file slap onto the desk and then a heavy sigh. "It's like she doesn't want to wake up. Like there's something in her mind that's stopping her from coming back to us."

There's a sad pause that makes my heart hurt.

"Have you spoken to her parents about it?"

"Kevin said he'd talk to them today." Donna sighs again. "I guess all we can do is keep talking to her and moving her around to make sure her muscles don't atrophy. When she wakes, we want to give her the best chance of a quick recovery."

*When she wakes.*

I have to cling to those words as I push off the wall and shuffle down the corridor.

I don't know how to feel about what I've just heard. Part of me is stoked that Skylar's brain is healing so well, but the doctor's confusion is unsettling.

Why?

Why would Skylar fight coming back to us?

I rub my forehead. A headache has been forming

since Lettie called me and treated me like an unappreciated mother.

A growl rumbles in my throat. At least I don't have to deal with her tonight. I don't know what I'm going to do with myself. Probably hang out here and talk to Sky, then be a support for her exhausted parents.

Shit, I feel drained already.

Is this how my summer is going to go? Days in this hospital?

The idea is kind of depressing.

Dad's right. I do need a hobby.

I thought surfing would be it, and I'm still playing with that idea, but I haven't found the guts to ask for Harley's help yet.

School has been a great excuse. If anything is going to distract me, it's finals week.

I hate to think how badly I've done this year. Studying has been near impossible. Hopefully I've done enough not to damage my future. The pressure around the school has been intense and only made worse by the Skylar rumors that have been flying—constant chatter and speculation. The stories have inflated to the ridiculous at some points, elaborate imaginings to keep students entertained. I've tried to ignore every theory and have resisted the urge to stand on my desk and scream at everyone to just shut the hell up!

No one knows what happened to Skylar...and no one will until she wakes up and tells us.

Officer Malloy is still trying to piece things together, but apparently Wyatt doesn't know anything.

His attendance at school has been kind of iffy over the last week. I saw him one time and willed my courage not to fail as I approached him.

I started sweet. "How you doing?"

He flinched when he heard my voice and kind of leaned away from me, glancing over his shoulder like I was setting up to prank him.

"I just want to know if you saw anything that night," I murmured. "I know you like keeping tabs on her. I know you were on the beach after..." My voice trailed off as I gave him a pleading look.

He swallowed, his skin paling as he shook his head. "I didn't see. I didn't do anything. I didn't even touch her!" His voice broke as he shouted out the last few words.

"I didn't say you did." Raising my hands, I backed off a little, studying his agonized expression.

"Well, you're about the only one," he muttered, tears glassing his eyes as he spun and ran away from me.

I haven't seen him since and have to wonder if he even showed up to complete his exams.

Man, I hope he *was* telling me the truth. He seemed pretty torn up about it. Surely he didn't do anything to harm Skylar.

Ugh. This whole thing is such a nightmare. I'm not sure how much I can take.

Rounding the corner, my steps slow as I approach Skylar's room. I want to go in there. I do.

It's my turn for the day. I have things to tell her. She'll want to know about the senior pranks and how Patty Milton and Glen Parker were busted hooking up in the girls' locker room. She'll want to know that Craig stood up in front of everyone just before our final exam and sang a song in her honor, making some of the girls swoon and the guys all roll their eyes. It really pissed off Mrs. Baldwin too. That was actually kind of funny.

Sucking in a breath, I'm surprised by how glad I am that school is over for a while and I don't have to see Craig or listen to hallway gossip. Being at Walton without Skylar has been nothing but hard work. I miss hiding behind her, trailing her around, not having to think about where I'm going.

Now I've just got this big wide space in front of me and I'm not sure what to do with it. Or I don't have the courage to do anything with it.

With a self-deprecating sigh, I slump against the wall outside Skylar's room. Soft music is playing from the speaker beside her bed. I don't know when Marlo brought it in, but I think it's a great idea. I read that music is really great for coma patients.

"Get Up" by Shinedown is playing.

What a perfect choice.

My lips are just forming a smile when I hear a voice.

I don't recognize it at first, but as I peer around the corner, I know exactly who it is.

Anger flashes through me.

It's that cleaner again.

I told him not to be talking to Skylar. I should march to the nurses' station and report his ass right now. He shouldn't be harassing patients this way.

He shouldn't—

"…come back. There are people here who love and care about you. People who want to see your pretty smile again. I don't know what your voice sounds like, but I bet it's bright and brilliant."

My body relaxes as I hear his sweet words, take in his posture and the soft timbre of his voice.

He's holding a mop, picking at the end of the handle while he gazes down at Skylar. His voice sounds so genuine and sweet. There's nothing creepy about the way he's talking. Tugging on the edge of his uniform, he pulls the fabric over his rounded belly and grins. "So, I was halfway through telling you my story yesterday. You know, the one about that time my Gramma made me wear a shirt and tie to church. I think you're gonna like this one." He chuckles, then goes on to tell Skylar all about his fat little butt rebelling halfway through the service and ripping off the tie, which he then turned into a lasso.

I grin as his voice rises and falls with the story. He sure knows how to make it entertaining.

"So yeah, watching Gramma try to sing 'Amazing

Grace' when she's about ready to kill me has to be the funniest thing I've ever seen in my life. I would have laughed if I hadn't been ready to pee my pants. In the end, I was sent to my room for the afternoon. It wasn't so bad. She never made me wear one of those choking ties again." He wraps up his story with a satisfied sigh, then rests his chubby cheek against his hand.

I swallow, emotion coursing through me.

The way he's gazing down at Skylar makes my heart hurt again.

He wants her to wake up.

He doesn't even know her and he's coaxing her back to us, because maybe he can see it too.

People have never understood why I've stuck with Skylar. She can be a dominating bitch who likes to manipulate, meddle and control everything around her. But underneath all that crap is a thick layer of goodness. You just have to get close enough to see it. You just have to stick around long enough to find out how loyal she is, how she'll secretly go out of her way to do anything for you.

"I know life can be scary. And I know my church story isn't a very good one, but taking off that tie took a lot of courage. If I hadn't protested that day, I'd probably still be wearing ties to church every Sunday. But I took my stand and my Gramma, she heard me, you know? We can't hear you if you don't come back. And there's people here who really need ya."

Resting his mop against the end of the bed, he

reaches out as if he wants to brush his fingers down Skylar's arm, but he stops himself just in time. Curling his fingers into a loose fist, he gazes down at her and whispers, "I don't know what's keeping you trapped, but please, find whatever ounce of courage you've got buried in there and come home. Even if it's going to hurt for a bit, it'll be worth it in the end. You'll see."

I don't know what it is about his voice today, but that cleaner is touching something in my heart.

A soft smile tugs at my lips and I lean my head against the wall.

Courage.

Just a little bit.

That's all it's gonna take.

## 14

## 99¢ GUM AND A $20 DEAL

## SAVANNAH

"Courage," I whisper to myself as I park my car and stare at the Freshmart sign.

I've been back and forth on this all weekend, but I can't keep putting it off. I need to make a change in my life or I'm gonna go crazy.

Skylar still hasn't stirred. According to Dad, all her vitals are good. She just needs to wake up now. I watched the nurse work her muscles today. Held Marlo's hand through the entire process. She's holding up pretty well, although she's losing weight and the bags under her eyes are only getting darker.

I wish there was some way I could force Skylar back to us. But my words don't seem to be enough. No one's do.

So I had to get out.

I had to leave the hospital and hit the sunshine.

And now I'm here, in the parking lot of Freshmart. I hardly ever come to this grocery store, but when I checked out the beach before, Harley wasn't around. So, I'm on a hunt to find her. I know where her house is, at least I think I can remember where it is, but Freshmart seems like a safer bet somehow, so I'm trying here first.

The chances of Aidan being here are pretty low. And that's a good thing, because I don't want an audience when I tackle this conversation. I'm nervous enough as it is.

I actually heard Aidan got a job working with Griffin at the rental place. Jonah told me. None of his friends can understand why he'd take a summer job. It's not like he needs the money, but there it is. He's working, which means he and Harley won't be attached for like a microsecond.

If they're both at work right now, then this is my chance.

I have to take it.

Holding my breath, I march into the store before I can change my mind. A cold blast of air hits me as I walk past the fruits and vegetables. My eyes are darting to all the stripy shirts, my breath on hold as I scan for a petite blonde.

And then I see her.

She's in checkout number five. My teeth pinch the edge of my lip as I head in her direction. She hasn't seen me yet, and I'm kind of relieved; if we make eye contact before I reach her, there's a chance I'll chicken out and veer down the baking goods aisle.

*Just do it, Savannah!*

Stopping at her checkout, I impulsively snatch a packet of gum off the shelf and slap it down on the belt.

Harley kind of jumps, then looks up at me, her eyes bulging like I'm the last person she wants to talk to. I can only imagine what she must be thinking, but she's got it all wrong. I'm not here to beg for Aidan back, or to yell at her for taking my man.

I need her help.

*Shit, this is humiliating.*

The thought irritates me and my eyebrows dip into a V.

Harley stares at me, silent as a goldfish, her eyes darting to the gum packet before landing back on me.

*This is ridiculous! SAY something, Savannah!*

Resting my hands on the edge of the counter, I let out a sharp huff and snap, "We need to talk."

Harley seems kind of frightened by this, her cheeks paling in the middle. And that's when I realize how intimidating I must look. To her, I'm her boyfriend's ex. A stranger who has marched up to her, looking pissed off and ready for a fight.

I swallow and take a step back from the counter. I don't know what to do with my hands, so I end up linking my fingers and blurting out the truth in double-time. "Dad says I need a hobby and I was thinking surfing. It looks like fun, and I really need to do something totally different to anything I've done before."

There's this long, dead beat of silence.

Harley's lips part, her eyebrows rising as she gapes at me.

Is she going to make me repeat myself?

"Um…" She licks her lips, the edges of her mouth curling as if she's about to smile.

I frown at her. "What?"

"Uh…" She shakes her head and struggles to speak. "Can… can you swim?"

"Of course I can swim!" I flick my arms up. They smack back down onto my thighs and I'm now thinking this is a big mistake. I should turn and split.

"I mean, strong enough that if you wipe out you can get to the surface again. Strong enough to battle a wave."

"Oh." I cross my arms and look down at my lone packet of gum on the belt.

Harley's tone is serious. I glance at her face to confirm that I'm right. She's not laughing in my face, she's actually being legit.

I clear my throat. "Well…" I fidget with my earring and force my head to bob up and down. "Yeah, I'm strong enough. I've been swimming my whole life. I mean, I'm no Aidan, but I can hold my own."

"Okay." Harley reaches for my gum. I wait in silent agony for her to say more.

She doesn't.

She just scans the packet, the beep sounding loud and intrusive. She rests it on the counter within easy reach of my hand, then starts nibbling her thumbnail.

Frustration bred from humiliation and doubt makes me snap, "Look, I can pay you, if that helps."

Why did I just say that?

Do I really want lessons that badly?

Why am I doing this?

I could just go home right now. Bury myself in a book and forget the whole thing.

Wriggling my toes in my sandals, I can feel my body rejecting that idea. I want the summer breeze on my face, the warmth on my skin, the sound of the water. It's all so appealing.

I want to try this.

I want to be a surfer chick.

Harley glances up at me, obviously checking to see that I'm serious.

"So, you'll do it?" I ask.

"Um...yeah, I mean, I guess." She cringes. "This isn't some rich kid prank or anything though, right? Like other people aren't putting you up to this just so you can slay me later?"

"What?" I'm shocked by this. I would never do something like that. I let out a slightly surprised and insulted laugh before shaking my head. "Okay, you've obviously watched too many high school movies. I just want your help. I need to destress. I need a hobby! Out of all the hobbies I can think of, this is the only one with slight appeal."

"Destress." Harley swallows. "I'm kind of sensing that."

"Well, you seem relaxed." I wave my hand at her. "Aidan's chilled out big-time. Seems uber happy. So, maybe it's the surfing!" I wince, well aware that it's probably way more than the surfing.

It kind of stings that I wasn't good enough to win him back.

It hurts that the fire died between us because we weren't the right match. Because Harley was out there somewhere—the better fit, the right girl.

My sadness is distracted by the smile on Harley's face. It's not a mean, triumphant one. It's genuine and beautiful...excited. "Surfing *is* the best thing in the world."

"Oh yeah?" I brush a lock of hair off my face. "So prove it, then. Teach me."

She chuckles, raising her eyebrows and biting her bottom lip. "All right. You can borrow my longboard to start. If you like it, you'll need to buy your own board or hire one from Mr. Dreads."

My face no doubt turns pink, my body tingling at even the mention of dreadlocks. She must be referring to Griffin. Any excuse to talk to him is a good one.

Her eyes narrow slightly, and I clear my throat, lifting my chin to hide my crush. "What else?"

"I charge twenty dollars a lesson."

"Fine." I nod.

"And you need to meet me on the beach at five thirty tomorrow morning."

"What?" I squeak and stare at her like she's insane.

Because she is insane.

Five freaking thirty?

She laughs at my no doubt incredulous expression. "At this time of year, it's the only time the beach will be empty, unless you want an audience for those initial lessons."

I cringe.

*This is a bad idea, Sav. Back out. Back out now!*

Harley shrugs and points to the screen in front of her. "That'll be ninety-nine cents for the gum."

"The gum?" I blink at her. "Oh, the gum." I pull out my wallet and hunt in the coin section for the right change. I end up paying her in dimes and pennies.

She gathers them into her hand with a little sigh and counts them out before dropping them into the right compartments of her cash drawer. Grabbing the receipt, she passes it over and says, "Look, I'll be there tomorrow in the middle point between the lifeguard chair and the pier. I guess if you show up that means you really want this."

"Will Aidan be there?" I cringe.

Harley grins at me. "Aidan will probably show up around seven. Now that school's over, he wants to sleep in for a change."

"But you'll still get up?"

"For you." She nods, then winks at me. "And twenty bucks." She tucks a lock of hair behind her ear, then crosses her arms. She looks so incredibly cool and sporty, even in her Freshmart shirt. I can't help but admire her.

"Thank you," I murmur.

She laughs. "Don't thank me until you've tried it."

"You think I'm gonna hate it?" I scratch the side of my nose. "You think I'll be bad?"

She gazes at me for a long beat then smiles. "I don't know a person in the world who has tried surfing and hated it. As soon as you catch your first wave, you're gonna be addicted." Her eyes travel up and down my body. "We'll make a surfer chick out of you yet, Savannah Green. Trust me."

And for some weird reason, I do.

## 15

## ONE WORD: DANGEROUS

## GRIFFIN

There's something about the fresh morning air that I love.

I think it's the cool crispness of it. The fact that it feels untainted by the day—it's trouble-free and refreshing.

That's the main reason I get my ass up each day and go for a run. For one, it gets me out of the house, and secondly, exercise is the best way to energize my body.

I start at the north end and jog along the hard-packed sand. My muscles are still complaining, but they'll get used to it soon, and by the time I'm done, my blood will be pumping and I'll feel great. A smile twitches my lips as I pound through the initial pain and find my rhythm.

I'm guessing it'll be a full-on day at Ryder Rentals.

It was great having Aidan to help me out yesterday. Now that summer is kicking in, it's only going to get busier. That's why Marshall hired me, and I'm grateful for the gig. It should see me out for a couple of months.

He's still trying to persuade me to think about life-guarding as a career. I'm not sure. Rescuing Savannah's little brother was satisfying, but I can't see how I'll ever make it. I don't even have the educational require-ments, and although I could probably pay a guy to forge all that stuff for me, do I even want to?

Lifeguarding. I love the idea, but there's something kind of permanent about it and I just don't know if I should. All that training only to have to split in the night. It's probably not even worth it.

I frown and push a little harder, picking up my pace as I try to dodge the reality of my life. The fact that I can never settle anywhere. The fact that I've gotta keep running. Most of the time I try not to let it bother me, but there are some days where it really eats away at me.

Today is one of them.

And the eating is the angry kind, the resentful kind that I can't let fester.

I will not feel sorry for myself. I will not blame my brother for being an asshole.

Yes, I felt forced to run, but it was still my choice.

"My choice," I mutter, not willing to give that power away.

Focusing on my breathing, I try to just be in the

moment—feel the early morning breeze on my face, smell the salt of the water, feel the sand give way beneath each footfall. I gaze out to the horizon. It's going to be a scorcher of a day. Clear blue sky and an unrelenting sun. I'll be pushing the sunblock today. Marshall just got a couple of new boxes in. I'll make sure they're front and center on the counter.

I jog past the lifeguard chair and glance up at the wooden structure, wondering what it'd be like to sit up there. The view would be pretty decent. I nearly stop to have a go, but I don't want to throw off my pace. Instead, I keep my eyes ahead and spot something I didn't expect to see.

My step nearly falters, but I catch myself before falling.

Two girls are out in the water. I recognize Harley right away, but it takes me a second to work out that the girl on the longboard is Savannah.

She's attempting to stand, but I can tell even from this distance how nervous she is. Her legs wobble, her arms flailing as she falls off the board and crashes into the water.

She rises back to the surface, spluttering and wiping her face.

"You nearly got up that time!" Harley yells. "That's awesome! Try again."

"I don't think I'm gonna get this," Savannah argues.

"Yes you are. I'm not letting you quit. We haven't even done a full hour yet. Get your butt back out here."

Harley waves her over and Savannah starts pushing the board back out a little deeper.

She hasn't noticed me yet and I'm kind of glad for it. I don't want to embarrass her. Learning to surf can make you feel like an idiot. It took me two full days to catch my first wave, but once I got my technique right, I was away. I spent every spare second that I wasn't working surfing those Mexican beaches and loving it.

I hope Savannah doesn't give up. I want her to experience that same life-changing thrill.

As much as I want to plant my feet in the sand and watch her, I force myself to keep running. I'm not allowed to stop until I've slapped my hand on a pier pole. Then I'll give myself a second to catch my breath before jogging back to the north end.

I'll be a sweaty mess, but I'll dive into the water at the north end and go for a short swim before facing the rest of the day.

I hear laughter behind me and have to resist the urge to peek over my shoulder. The girls sound like they're having fun, and once again I find myself in awe of Savannah. I don't know who initiated the surfing lessons, but it takes guts to spend time with your ex-boyfriend's new squeeze.

Harley's a really cool chick though, and I'm glad Savannah is hanging out with good people.

I wish I could be one of them, but that's not likely to happen.

It doesn't matter how badly I might want something. It's not right. I can't afford to go hanging out with a hot chick whose eyes and smile make my insides turn to putty.

There's only one word for it: dangerous.

And I can't afford to put myself in a position of not being able to leave at a moment's notice.

# 16

# EMPOWERMENT

## SAVANNAH

I've been out here for over an hour and I still haven't caught one wave.

I'm not sure surfing is going to be my thing.

Aidan will be showing up soon, and I want to be gone before he arrives. I don't want him thinking I'm trying to sabotage his relationship or win him back. That would be so humiliating.

I'm still hurting a little, and when I do eventually see him, it'll probably suck, but the only reason I asked Harley for help is because she's the only surfer I know.

Well, there is Griffin, but I'm not about to embarrass myself in front of him. I'd be mortified if he saw me trying and failing to catch a wave.

"I think I should probably call it quits," I yell to

Harley, sensing the building busyness on the beach behind me.

"What?" She frowns and starts paddling toward me. "You can't give up now. You're so close."

"But I'm not getting it."

She sits up on her board and gives me a pointed look. "You're not leaving until you've caught one wave, even if it's just for ten seconds."

I grimace and have to fight the urge to whine like a little kid. "But Aidan will be here soon."

"Then you better get on with it."

"We've gone over our hour."

Harley snickers. "I won't charge you extra. Now come on. You're catching a ride if it kills me."

"But—"

"Get moving!" She cuts me off like a drill sergeant, and I've got no choice but to push the board back out until I'm waist-deep in the water.

Harley smirks at my scowl, then points out in the distance. "There's a set coming. I can feel it. Get yourself ready."

With a reluctant sigh, I make sure the board is facing the right way, then jump onto it. I nearly topple off the other side but manage to right myself and stay centered on the board.

"Here we go, here we go." Harley jumps off her board and wades over to me.

Gripping the edge of the longboard, she keeps her

eyes on the water while going over what I have to do again.

"Okay, start paddling."

I do as she tells me, my tired arms moaning.

"Go, go, go. Push until you feel it catch you."

I concentrate, carving my arms through the water until I feel the board lift slightly beneath me.

"Now stand!" Harley yells.

With a nervous kind of wail, I turn my ankle like she showed me, plant my front foot on the board and then pop up, keeping my knees bent. I wobble off balance, flailing my arms and nearly falling off again, but I grip my toes to the board and force my body back in line…

And I'm riding a wave.

I gasp, shocked that I've managed to stay centered.

"You're doing it!" Harley shouts behind me.

I nearly lose my balance as a laugh scuttles out of me.

I'm doing it.

I'm riding a wave!

A delighted scream punches out of my mouth as I stay upright, feeling the water carry me forward. The wave is starting to die out and my ride will soon be over, but it's enough.

I rode a wave!

And I loved it!

As the wave disintegrates into the shore, I jump off

the board and spin around to see Harley racing toward me.

"You did it!" Her smile is huge, and I just can't help myself.

As soon as she's within reach, I wrap my arms around her and hold tight. "I did it! Thank you!"

She laughs and awkwardly pats my back. "No problem." She pulls out of my grasp and steps back, crossing her arms with a grin. "Can't wait to see you do it again."

I squeal and jump on the spot, nearly telling her I'll head back out right now.

But I don't want Aidan to see me.

It'll be too awkward and weird.

At least I think it will.

He'll find out soon enough. That's inevitable. But I'd like to keep my first lesson ex-boyfriend free.

Harley glances over her shoulder, like she can read my mind or something. "You probably better get going if you're worried about Aidan showing up. He'll be here soon."

"Yeah." I nod and give her an embarrassed smile.

"You know he's going to find out eventually, right?"

"Yeah." I sigh.

She snickers. "If you fall for surfing the way I have, you won't care who knows. All you'll care about is being out in the water."

My lips rise into a broad smile. "Same time tomorrow?"

"You got it." She winks at me, then heads back out to the waves.

Rushing up the beach, I drop her longboard next to her bag and, after drying off, slip a twenty into the front pouch. We exchanged numbers before the lesson started, so I'll text her to let her know where I left the money.

Grabbing the rest of my things, I start walking up the beach, then take off running when I notice Aidan appear at the top of the stairs, near Ryder Rentals.

Changing direction, I head north and decide to run/walk home along the sand. Hopefully Aidan's eyes will be on the water, checking out his surfer girl rather than noticing my retreat.

I'm still kind of sad that he's not mine anymore, but Griffin's words really rang true for me. Aidan and I weren't meant to be. Yes, that leaves me out in the cold, but I don't feel so chilly today.

I surfed a freaking wave.

A smile takes over my face as I relive that empowering feeling.

Harley's so right. If I can keep catching waves like that, all I'm gonna care about is getting out there on the water, no matter who sees me.

# 17

## STEP BACK

### GRIFFIN

Savannah has been at the beach every day this week, practicing. Practicing. Practicing.

She is one determined chick.

I've been subtly watching her, falling just a little further each time she laughs, whoops or smiles. Falling just a little harder each time she wipes out and rises, coughing and spluttering, only to get back on the board again.

I love that she's not quitting.

And each day, she's getting just a little better.

Harley's given her so much time but seems to be loving the gig. Aidan offers her services to every single person who rents a surfboard, and he's managed to score her two new clients this week alone.

"At this rate she can quit Freshmart soon. She'll be

stoked." Aidan had the biggest grin when he said that. It's obvious how much he cares about his girlfriend, and how much he likes looking after her.

He nearly fell over a few days ago when he spotted Harley and Savannah working together.

"What are they doing?"

I snickered and crossed my arms, planting my feet in the sand and enjoying the chance to openly watch them. "Your girlfriend is teaching your ex to surf, man."

His expression cracked me up. I laughed so hard I scored a punch in the arm.

I guess it would be kind of weird, but for some reason Harley and Savannah seem to be getting along great. I credit Savannah for that. It must have taken so much courage for her to get over herself and ask Harley for help. Yet another thing to like about her.

I frown and turn back to the shed.

"Don't like her, man. Watch yourself," I mutter under my breath.

Aidan left work a couple of hours ago. He and Harley had a date, and by this time of day, the traffic for Ryder Rentals really slows down anyway. The last customer returned his board about ten minutes ago, so I focus on counting the stock and making sure everything is in its place, filing the signed disclosure forms, and locking up the cash. I'll need to take it up to Devon at the main building and make sure it's safe for the night.

I do that first, making a quick run up before returning to properly lock and secure the gear.

Just as I'm walking out the shed door, I spot Savannah trotting down the beach. She's dragging the yellow longboard behind her.

I glance past her to see where Harley is, but there's no sign of the blonde surfer girl.

With a slight frown, I check that the door's secure. I hope Savannah's not planning to surf alone. She may only be riding the peewee waves, but I still don't think anyone should surf alone. The lifeguards aren't even on duty at this time of day. All it takes is one bad wipeout. You could get hurt, hit your head—anything could happen that would stop you from rising to the surface.

I'm surprised Harley has happily loaned out her board without even being around.

Date night has obviously taken precedence...and maybe a little of her brainpower. I'll have to talk to Aidan tomorrow, pass on the message that Harley shouldn't be letting her clients surf alone.

Once the building is secure, and I've checked the back window as well, I walk around to watch Savannah. I won't get in her way; I'll just watch her from a distance to make sure she's all right. I'm sure she doesn't want me muscling in on her session.

When she spotted me yesterday—the one time I just could not drag my eyes away from her—her cheeks went bright red and she quickly looked out to the horizon. I don't know what I did to embarrass her, but I felt kind of bad about it, so I put in a concerted effort to look at anything but her for the rest of the afternoon.

It was really hard.

Clearing my throat, I get busy tying my dreads into a ponytail while scanning the surf for Savannah.

That's when I spot something that makes my stomach curdle.

There's no way I'm going to be able to watch from a distance now.

That guy from Hatchet Cove—I asked around and found out that people call him Ripper—is standing right next to Savannah, saying who knows what. He skims his fingers down her arm and she shies away from his touch. The awkward look on her face tells me she's not interested in whatever he's proposing. The leering smile on his face and the way his hungry eyes are undressing her sparks an instant anger in my chest.

Damn, he reminds me of Phoenix. Guys like that seem to walk and breathe intimidation and dominance, like it's part of their DNA. But Ripper has something else too, this creepy, lusty vibe that grosses me out.

Savannah tries to turn away and walk into the water, but he stops her. The second his large hand wraps around her upper arm, I'm sprinting.

As soon as my feet hit the water, I force myself to walk the last yard. The salty spray splashes my ankles as I breathe deep and try to control my inner trembling.

I need to be calm.

My anger will only spark his.

I need to come in strong and resolute, not feisty.

Ripper hasn't seen me yet, and he actually flinches when I appear on Savannah's left and quietly order, "Step back."

His head jerks in my direction, and I eyeball him, refusing to back down.

I'm not afraid.

I may be shorter than this guy, and he may be stronger than me, but I learned to fight for survival in juvie, and that kind of skill outweighs size and power.

Ripper's upper lip curls. "This is a private conversation."

"This is a finished conversation," I retort, stealing a quick glance at Savannah.

Her arm is still trapped within Ripper's grip, and I can tell she wants him to leave her the hell alone.

"Let her go." I move in a little closer and rest my hand on Savannah's lower back, silently letting her know that I'm not walking away from this one. I've got her.

She shoots me a grateful look and makes it a million times easier to stand my ground.

"Dude, let her go or this is going to get ugly." I don't like using threatening words. Guys like Ripper rise to that kind of thing.

His eyes narrow as he sizes me up. I refuse to break eye contact. I am seriously not afraid, and I think he can sense it.

With a little growl, he lets Savannah go and steps back.

"Stay away from her," I warn him.

"She's not your property, asshole."

"She's not yours either." I glare at him. "And if I see you talking to her again, I won't be so damn polite."

With another lip curl and a snarl, he spins and stalks off.

I drop my hand off Savannah's back and give her a little space, not taking my eyes off Ripper as he heads south. His fists are curling in and out and I'm pretty sure he'd like to beat the hell out of me, but he probably won't do that without his crew for support. God forbid he gets a bloody nose.

Man, I'd love to give him one.

But I'm glad I didn't get the chance.

Even the conversation we just had could come back to bite me on the ass.

Glancing down at Savannah, I catch her eye and give her a soft smile. She returns the look and I instantly know it was worth it.

Even if it got my ass thoroughly kicked, I'd stand up for her again in a heartbeat.

# 18

# THE MOST FUN

## SAVANNAH

Thank God for Griffin.

My insides are shaking like a series of minor earthquakes are rippling through me. One aftershock after another. Crew Cut creeps me out. He may be tall and muscly, but his inner sleaze makes him the ugliest guy I've ever seen.

I think back to Skylar's party and the way he was all over my best friend. I tried to warn her away from the guy, but she was drunk and wouldn't listen to me. So instead, I found a perch on a rock and watched her make an absolute fool of herself.

I'll always regret leaving her that night, letting her slink off into the shadows with Mr. Hands and get up to who knows what. I should have stayed, been her wingman, even though she told me she didn't want me. I've learned to take Skylar's pissyness with a grain of salt, especially when she's drunk, but it hurt that night, so I asked Aidan to walk me home.

But I should have stayed.

Skylar was never the same after that party, and I can't stop wondering if something happened that night. Something that crossed even her line. I've been too afraid to tell anyone that. I don't want everyone assuming the worst about my best friend. They do that already without my help. I can't bad-mouth her while she's in a coma and unable to defend herself. I'm desperate for Sky to wake up and tell us what the hell happened.

What if she and Mr. Hands did have sex at the party? What if he wanted more and coaxed her to the pier? What if she had a change of heart and he got pissy the way Craig did, but rather than a screaming match, he pushed her?

I shudder at the thought, but Griffin distracts me, his hand skimming down my back. "You know you should never surf alone."

I shrug, keeping my eyes on my sandy, wet feet and trying to hide the blush that is no doubt storming my face. "Harley does it all the time. Besides, I need all the practice I can get."

"I get that, but it's more fun with company. And a hell of a lot safer."

I glance up in time to see his smile and feel my insides quake some more. But in a good way this time.

Damn, his smile is so gorgeous.

I've been spying on him every time I come to the beach, admiring the way his body moves, the way he interacts with people. I haven't been able to hear what he's saying, but his smile always comes readily. He has a relaxed style about him. The way he stands and moves. He just seems unfazable. I wish I could be that cool.

He's gazing at me now, his dark brown eyes trying to read my mind.

I give him a half-smile and decide to be brave. "You want to come join me, then? I'm pretty sure surfing with you would be safe."

His lips twitch with a smile as he scans the beach up and down, then looks over his shoulder at the shed. After a long beat where I manage to convince myself that he's going to say no, he bobs his head and agrees. "Let me grab a board."

I wait in the water, watching him unlock the shed and pull a board out. It's shorter than the massive long one Harley has loaned me. She's been so super nice to me over this whole thing. I like her a lot more than I'm willing to admit. I'm trying to keep her in the surf instructor zone, but my heart wants to make her my friend.

Which is so weird.

She's Aidan's girlfriend!

But I can't help liking her spirit. Her passion for surfing is contagious, and her sunshine smile is heart-warming. It's been cool hanging out with someone I don't have to check myself around all the time. I'm not worried that she'll criticize or tell me off. I can just be Savannah—the girl who's learning to surf. It's an easy gig.

Griffin leans the surfboard against the shed, then locks the door.

And then he takes his T-shirt off.

My mouth dries up like the Sahara and I couldn't look away if I wanted to.

He's ripped.

Not in that big, bulky, I-live-at-the-gym kind of way. Just in a sporty, I'm-a-physical-guy kind of way. And damn if it isn't hells sexy.

He notices me gawking at him and gives me a friendly smile as he tucks the board under his arm and comes to join me. His blue-and-green board shorts match the bright green of the board he's borrowing, and I'm pretty sure I'd be happy to just gape at him for the rest of my life.

"Shall we do this?" He stops beside me and I'm suddenly aware of his height, his strength, his manly smell.

I wonder how old he is?

I feel like asking would be dumb, so I just give him a closed-mouth smile and nod.

"All right. Let's go."

I follow him out into the water, raising my knees to get over the baby waves, before lowering my board and pushing it out until I'm waist-deep.

And then the fun begins.

As I focus on the waves and catching them, my nerves start to ease, and I'm transported into that place Harley always talks about—sensing the energy in the water and being one with the board.

It's easy to forget about everything else when you're doing something so thrilling and all-consuming.

I grip my toes and lean forward just a little, letting the wave carry me. It's a sweet, straight ride into shore. As I jump off, I spin to see what Griffin's up to. He caught a wave out a little deeper and is carving it up with little twists and snaps that give away how good he is.

I wonder how long he's been surfing for.

I wonder who taught him.

I wonder a lot about the guy.

He jumps off the board, splashing into the water and ending his run. As his dreads pop back into view, he starts looking for me. I wave my hand to acknowledge him and his beautiful smile appears.

Grabbing my board, I race back out to join him again.

I'm aware the sun is going to set soon.

I'm aware that I should be heading home to my family.

But I'm having way too much fun to stop now.

Griffin is sweet and easy to be around. I'm not about to walk away from the most fun I've had in a really long time.

# 19

# A SUNSET INSIDE THE BODY

## GRIFFIN

As the light starts to fade, I wrap up the surfing session.

I don't want to be surfing in the dark.

Savannah seems disappointed when I tell her and then start to walk out of the water. I get it. I've been having fun too. Watching her enthusiasm, listening to her laughter...it's been a sweet afternoon.

She's got grit, albeit in a quiet way. But she's stronger than she thinks she is, and I love that about her. I love that she doesn't know how amazing she is. That's a weird thing to think, but it gives her a humility that makes her even more beautiful.

I wipe down the surfboard and store it back in the shed. Marshall said I can use them when I'm off duty. A perk of the job. I make sure it's returned exactly as I pulled it out before locking up the shed.

The sun will set soon, and the sky is looking brilliant, streaks of orange and pink flaring out from the horizon. It's casting a golden glow onto the beach and making Savannah's body shine.

She glances up from drying off and gives me an impish smile.

So cute.

"Do you need a towel?" she asks, holding hers out.

"Nah, I'm good. I'll just drip dry." I walk back to her and perch on the end of Harley's longboard, resting my feet on the sand.

Thankfully it's not too cold. My body should be dry by the time darkness envelops us, and I still have my dry T-shirt to throw on once that happens.

Savannah wraps the towel around her shoulders and takes a seat beside me.

"That was awesome. Thank you so much for joining me. I had fun."

I grin at her. "You seemed to be having fun."

"It's so weird, you know? Because I've never been a huge fan of the water. I mean, my parents made me learn how to swim because I live by the beach, but in the last couple years, I only tend to come here to sunbathe. I never usually get in. But surfing brings a whole new dimension to it." Her dimples appear as she shakes her head, gazing out at the ocean and suddenly going quiet.

I nudge her gently with my elbow. "You okay?"

"Just thinking about Skylar." She picks up a shell and starts drawing patterns beneath her bent knees. "She was my tanning buddy."

"And now she's in a coma," I murmur, making sure I've got the right person.

"Yep." Savannah bobs her head repeatedly and lets out a heavy sigh. "I really hate hospitals. When my mom got sick a few years back, we had to spend a lot of time in them, and Sky would always make it better, you know? She'd come with me and make up games to pass the time."

My gut clenches as a thought hits me—is her mom dead?

I swallow and have to know. "What was wrong with your mom?"

"Cancer," she whispers. "It just ripped right through her. From stomachaches to dead in less than a year." Her lips wobble as she tries to give me a sad smile.

I rub my hand down her back, trying to comfort her. Wishing I knew what to say.

"That's rough," I croak.

"She was a really beautiful person. Left this gaping hole, and I thought I could manage it, you know? I've been trying to manage it, but now Sky's where Mom was and if she doesn't wake up…" She bites her lips together.

"She'll wake up," I reassure her.

She gives me a worried frown, then rests her chin

on her knees, wrapping her arms around her legs and kind of rocking back on her butt.

"And then you can teach her how to surf. Soon enough, this beach will be overrun with gorgeous surfer girls."

This makes her chuckle and I feel like I've just won a gold star.

She smiles at me and I'm struck again by how pretty she is. Pretty and sweet.

"Where'd you learn to surf?" she asks, and I'm grateful that I can answer the question.

I perch my elbows on my knees and stare at the water while I talk. "Mexico. I met a guy down there who took me under his wing and taught me everything he knew." My voice grows thick as I think of Pedro and how I'll never see him again. It hurts. It sucks. But I guess his death brought me here, and maybe I should be grateful for that. I glance at Savannah's pretty face and can hear Pedro's voice in my head.

*"All things work for good if you let them. It's all about perspective. Do you want to focus on the bad or the good? What you don't have or what you do have?"*

"I bet you picked it up fast." Savannah's dimples appear and I study the shape of her face, memorize the nutmeg color of her eyes, then give her a modest smile.

"It did take me a couple days to actually get up on the board, but after that I was away."

She grins and nudges me with her elbow. "What were you doing in Mexico?"

My insides rattle, nerves kicking in as I enter the dangerous part of the conversation. I have to check myself before I say anything, not wanting to give my past away. "Working." I nod.

"And how long ago was that?"

"Uh…" Scratching my scalp, I rearrange my dreads. "Not too long ago. I worked at a couple of resorts before I decided to come back."

"Are you originally from California?"

It's an innocent question that I should be able to answer with confidence, but all I manage is a small headshake.

"So where are you from, then?"

Why the hell didn't I just say yes to California? My ID is California-based. I'm such a freaking idiot.

Truth is, I *am* from California, but I just don't want to have to elaborate on where. That's what she'll ask next. She'll want to know which city I was born in, where I was raised. I can't tell her any of that stuff.

Clearing my throat, I put on a smile, but shake my head again.

Her forehead wrinkles with confusion.

Shit, now I have to explain.

Fudging as best I can, I go for vague. "I travel around a lot. I don't really have a solid base, so to speak. I'm not from anywhere."

"Right." She still looks confused, but maybe she senses not to probe too hard.

My jaw is clenched, my muscles are wound tight. I'm no doubt oozing *don't ask* vibes.

Clearing her throat, she picks her shell back up and resumes her sand drawing. "So, you're a bit of a nomad."

"Yep." I thread my fingers together and tap my thumbs against each other. "I like to keep moving."

"I wonder why," she murmurs, but doesn't outright ask.

I'm grateful that she lets me get away with not saying. Like I can tell her that I ran away from foster care after a stint in juvie. That my psycho brother is an ever-present danger in the back of my mind, and how I constantly worry that my ID won't hold up and I'll get busted and sent back to Vallejo.

"You have any family?"

My shoulders deflate as she steals my relief with another innocent question. I hedge and keep it brief. "I used to, but not anymore."

"Did they die?" she barely whispers.

"Um." I lick my lips, then croak, "Mom died when I was just a kid and well…I'm pretty sure I'm dead to… to the rest of my family, so yeah, metaphorically, they died."

"Wow," she murmurs. "There's a big story there."

I bob my head, then give her a pained grimace. "Can't tell you. Sorry, I just… I never talk about it."

"That's okay." Her smile is sweet and way too understanding.

Resting her hand on my arm, she gives my bicep a gentle squeeze and then surprises the hell out of me. She should be getting up and walking away, but instead, she leans her head against my shoulder and lets out a contented sigh.

"It's so peaceful, isn't it?"

I breathe in through my nose and silently agree with her. With the waves gently lapping onto the shore, the sun setting, a few people ambling along the beach... there's no tension. No fear. Just calm contentment.

I close my eyes and relish the emotion, soaking in it.

"How old are you?" she murmurs.

A smile curls the edges of my lips. I wish I could tell her the truth, but instead I lie and tell her the age on my Griffin Ayala ID. "Twenty-one."

She doesn't respond, and I wonder what she's thinking.

Clearing my throat, I figure I'll break the tension with my own question. "How old are you?"

She sits up and grins at me. "Seventeen. One more year of school to go." She purses her lips, then gives me a sad smile. "It's strange how I sometimes feel so much older than seventeen though. Since Mom died, I've been forced into this weird pseudo-adult life. Trying to be a mother to my siblings and a support for my dad. Sometimes I feel like a full-blown adult, but then other days I feel like a kid playing pretend."

The light hits the edge of her cheek, illuminating

her beautiful, smooth skin, and I have to touch it. Tracing my fingers lightly down the curve, I brush her right dimple and whisper, "There's nothing pretend about you."

Her gaze jumps to mine, and I hold it, drinking in those pale brown eyes. Damn, she's beautiful the whole way through. I can sense her good soul, feel my heart being pulled toward it.

I need to back out.

Back out now.

But then she leans in.

It's just an inch at first. Lean in. Pause. Hesitate.

Skimming her tongue against the edge of her mouth, she brushes her teeth over her bottom lip, then leans in again.

I should move back. Away.

But I can't.

My fingers are glued to the side of her face; I can't let go. All I can do is trail them around her cheek until they're resting on the nape of her neck.

She's close now, our lips only an inch apart.

The tip of her nose skims against mine and I can't pull away now.

As soon as our lips connect, I touch the edges of heaven. Her mouth is soft and supple, her taste a salty sweetness that warms me all the way through. It's like the sunset is suddenly inside of me, lighting the edges of my dark, gray mass with streaks of pink and orange.

She wiggles on the board, inching closer as I lightly dig my fingers into her neck, grasping the back and not wanting to let go.

But I should.

I have to pull away.

Her lips part, the tip of her tongue seeking mine, and I give it to her, needing a deeper taste. I only give myself the smallest nibble, but it's like tasting chocolate for the first time. Her tongue is warm and it's tempting to dive right in. To spend the rest of our time together lost in this addictive dance.

But I have to pull back.

Forcing my brain to override my instinct, I ease out of the kiss, softening the move with a gentle smile.

She grins back at me, her cheeks tinging pink in the dying light.

I snap a mental picture of her, something I can keep with me forever.

Because I can't kiss her again.

If I let myself go, I'll want more and more. I'll want to hold her hand and meet up with her any chance I can get. I'll want to be her boyfriend and call her my own.

And I can't do that to her.

To myself.

I told her I was twenty-one. I shouldn't be kissing or dating a seventeen-year-old. Just because I'm really eighteen doesn't make it okay. As far as my ID's concerned, I'm playing with molten fire right now.

Besides, I live a temporary life for a reason. I can't have anything permanent in it. And I've got the feeling that if I let her, Savannah would burrow her way into the center of my heart, making it impossible to walk away when I need to.

## 20

## COLLIDING OCEANS

### SAVANNAH

I float home from the beach.

Griffin's kiss is still tingling on my lips as I park my car next to Dad's and hum my way into the house. I feel like twirling. I can't stop smiling.

All I can hear is Griffin's soft voice warming my brain, his slightly rough hand gripping the back of my neck. Perfect pressure.

And his lips.

Oh man, his lips!

He tasted amazing.

I wish he hadn't pulled back. I wish he'd initiated another kiss, but it was probably the right thing to do.

I left about ten minutes later. Well, I tried to. He helped me carry the longboard up to my car, and we then spent the next hour saying goodbye.

He leaned against my car, his ankles crossed as we talked about everything from hot dogs—he doesn't like mustard either—to his time in Mexico to how I came to live in Ryder Bay.

I could have stayed there all night talking to him.

He's so different to the guys at Walton. There's a depth to him, a maturity that comes from not being raised as an entitled rich kid. I don't know what he's suffered in his past, but he definitely has suffered. I steered clear of my curiosity. Talking about painful histories can be hard. I've learned to talk about Mom because it's helped me process, but some people don't work that way, and Griffin is obviously like that.

I can respect that.

If and when he's ready, he'll tell me.

A smile blooms over my face as I imagine future conversations. If I'm lucky enough, I may even score a date or two.

The thought makes me giggle.

I can't believe how wonderful I feel. A warm, buzzing energy is taking over my body, my heart, my mind. I'm crushing big-time and it feels so freaking good. I don't remember feeling this way with Aidan. I know I shouldn't compare, but there's something about Griffin that has captured me in a way nothing ever has before.

"Savannah!" I flinch at Dad's sharp bark and let out a small gasp. "Where have you been?"

He looks tired, his hair disheveled, his T-shirt stained in the middle.

"Have you been cooking dinner?" I point at his shirt.

"Dinner has come and gone, young lady. I'm now doing the dishes. *Where* have you been?"

"Uh…" I blink, trying to figure out why he's so annoyed with me. Dad never gets annoyed with me.

"You know I don't mind you being out, but you could at least have the courtesy to keep me in the loop. I've texted you four times and heard nothing in response. I was starting to get really worried! And I didn't even know where to start looking for you. You weren't at the hospital. You've broken up with Aidan, so I knew you weren't with him!"

"Dad." I raise my hands, trying to calm him down. "I'm sorry. I didn't get any of your texts."

Rummaging in my bag, I pull out my phone and notice the battery has died. Crap, I never let that happen. Griffin was more of a distraction than I realized.

My lips want to smile, but I force them into line so I can make things right with my dad.

"My battery died." I show him. "I'm really sorry."

He sighs and calls me to his side with a flick of his hand. Wrapping his arm around my shoulders, he kisses my forehead and mumbles, "At least you're home safe now."

I squeeze his waist, then pull back, grateful that he's being so nice about it.

"Come on, help me finish up the dishes and you can tell me what you've been doing."

Following him into the kitchen, I place my bag on the floor and try to figure out how much to say. I'm not going to lie, but do I go for full disclosure?

Grabbing the dishtowel off the oven door handle, I start drying the Tupperware while Dad continues washing. It won't take long—all the plates, glasses and cutlery are in the dishwasher.

"Did Rosalie not come today?"

"I sent her home early. She's got a cold but came anyway to cook us dinner. As soon as I saw her, I ordered her home to bed."

"Poor thing."

"At least it's Saturday tomorrow. She can take the weekend to recover. The woman is such a hard worker. We're lucky to have her."

"I know," I murmur, dropping the dried container into the plastics drawer.

"So, other than promising me that you'll never let your phone battery die again, tell me what you've been doing."

I snicker and promise, "I won't let my battery die again." Clearing my throat, I grab another container and start drying, hoping to sound casual enough as I admit, "I was doing my hobby."

He turns to me with narrowed eyes. "Surfing? Again?"

This makes me laugh. "You told me to find a hobby! And I seriously love it."

"You've just been doing it so much this week." His eyebrows rise, like he's stoked his child has actually done something he suggested.

Biting the corner of my lip, I drop the container into the drawer and quickly say, "You have to practice *a lot* to get better."

"Surfing." He stops washing and glances over his shoulder. "That's seriously the last thing I thought you'd go for."

I can't help a smile.

Dad grins at my expression. "And who's teaching you again?"

"A girl from the beach. Harley. Aidan's girlfriend."

I wince when his smile fades. Maybe I should have left out the last part...like I did the first time we had this conversation.

"You're..." Dad swallows and gives me a pained frown. "You're hanging out with your ex-boyfriend's girlfriend? Honey, what are you doing?"

I blink, mildly offended that he might think I was scheming. Skylar's not around to encourage me to do that type of thing. Besides, I wouldn't. Harley's too nice. She and Aidan are too happy together.

My eyebrows dip into a sharp V as I defend my position. "I'm learning to surf. Swear, Dad, that's it. I'm not trying to muscle in between them. I like someone else!"

Whoops. Too much of a defense.

Dad frowns. "Who?"

"Oh, um…" I shrug, quickly trying to back-pedal and go for casual. "He's just a guy who works at the beach. Ryder Rentals? He…" I snap my fingers and point at Dad. "He's the one who saved Louis's life." Dad's lips twitch, no doubt amused by the fact that I'm getting all flustered. "I mean, I like him, but it's not like… it's just a crush, Dad. No big deal."

I swallow and force a smile. I feel like I'm blushing big-time, giving away some of this warm energy inside of me.

Dad's eyes mist as he gazes at me. "You look so much like your mom when you smile that way." He brushes one of my dimples with his sudsy finger. "I love you, kid."

I laugh and wipe the moisture off my cheek. "Love you too."

We resume the dishes and finish tidying up the kitchen in companionable silence. I spend most of that time thinking about Griffin, and just a few minutes lamenting the fact that poor Dad is alone. As far as I know, he hasn't even liked anyone since Mom, let alone gone on a date. He's filled up every spare moment with us kids and work. He survives by keeping busy.

But how long can he sustain that?

I wish there was an easy answer.

I wish death didn't exist.

At least unfair death where the heart of the house can be ripped out, leaving a shell behind. A shell that's supposed to keep functioning.

We have in some ways.

We've pushed through, but I wish I could do more.

As Dad walks out of the kitchen, I lean my arms against the counter, my insides split through the middle. An ocean of warmth crashing against an ocean of deep, blue sadness.

## 21

# HIDING PLACES

## GRIFFIN

I shouldn't have kissed her.

I mean, she made the temptation pretty damn hard to resist. I could argue that *she* kissed *me*, but I'd be kidding myself the whole time. I wanted it just as badly as she did, and I gave in. I tasted her. And now I want more.

"Idiot," I mutter to myself as I drive north to where I'm staying.

I can't give in again. I have to be strong.

More is not a word in my vocabulary right now.

Strong. Resilient. Survival. Those are the words I should be focusing on. Words that will get me to next week. Next month. Next year.

I don't have the luxury of more.

Swallowing has suddenly become hard. I grip the wheel and slam back in my seat.

"Come on, man. Pull it together!"

She's a seventeen-year-old kid.

*You're only eighteen! If you think about it, you're a kid too.*

I squeeze my eyes shut against my mental taunts, then remember I'm driving and quickly open my eyes. Flicking the blinker, I turn on to my street and one minute later realize that it's not my street anymore.

Lights are on in the house. There are two cars parked in the driveway. And all I can be grateful for is my rigid routine of always packing up my stuff before I leave every morning. My sleeping bag and pillow are wrapped up in the plastic sheet in the pickup bed. My meager supply of food is hidden beneath it.

Looks like I'm suddenly homeless again.

The vacationers have returned.

With a heavy sigh, I spin the truck around and head south, then spend the next two hours parked at the beach, just sitting in my cab and staring out at the ocean…waiting. And trying not to think too hard.

It's impossible.

My brain tortures me with everything from memories of the past, growing up on the streets with Phoenix, to hearing Savannah's voice when she spoke of her mother's death.

My mom died when I was six. After that, shelters became foster homes. Being a ward of the state was supposed to keep us safe, but we ran away more than we stuck around.

And then came the gang life.

Again, it was supposed to offer a sense of safety, but brought with it a whole new meaning to the word danger.

I was just fourteen the day Phoenix stole that money.

He put me on lookout duty, but when I heard the screaming, I left my post to check that everything was okay.

I didn't expect to see what I saw, and it froze me.

"What the hell are you doing, man?" Phoenix was pissed.

But all I could do was stare at the woman's bloody face, her limp body unmoving on the concrete.

Police sirens snapped me out of my trance and Phoenix started freaking out. He shoved the box of money into my hands and told me to hide it. I was still a small runt at that stage, but I was fast.

So we split up, diverting two different ways in order to make our escape. The cops nearly caught Phoenix, but I managed to distract them. I'd hid the money already and came back to help my brother.

And help him I did.

I got cornered and caught.

He got away.

And then because I was loyal to a freaking fault, I kept my mouth shut. About everything.

Turns out pleading the fifth does you no favors.

My silence cost me seventeen months in juvie. I was blamed for assault and robbery, even though Phoenix was the one who attacked her. Thank God the woman survived.

It makes me sick that we stole from a school. They'd been running a huge fundraising fair all day—raising money to refurbish the library. We even paid a couple bucks to go to it…so we could keep an eye on the money. At the end of the day, the organizers got together and put the money into a lockbox for banking. We followed that poor woman and stopped her three blocks from the bank. She didn't even know what hit her.

It was a shitload of money. I never had time to count it, but it must have been several grand. Too bad the school never got it back.

I wriggle in my seat, guilt churning through me. I always meant to pay them back, but every time I think about saving, I end up spending the money or splitting to a new town.

Phoenix only visited me once when I was locked up. He wanted to know where the money was, but I refused to tell him, so he left me alone to rot in juvie.

After that, the first contact I had with him was the day I got out on good behavior. He was there to collect me. Ready to pull me back in.

To hell with that.

I'd learned my lesson.

He wanted to know where I hid the money. I told him I couldn't remember, so he tried to beat it out of me.

And that was the final straw.

A couple nights later, I stole every last penny from my foster parents' wallets, and I ran. Their fifty bucks got me as far as an old friend, but Phoenix still found me, and the fear of getting caught has been chasing me ever since.

Grabbing my cheap phone off the dash, I check the time. It's after ten now, safe enough to settle down for the night. I start the engine. It coughs and groans, but remains faithful, taking me down the road to Freshmart.

My muscles are coiled tight as I pull into the darkest corner of the lot. I discovered it on my second or third night in Ryder Bay. There's a small space for staff parking around the back of the building, and after ten, when the grocery store closes for the night, it becomes deserted.

I cut off the engine and just sit, scanning the dark lot for anything I may have missed.

But it's empty.

I'm safe. For now.

Setting the alarm on my watch, I go for four thirty. It's not like I'll sleep well, so getting up early won't be a problem. I'll be able to fit in a morning run and maybe even a surf.

As I settle down in the bed of the truck, I tuck the

sleeping bag under my armpits and gaze up at the night sky. The stars are playfully winking at me. I move my hand behind my head and try to find that sense of peace I've been working so hard for.

Since coming to Ryder Bay, the peace has been easier to snatch. Just moments of it here and there, but tonight has unsettled me.

The whole day has.

Being with Savannah was the best, but in some ways the worst as well.

It's like staring at a three-layer chocolate cake when you're starving and knowing you can't have any of it.

Usually I run from temptation like this.

Shit, I should probably be driving out of Ryder Bay right now.

But I love it here.

I have a good job. A great boss. This place is freaking beautiful.

It's the first place to ever truly feel like home.

So I'll stay for a little longer. Even just the summer.

But I won't get attached.

Not to Savannah. She'll make it impossible to leave.

And I don't have the luxury of throwing anything impossible into my life right now.

## 22

## LIFE CAN BE WEIRD SOMETIMES

## SAVANNAH

So Griffin hasn't spoken to me, let alone looked at me, since we kissed.

I don't understand.

Our kind-of-date ended on such a sweet note. I floated home. I dreamed about him. I rushed down to the beach as soon as I could on Saturday to see him again, but he kept himself so busy and sent off such strong "leave me alone" vibes that I never got a chance to talk to him.

Was it something I did?

I've replayed our kind-of-date over and over in my mind, trying to work it out. But I come up blank every time. For me, it was perfect.

Scuffing my feet in the sand, I shuffle down the

beach, wondering what I'm supposed to do with myself.

It's Monday and the weekend was decidedly average.

After my Friday night bliss, my Saturday crash landing sucked. I went to the hospital in the end, to hang out with Skylar. That black guy was in her room again, chatting away. He always says the nicest things, but because I was in a foul mood, I made my presence known really quickly. He got my silent hint and took off.

I stayed there until dinnertime, then went home and managed to get into an argument with Scarlett about who knows what. I can't even remember now, but we were both yelling. Dad and Louis weren't home to stop it, and in the end, we slammed our bedroom doors in unison and that was that.

Louis left on Sunday. He's spending summer with Mom's parents and I'm gonna miss him. His sweet little smile tempers Scarlett's grumpiness. I don't know what the hell is going on with her right now, but puberty has not brought out the best in my sister. Talk about mood swings. I don't remember being that bad, but maybe I was and I just didn't realize it.

I groan and slump into the sand, wondering how many other seventeen-year-old girls in the world are worrying about their sisters going through puberty.

Pushing the shades higher up my nose, I stare at the ocean. I don't even feel like surfing today. Not that I really can. The waves are mush. Aidan and Griffin won't be very busy today, but there's no point wandering down there. Griffin will just do his polite smile and turn away thing. It freaking hurt on Saturday, and I'm not in a good enough mood to cope with it right now.

"You okay?"

I flinch at the girl's voice and glance over my shoulder to see Harley. She's walking toward me with a curious smile. Her blonde hair is bunched at the back of her head in a messy knot, lumps bulging on the crown of her head. I'd never leave the house like that. She plunks down beside me, and I notice a small stain on her jean shorts, plus she has a mark on her shirt that needs washing off.

My lips twitch with a smile. She's so different to me. I always take my time getting ready, making sure I look good for the world. It makes me feel confident, but Harley just doesn't seem bothered by that kind of stuff.

How is it that Aidan went from loving me to adoring her?

"I don't understand guys," I murmur.

Harley stills, no doubt regretting the fact that she took a seat beside me.

I sigh and let her off the hook so she doesn't worry that I'm referring to her boyfriend. I was thinking about him when I said that, but I'm now thinking about Griffin...who is just as confusing.

"I kissed Griffin." I frown while Harley nudges me and grins.

"When?"

"On Friday. I was out here surfing, and he stepped up and helped me out when that crew cut guy tried to flirt with me."

"Ripper?"

I shrug, but then nod when I see Harley's expression.

"That guy's such a creep." Her scowl starts to fade when she looks at me and nudges me again. "But Griffin's not."

I scoff and shake my head.

"What?" she asks.

With another heavy sigh, I tell her about our epic date and how every moment of it was perfect.

"So what's the problem, then?"

"He hasn't looked at or spoken to me since!" I throw my hands up. "I don't get it. I thought we had the best time, and now he's just ignoring me!" With a frustrated huff, I hug my knees to my chest and mutter, "Why are guys so confusing?"

Harley shrugs. "Because they're guys?"

I cough out a short laugh but end up shaking my head again.

Harley stretches out her legs in the sand. "There's only one guy in the world who doesn't confuse me."

"Aidan?"

"No way, that guy can still throw me for a loop."

She snickers. "I'm talking about my best friend. His name's Jed and he's kind of like the brother I never had." She grins. "He's honest to a fault, but I love that about him. What you see is what you get."

"Aidan's kind of like that." It's weird that I'm standing up for her boyfriend.

"Yeah, true." Harley nods. "But I guess it's different when you feel more than just friendship for a guy. With Jed, he's just Jed, you know? I'm not second-guessing myself because I don't get the tingles when I'm around him."

"The tingles?"

Harley blushes. "You know. Those warm fuzzies that make you feel light-headed and slightly nauseated. That emotion that rockets through you every time you're around someone you really like."

My lips twitch with a smile, but I can't make it grow. I know exactly what she's talking about, because I'm pretty sure Griffin could make me tingle all over, if he'd just talk to me again.

"Sorry." Harley wrinkles her nose. "I shouldn't be talking to you about Aidan. Let's go back to Jed. My BMF. That's what he calls himself. He's all about the acronyms. BMF is 'best male friend,' and his latest that I actually love, but will never admit to him, is OTD."

I think on it for a second, then give her a perplexed shrug.

"Oh, totally dude."

I laugh. "I never would have gotten that one."

"I know, right?" Harley laughs with me. "He's the only person in the world who can cheer me up or talk me out of a bad mood."

"He sounds awesome."

"He is. You should meet him some time." She clicks her fingers then points at me. "Actually, you may have already seen him. He works at the hospital. He's a cleaner."

I pause and then glance at her. "Is he black?"

"Yep, black and big." She grins.

"I know him. He talks to Skylar all the time. Whenever he's cleaning her room, he's chatting away to her. He says really nice things, although the first time I caught him, it really threw me." I cringe. "I told him I'd call security. I think he's kind of nervous of me now."

Harley laughs, tipping her head back. "Oh man, I'm going to have to give him grief about that one."

"Please don't." I nudge her, but can't help a smile.

Harley licks her lips and looks at me. "You should let him talk. The guy has a heart of gold, and he'll only have good things to say to her."

"Yeah, I think you're right." My eyebrows crinkle as I think of my best friend. I should probably head to the hospital soon and do my daily shift, but I'm really enjoying myself here.

I'm guessing Harley is waiting for Aidan to get off work, which might happen sooner rather than later with this flat surf. There are still some kids boogie boarding in super peewee waves though.

"Do you want to go for a walk?" I spontaneously ask.

"Um." Harley glances down toward the Ryder Rentals shed, then turns back to me. "Sure." Her smile is sweet, and I grin back at her, standing tall and brushing the sand off my shorts.

We head south, ambling down to the pier.

At first, I'm a touch nervous, wondering what we'll talk about. We've only ever surfed together, but she starts up a conversation about surfing, which then leads to other things. We keep it light and breezy. It does come up that my mom isn't around anymore, and she does hint at the fact that her mom doesn't really care about her.

I find that a hard one to get my head around. How could a mother not care about her own flesh and blood? But I guess not everyone is as lucky as me when it comes to parents and family. In spite of my loss, I'm rich. It's good to be reminded of that.

We end up talking the whole way to the pier and back.

I can't remember the last time I've felt so relaxed with another girl my age before. Harley is so easy to hang out with. No fuss. No pressure. I didn't realize how liberating it is to be with someone who isn't demanding anything more than a little conversation from me. She's not trying to manipulate me to say and do anything.

I mean, Skylar doesn't always manipulate me. I definitely have some sway, but compared to Harley, she's a force to be reckoned with.

By the time we get back to our starting point, I'm relaxed and happy. I want to try and stay that way, so I stop before we get any closer to Ryder Rentals.

"I'm gonna head off now." I point my thumb over my shoulder. "Have a nice date with Aidan."

Harley grins. "I will, and I hope things get figured out with Griff."

I scoff and brush my hand through the air. "Yeah, whatever. I'll just keep my distance for now."

With a kind smile, she reaches out and squeezes my arm. "Thanks for a cool afternoon."

I can tell she means it and I smile back at her, my throat suddenly thick with a gratitude I can't express.

Life can be weird sometimes.

Who knew that I'd have so much fun hanging out with my ex's new girlfriend?

## 23

## NOTHING MORE THAN A VAGABOND

## GRIFFIN

Today has been a hard slog.

The waves were practically nonexistent, which made renting surfboards nothing but a drag. We managed to get a few boogie boards out, and Aidan and I had some laughs watching the cute little kids trying to dominate the peewee waves.

I stayed in the shed mostly, watching through the big open space. I moved there as soon as I saw Savannah arrive on the beach. I'm a coward, I know. I should just make up some bullshit excuse about how I don't want to get attached, but there's no way I can pull it off. I can't stand there, look into those beautiful eyes and tell her I'm not interested. I'm not that good of an actor.

So I'm going with avoidance.

"Time to wrap this up?" Aidan asks as he wipes down the last boogie board and stores it behind me.

"Yeah, we'll close up shop. It's been a slow day. I should have let you go earlier."

"Nah, that's cool. Harley wasn't around anyway. She and Sav took off for a walk down the beach." His forehead crinkles with concern and he pokes his head out the door. "Here she comes."

I can't help smirking at the way his voice pitches. Seeing Harley always makes him goofy. I don't think he's aware of just how sappy he is when it comes to that chick.

"Hey, fellas." Harley grins as she stops outside my window.

"Hey, you." Aidan slips out the door and gathers her against him, kissing her softly before leaning back to smile down at her.

I turn away, letting them have their little moment. May as well straighten out the already tidy and organized shed. I start shifting boards an inch this way and that, making no real difference.

"So, I just took a walk with Savannah."

I wait for Aidan to respond. When he doesn't, curiosity makes me glance over my shoulder.

Harley's talking to me, her blue eyes shimmering with something I don't want to know.

Shit, Savannah told her about the kiss and the fact that I'm acting like an asshole.

I swallow.

"I've got her number if you want it." Harley pulls her phone from the back pocket of her jeans.

I shoot Aidan an edgy smile then brush my hand through the air. "That's cool. I don't need it."

"Yeah you do." She nods, holding out her hand and snapping her fingers. "Give me your phone, I'll put it in for you."

I cross my arms and stare at her.

She tips her head and gives me a pointed look. "What is your problem? It's just a phone number. You don't *have* to call it. You should, but you don't have to. I'm just giving you options, man."

"I don't want options."

She huffs. "Then you're an idiot."

"Maybe," I counter quietly.

"Uh...what's going on here?" Aidan looks between us.

I wince and glance at the floor, scratching the back of my neck and wondering how to politely shut her up.

"I'm not always available to go surfing with Sav, so I thought it'd be nice for Griffin to invite her sometimes. She really wants to get out into the water as much as she can."

My head pops up. Is that what Savannah said? Is that *all* she said?

I can tell by Harley's subtle wink that it's not, but then Aidan goes and backs her up.

"That's a cool idea. She'd love that. Thanks, man."

*Shit. How the hell am I supposed to get out of this now?*

They're both staring at me, expectantly waiting.

With a sharp sigh, I snatch out my phone and ignore Aidan's confused frown. He probably thinks I'm acting like a douche, but isn't rude enough to call me on it.

Harley programs in Savannah's number, which I cannot call. As soon as she's gone, I should probably delete it.

"There you go." She hands the phone back with a smile.

I take it, not returning the cheerful sentiment. I wish I could tell these people why I have to be so careful. But I can't.

"Hey, so what's our plan, babe?" Aidan runs his hand around Harley's lower back.

A flash of jealousy scorches me. I wish I could run my hand around a girl's back, pull her close, talk to her like she was mine.

Savannah's pretty smile tortures me and I turn away from the lovebirds, checking to make sure the back wooden shutter is bolted down.

"Why don't we walk until the sun sets? Then I'll head home, shower up and we can go out for dinner or something."

"Sounds good. I'd like a shower too, so why don't I drop you home, then come back and get you? There's this great place about thirty minutes south that I want to try out."

"Mexican?"

"Of course."

I spin around in time to see their smiles connecting. They deepen the kiss and I grimace, not sure how much more I can stomach.

"Okay, okay, get walking, lovebirds. I'll lock up and check in with Devon."

"Thanks, man." Aidan's smile is loved up and dopey.

I roll my eyes and send them away with a flick of my hand.

Snatching my phone off the counter, I gaze down at Savannah's details.

*Delete!*

I rub my thumb over her name and slip the phone into my back pocket.

I'll delete it later. Right now, I need to get this money and these receipts up to Devon.

---

I walk through the glass door and find Marshall behind the counter.

"Hey, man." I grin at my boss. I really like this guy.

He's older than he looks, with weathered skin from being outside so much. He loves the ocean, the wind, the sand, the sun. Anything to do with nature invigorates the guy, and I can absolutely relate. Being in the outdoors does something to my spirit, heightens it in a way I can't even explain.

"I've just sent Devon home. How'd your day go?"

I wince and hand over the lockbox. "It was kinda slow today."

"Yeah, Trinity said it was a slow shift."

Trinity Cable is one of the other lifeguards. She's one strong, confident chick. She's tall and muscly. When she's not at the beach, she's working out at the gym—the CrossFit queen.

"I'm sure she's burning off the energy at the gym now."

Marshall laughs and points at me. Opening up the lockbox, he counts the money and checks each receipt while we talk about the weather and hope for better surf tomorrow.

"So, how's Aidan working out?"

"Yeah, really well. I probably didn't need him today. Business was slow, but we just talked, and the time passed by."

"He's a good kid. Make a great lifeguard." Marshall's gaze brushes past mine. "Like you."

I give him a lopsided grin. We have this conversation a lot. I wish I could tell him that I'm not qualified, and I don't want to spend my money on a forged high school diploma.

I want a real one.

I just haven't found the courage to go for it. I don't even own a computer, so it's not like I could do it online. I don't want to be online. It feels too traceable somehow.

Marshall lets his comment hang, locking the box into the safe and turning to face me.

"You up to anything tonight? You're welcome to come and have dinner with me and Denee. I don't know what she's cooking, but it'll be good, whatever it is."

He always gets this adoring look on his face when he's talking about his wife. I'm pretty sure those two are soul mates, destined to be together before they were even born.

I wonder what that kind of love must feel like, then shut the question down before it can fester. I don't want to be that guy. The romantic one who thinks that kind of shit.

Clearing my throat, I cross my arms and politely decline.

As much as I would love a home-cooked meal, I need to spend my evening looking for a new place to stay. I can't keep sleeping at the back of Freshmart, and I need time to scope the neighborhoods with a higher percentage of vacation homes.

"Maybe some other time." Marshall smiles. "You're always welcome at our place."

"Thanks, Marshall." I give him a wave and head out the door, overcome by a deep sense of loneliness that tries to take me out at the knees.

I force myself to stand tall and keep walking.

I won't give in to self-pity.

It was my choice to flee, my choice to lie, my choice

to live this false life. I can't have it all, and I need to accept that and focus on the good things around me. A great job, the chance to surf...

My list peters out as Savannah's name flashes through my mind and I'm forced to keep it moving. After that, I can't think of anything else to celebrate, so I focus instead on finding a place to sleep, and try to ignore the fact that I'm nothing more than a vagabond.

## 24

## TRASHY MAGS DON'T CUT IT ANYMORE

## SAVANNAH

I decide to spend Tuesday hanging out at the hospital. When I texted Harley first thing, she said she was busy, and since surfing by myself isn't safe, and I don't want to spend my time on the beach being blatantly ignored by Griffin again, I may as well hang out where I'm wanted and needed.

So far, I've run a few errands for Marlo, talked to Skylar for a while, gone home to check in on Lettie, eaten lunch with Dad, and I'm about to settle in again for another afternoon session with my best friend. I'm armed with the most gossipy magazines I could find and am prepared to spend my time reading them to Sky.

Scarlett is spending the night with her friend Johanna. Together they make the perfect bookworm pair. They'll stay up late talking book boyfriends, plot twists, and characters they despise. Then they'll spend the rest of their time scrolling through Instagram for inspiration.

I've checked out Lettie's account before. It's gorgeous. She has a real talent for photography, and her passion for books comes through loud and clear. Not that I can tell her that. Last time I tried, she shot me down and twisted what I said into a negative.

I give up!

Surly Scarlett is too much for me to handle right now.

*Yes, even after all the training I've had with Skylar.*

I grin at my internal joke. I'm only teasing my best friend. She can be so extra and a lot of work, but I understand how she ticks. I know how to win her over, make her laugh, and I know she cares about me. Yes, she has occasionally done me wrong, like the way she ditched me at her party. But if she'd been acting like her normal self, she would have made up for it on the Sunday afterward.

She didn't.

And that's another niggle that won't stop scratching.

Something happened to my best friend, something that changed her, and I wish I knew what it was. I should have gone around and seen her on Sunday, but I was still pissed off with her and super down about Aidan not kissing me. I just didn't want to face Sky.

And look what happened.

Clearing my throat, I round the corner and try to shake off my black mood. Skylar needs my voice to ring with cheerfulness and hope. I want to give her reasons to wake up, not stay buried in her coma cocoon.

According to my dad, her body is healing just the way it should. He's mystified by what's keeping her trapped, but every time he talks to neurosurgeons, they give him the same message: As long as her vitals are fine and there's no infection, give it time.

Dad's been monitoring her so closely.

He's hoping she'll wake up any day now.

We all are.

I slip into the room and run my hand across Marlo's shoulders. "How you doing?"

She gives me a tired smile.

"Hey, why don't you go home, have a bath, something to eat? I'll stay with her until you get back."

Marlo pulls in a breath, then turns to stare at Sky.

"She'll be okay, and you know I'll call you if anything changes."

Another tired smile and finally a reluctant nod. "You're probably right. I need to freshen up."

"This place can make you crazy. You need to get out."

"I know." She sighs. "It's just hard to leave her."

It's hard not to wince at the wobble in Marlo's voice. She's stressed beyond coping, and I worry that she's going to fracture and break apart.

Helping her stand, I pull her into a quick hug. "Just pretend she's at a sleepover at my house. We're gonna read gossip magazines and just hang out."

Marlo's laughter is tired and halfhearted, but she pulls back and gives me a glassy smile.

"Sweet, precious girl. What would we do without you?"

I shrug. "I'm not going anywhere."

"Thank God for that." She pulls me back into a hug and kisses the side of my face.

"Get going." I pat her back. "I've got this."

Pulling in a shaky breath, she lets me go and grabs her things. Pausing one last time at the doorway, she blows her daughter a kiss. "Back soon, honey."

"Take your time." I point at her, sounding more like the mother.

She snickers and shakes her head, slipping out the door while I make myself comfortable.

"I've got pure trash for us today, Sky. I thought we could do that thing where we try to figure out how much truth there is in each article." I flip the magazines over, scanning the covers. "So, what do you want to start with? The latest celebrity breakup? The lip-syncing scandal? Or the...saucy new reality show that's going to blow our minds?" My eyes bulge as I look at the scantily clad rock divas and their muscly bodyguards.

I spend the next hour reading to her but find her lack of response to all the juice kind of depressing. In the end, I snap the mags closed in frustration and rest my elbow on the bed, staring glumly at my mute bestie. We'd always laugh our asses off over these magazines. We'd make up stories, pretending we were celebrities and what we'd do with all our money and time.

But there's no laughter right now, unless you count the forced, canned stuff I've been trying to produce.

I'm tired.

I know that's selfish, because it's not like Skylar can help being in a coma, but I want her to wake up. I want her to listen to my problems and tell me how to fix them. I want her to distract me with nail polish and fashion and stories about her rocky relationship with Craig.

I want—

A flash of movement past the door distracts me and I glance up in time to see a cleaning cart.

"Hey!" I stand and run to the door.

The cart jerks to a stop and I peek out to see Jed.

At least I think it's him.

He's in his cleaning uniform and is pretty much how Harley described him.

"Uh…" His forehead wrinkles. "Is everything okay?"

"Yeah." I grin. "I just wanted to introduce myself. I'm Savannah." I point to myself and his confusion starts to fade.

"Harley's teaching you to surf."

"Yep. That's me."

His smile takes over his round face, a flash of beauty. "Harley's stoked to be getting a little business. I think Aidan's lined her up with two other lessons this week."

"Oh really? She didn't tell me that." I cross my arms and lean against the doorframe. "I hung out with her yesterday afternoon. She says you're the best. Her BMF."

He laughs and slaps the handle of his cleaning cart. "That's me. She's one cool chick."

"OTD." I screw up my nose. "Did I get that right?"

He laughs again. "Damn, that's fire. I told her it would catch on."

We laugh together and I instantly see what Harley loves so much about him.

He's a sweetheart.

Walking around the cart, he comes to a stop beside me and glances over my shoulder.

I gaze right at him. He's only half an inch taller than me, so it's easy to see his expression. His eyes soften with a look of sadness that breaks my heart.

"How's she doing?"

"Same." I'm struck by the look of affection on his face. Considering he never knew her, he seems to have taken a liking to her. Is it just because she's pretty? I'd hate for him to be that shallow.

"Did you…?" I swallow and turn to gaze at Skylar's petite body. She makes the bed look huge. "You didn't know her before…did you?"

He shakes his head. "First time I laid eyes on her was when I came in here to clean her room." His mouth curls up on the right. "There's just something about her that..." He starts patting his chest, right where his heart is.

My eyebrows rise, and it's not until he glances at me that he must realize what he's doing.

Snapping his gaze to the floor, he shuffles back and murmurs, "I should get back to work."

I'm fighting a grin as I raise my hand in a wave. "It was nice meeting you."

"You too." He bobs his head, but keeps his eyes down. He's obviously super embarrassed to be caught crushing on my best friend.

I don't have the heart to tell him it will never happen.

If—I mean *when* Skylar wakes up, she won't be interested. Appearance is important to her, and as much as I hate to say it, she wouldn't be caught dead dating a guy like Jed. A guy with chub instead of muscle. A guy who blatantly wears his heart on his sleeve.

Skylar's always gone for good-looking hotshots. She's not interested in depth and inner beauty. And in fairness to her, I've never thought to consider it either. You tend to like the way someone looks before you get to know who they are.

As I take a seat next to Skylar, I gather her fingers in mine and think about Craig and that asshole

Ripper. Both super-hot guys with hearts the size of peanuts.

"Maybe we've got it all wrong, Sky," I murmur, even throwing Griffin into the mix.

Although I can sense he's not a total jerk, he did kiss me and then make a point of ignoring me. He may not be a Craig. He's definitely not a Ripper. But in no way is he the perfect guy.

## 25

## AN IMPOSSIBLE PHONE CALL

## GRIFFIN

The day was long and hard.

In spite of the brilliant sun, the perfect surf and the busyness of the day, it still felt like a hard slog. As far as I could tell, Savannah didn't even set a toe on the beach, and it consumed me all day.

I couldn't stop looking for her. It drove me nuts.

Her number is still on my phone.

I can't seem to delete it, even though I've tried a few times.

With an irritated huff, I slap the steering wheel. This is ridiculous. I have more important things to worry about than a girl.

Not just a girl.

I shake my head, unable to put her into such a simple box.

Clenching my jaw, I check my speed and continue cruising the streets. I didn't find anything suitable last night and got sick of scouting, so just ended up at Freshmart again. I can't give up so easily tonight. I need a roof over my head. A soft mattress underneath my body.

I'm at the north end of Ryder Bay, down near the base of the cliffs. This is where a large chunk of the vacation homes are. A mix of the old and the new. I've tried out both. My last place was one of the new condos. As nice as it was, I found it cold and sterile. But hey, it was a roof over my head, right?

This time, however, I'm gonna try one of the older places.

It's getting harder and harder as vacation homes are taken over by families for their summer break. School's been out for over a week, and my time is getting more and more limited.

Maybe I should just slip out of town now?

But where would I go?

North to LA just takes me closer to Phoenix. East to Arizona just takes me away from the beach.

My nose wrinkles.

I could head south again.

Back to Mexico.

Working in those resorts wasn't too bad, but I don't know. I was restless. Seeking a sense of home, which I never felt down there.

I've never really felt it anywhere...until I reached Ryder Bay.

Shit. Why do I have to love this place so much?

Why do I even want a sense of home? It'll cause me nothing but trouble.

I spot a section of darker houses up ahead. Lights aren't on. I check my watch—9:03pm. It's too early for all the lights to be off, which means these places are still empty.

It may only be for a night, but I'll take it.

Slowing my truck, I amble past the row of five identical beach houses and pull up beside the one at the end. I idle there for a moment, studying the house. After a few minutes of nothing but the low rumble of my engine, I figure the place is empty and pull into the driveway.

It curves around the back of the house, so I can hide my truck in the carport. Usually I park a few blocks away, or leave my truck at the beach, and just walk to where I'm sleeping, but tonight I'm gonna risk it. Let's hope whoever vacations in this place doesn't show up at dawn.

Easing out of my truck, I grab my stuff and cautiously head into the house.

The back end of the carport is rough concrete while the other has been lined. A temporary wall has shrunk the carport, and I'm assuming the space is used for storage. Treading back up the driveway, I check the street before inching my way to the door. It's not hard to jimmy the lock. I've been doing it my whole life. I can't even remember learning to do it, which means I must have only been a little kid when I was taught.

Easing the door open, I wince when it creaks and freeze still, holding my breath as I count to twenty and order my pounding heart to slow the hell down.

When no lights flick on and nothing jumps out to grab me, I slip through the door and take my flip-flops off. Wandering through the house, I use my flashlight to establish a quick layout of the place and work out my fastest exit. Hopefully I won't need to use it.

What I need is to sleep like the dead.

Dumping my bag on the kitchen floor, I set about making myself a peanut butter sandwich. I make sure I wash everything and replace it before even sitting down to eat.

Perching my butt on the edge of a dining room chair, I gaze out through the glass sliding doors, mesmerized by the dark ocean. It's there, just beyond the black patch of sand. I can hear it moving and sway-ing, calling me in.

I won't listen to the call tonight. As tempting as a pre-bed swim would be, I don't want to leave this place tonight. I need sleep.

Swallowing down the last of my very unsatisfying dinner, I finish off with a big glass of water, then wash and dry the two dishes I used. The kitchen is now just as I found it. The dull light bulb in the center casts a dirty yellow glow over the old countertops. Man, this place has to be an original.

The black-and-white checkered floor, the stained white bench tops, the old cabinetry. I grin as I slip the plate back in the cupboard, noting the mismatched dishes. The cutlery drawer is the same. This beach house is full of the stuff the owners no longer want in their everyday house. I kind of love the rustic nature of it.

If I had a home, I can imagine it being a little like that. A collection of secondhand bits and pieces.

A home.

Shit, I can't even imagine what that must be like.

The longest "home" I've ever known was juvie, and that's a place I never want to see again.

My heart squeezes uncomfortably as my mind tries to torture me with dreams that will never come true—a little house I can confidently walk into, because it's mine. A couch with my butt print on it, a bed I can really relax in, a shower that will have my favorite soap sitting on the shelf.

"One day," I murmur, but know it's a lie.

Closing my eyes, I rest my hands against the counter.

I need sleep.

I need rest.

I want peace.

Snatching my bag off the floor, I traipse through the house, looking for the right bedroom. The one at the end is full of kids' toys and bunk beds. Although it's got an easy escape route, I decide to go for the room next to it. There's a nice double bed and not much else. I check the window, opening it just a crack in case I need a quick escape in the night.

Damn. I probably should have left my truck a few blocks away. I nearly go move it, but as soon as my butt hits the edge of the bed, laziness kicks in and I spend the next ten minutes convincing myself it'll be fine.

I'm tired.

Not physically, but mentally.

I just want oblivion to take away this ache inside my chest.

I don't know what's up with me today. I feel weighed down and heavy.

Pulling out my sleeping bag, I lay it down on the bed then grab my pillow. I don't bother getting changed. T-shirt and board shorts have always made good pajamas. Crossing my ankles, I lie on my back and gaze up at the ceiling. I should get into the bag and settle down, but as tired as I feel, I'm also wide awake.

I lean over the side of the bed and pull my phone from the front pocket of my bag.

The screen lights up as I press the button. I stare at Savannah's number. The one I can't delete. Brushing my thumb over her name, I scratch my chest and wonder if this is why I'm feeling so unsettled.

Not because I haven't deleted her, which is something I really should do.

But how can I when I've left things so unfinished between us?

I've acted like an asshole, and it's eating me up.

I can't just kiss a girl like Savannah and then pretend she doesn't exist. It's not fair to her, and I'm pretty sure I'll have a snowball's chance in Hell of getting over her unless I make this right.

One phone call.

One apology.

A short explanation.

It doesn't have to be the whole truth, just a small enough morsel for her to understand.

"I can't get attached because I may have to leave soon, and I don't want to hurt you." I test out a few more options. "I think you're amazing, but you're still in high school. The age gap is..." Bullshit, because I'm only eighteen, not twenty-one!

I sigh and nearly drop the phone down. I need to forget this, but my fingers resist, gripping tight to the device.

"Call her, or you'll never sleep," I mutter, my thumb hovering over the green button.

But I can't call her until I've figured out exactly what I'm going to say.

With a grimace, I shake my head and wonder how I'm supposed to do the impossible.

# 26

# THE HQ CRISIS

## SAVANNAH

I t's getting late.

I've run out of words to say, and Marlo is now back with Jeff. They're sitting on either side of their daughter, murmuring softly to her and then each other. Although they'll never intend to do this, I'm feeling completely unnecessary right now.

"Good night, you guys," I whisper softly.

Marlo looks up and gives me a tired but grateful smile.

Jeff's eyes are glued to his daughter's face, his expression kind of desolate.

It hurts to look at him, so I turn my back and slip out of the room.

Dad's already left. He swung past to say goodnight and told me not to be too late. Poor guy looked exhausted, but he probably didn't want to go home to an empty house either. Or maybe he did. Maybe he's taken a long shower and is watching a movie in bed.

I hope he's doing something to relax.

I should probably follow suit.

A shower and a movie would be the perfect way to end the night. Or maybe I could binge-watch *American Vandal* until I fall asleep.

I'm just starting to like that idea when my phone buzzes with a text. I pull it out and glance at the screen, then jerk to a stop and gape at the message.

It's from Aidan.

*Harley just dumped me.*

*Did she say anything to you yesterday?*

I have to read the message three times to really absorb it.

What the hell?

I poise my thumbs over the screen to type back, but I can't think of what to say, so in the end, I call him.

"Did she say anything to you?" Aidan greets me.

"No," I sputter and shake my head. "I can't believe this. It feels so random."

"She's not answering her phone." I can feel his stress, hear it in the tight pinch of his voice. "I don't know what the hell I did wrong. You didn't say anything to her, did you?"

"What?" I hiss, highly offended. Like I would try to break them up. I'm not a total bitch.

"Sorry," he mumbles. "I'm just trying to figure this out."

My quick anger dissipates, and I let out a sympathetic sigh. "Well, what happened today? Did you guys fight or anything?"

"No! It was awesome!" Aidan's voice pitches. "We surfed, we both went off to work, and then we met up later. We had dinner at my house, and then I drove her home. She kissed me good night and I waited until she'd stepped inside before driving away. Then an hour later, she's breaking up with me and I don't know what the HELL IS GOING ON!"

"Okay, okay."

"I'm thinking I might drive back to her place and see if I can't talk to her." He sighs. "I just wanted to get your take on it first. Maybe she gave you a little hint when you were together yesterday."

"No hint." I shake my head. "She seemed as loved-up as you."

He doesn't say anything, and my heart squeezes with sympathy. It's weird how quickly my feelings for Aidan have changed. A couple of weeks ago, I would have been happy that he and Harley broke up, but now I just want to help.

"I could try calling her if you want. Maybe she'll talk to me?"

"You sure? That's probably kind of awkward for you."

"I just think turning up at her door might be a little too much. She's obviously broken it off for a reason. I'm guessing it's a really crappy, spontaneous one and maybe she just needs a day's grace or something."

"Yeah, maybe," Aidan murmurs, sounding like a sad puppy dog.

"Let me find out what's going on. She might tell me something she's not willing to say to you."

"Thanks, Sav."

"I'll call you back soon, 'kay?"

He hangs up after a murmured goodbye and I immediately call Harley.

She doesn't answer.

Gripping my phone with an annoyed huff, I consider showing up at her place myself, but one, I'm not sure I can remember how to get to her house, and two, I can't tell Aidan not to show up and then arrive unannounced myself.

Scratching my forehead, I stare at my phone screen and try to come up with the perfect text to coax her into replying.

I'm coming up blank as I round the corner and bump straight into Jed.

"Woah." He catches my arm to steady me and I give

him a fleeting smile, then gasp and snatch his wrist. Maybe he can help.

"Uh…" He looks down at my hand and gives me an awkward smile. "You okay?"

"Harley just broke up with Aidan." I rush out the words.

"What?" His head jerks back, giving him a double chin. "No way. She's totally in love with the guy."

"Right? It's so weird." I let go of his wrist and point at him. "We've both tried calling her, but she's totally ignoring us."

He shakes his head and yanks out his phone, pulling up her number. He starts clicking on the screen, then stops. "Wait. When did this happen?"

I shrug. "About an hour ago, I think."

"And she just out of the blue texted Aidan and broke it off?"

"Yeah."

"No pre-warning?"

"Nothing."

Jed goes very still, his round face crumpling with a look of anguish as he runs a hand over his head. "Shit. Shit!"

"What?"

"Her mom's boyfriend must be back in town."

I give him a confused frown. How would he know that?

And… "Why is that a problem?" I ask.

Jed shakes his head. "The guy's a total jerk. He..." A flash of dark rage takes over his expression.

"He what?"

"He tries to..." Biting his lips together, a sharp breath puffs out his nose before he grits out, "He tries to touch Harley. You know, when her mom's not around."

"Touch?" I'm confused until I suddenly get what he's saying. I grimace. "Like..."

"Like he wants in her pants." Jed spits out the words.

"Ewww!" I cover my mouth, horrified. I've never been around sick adults like that. I just don't understand how people can behave that way.

"I know," Jed mutters and starts texting again.

"Has she told her mom about it?"

"She's tried, but her mom won't believe her. Every time he comes into town, Harley takes off. Last time I found her walking to SD." He rolls his eyes, then sends a text, then immediately starts typing again.

Looks like he's sending Harley a chapter book.

"Walking to San Diego?" My voice is skeptical.

He nods but doesn't look up at me. "Yeah, she was trying to hitch a ride down there. I convinced her to come back, and she hid out at my place until he left. Don't think I can get away with it again though. My grandma would hit the roof if she caught her in my room."

My eyes bulge. "Where do you think she's gone?"

"Don't know, but she's not replying to any of these." He hits Send again. "She's probably turned off her phone." He runs a hand over his head again. "Shit. We've got to go find her." He checks his watch and winces. "She could have gone any direction."

"Well, I'll help. And she can totally stay with me. We've got room."

The edge of Jed's mouth lifts into a half smile. "You know, HQ's never had a friend who's a girl before."

I swallow and bob my head once. "Well, she's got one now."

"PC." He smiles.

"PC?"

"Pretty cool. It's gonna catch on."

I grin. "OTD."

Patting his chest, he murmurs, "I'm so proud," then starts walking for the exit, giving me his number at the same time.

I record it on my phone. "So, where should I start looking?"

"I'm gonna drive past her place first and see if I can't get that dickwad to tell me something. You start driving south and keep me posted."

As soon as we exit the building, I run for my car. I'm about to slip behind the wheel when my phone rings.

I don't recognize the number, but it could be Harley, so I quickly answer it. "Hello?"

"Hey, uh... shit," a male voice mutters.

I go still, trying to work out who the hell is calling me.

"I'm sorry to just call like this."

And then I know. "Griffin?"

"Yeah."

My body reacts to that knowledge, flashing with a tingling desire. I swallow and can't find any words.

"Harley gave me your number and...well, I was going to call, but then..."

I dump my bag on the passenger seat. I'm kind of annoyed by my total elation at hearing from him. He's been cold-shouldering me, and I'm dealing with a crisis right now.

I should really tell him I don't have time for this, but instead I say, "What's the matter?"

"I just wanted to apologize for what I did. For ignoring you. I was an asshole, and I should have explained myself."

Aw. That's kinda sweet.

But do I really want to hear the explanation? What if he's just going to say that we can never kiss again? That he doesn't really like me at all?

I don't think I can stomach that right now.

Biting my lips together, I sniff in a breath and tell him, "Look, can we talk about this later? I'm kind of in the middle of a crisis right now."

There's a quick pause and then his voice changes. "What's up?"

I can't help a fleeting grin. Gone is that remorse-filled mumble. His voice is now alert, concerned. I can't see his face, but I can already tell he wants to help me.

What does that say?

Maybe his explanation won't be so bad after all.

I swallow down the tingling jitters that are trying to take over my throat and manage to quickly spill my story about Harley.

He doesn't even hesitate.

"I'll come help you." I can picture him moving, quickly looking for his keys. He explains where he's going to go and suggests which route I should take.

I agree with him and hang up a few minutes later.

I'm smiling.

I shouldn't be smiling. Harley could be in trouble.

But I am.

I'm smiling because Griffin is helping.

And I instantly feel a million times better.

## 27

## A FLASH OF BLONDE

## GRIFFIN

The second Savannah said she had a crisis, I felt it —right in the middle of my chest.

It made me realize that I'd drop anything, do anything, to help her out. I was in dangerous territory, but I wasn't turning my back on her...or Harley.

I want to maim that guy for driving Harley out of her own home. If he's touched her, he deserves to be pummeled. That kind of stuff makes me sick. The whole objectifying women thing. Nonconsensual sex. It's wrong on so many levels. Some things get to me more than others, and that's one of them. I just can't tolerate assholes with no respect.

I swallow as I drive the main road hunting for Harley.

I've been at it for nearly an hour, checking in with

Savannah every ten minutes or so. She's contacted Aidan and clued him in. Harley's friend Jed has had no luck with the douchebag boyfriend, so we're all just roaming Ryder Bay and hoping she hasn't hitched a ride out of town already.

I'm actually out of Ryder Bay. I've cruised north and am wondering how far I should go before I turn back.

And that's when I spot her.

A flash of blonde.

She's walking on the edge of the road, right against the barrier, her arms crossed, a bag on her back, her shoulders hunched.

As soon as she hears me, she sticks out her thumb and my gut sinks. She's hitching a ride. Shit, I could be anybody. What the hell is she doing?

I slow the truck and pull up beside her, winding down my window.

She glances at me, blinks in surprise, then asks, "You heading out of town?"

"Nope." I shake my head. "Just coming to get you."

She scowls and spins on her heel, storming away from me. I lightly rev and give chase, my truck sputtering and coughing as I amble along beside her.

"I'm not going home," she growls.

"I'm not taking you home."

This stops her. With a swift jerk, she turns to face me, resting her hand on the edge of my window and silently asking for an explanation.

"Savannah's looking for you. Jed told her about Bryson. She said you could stay with her."

She shudders, then starts blinking. She's fighting tears and my heart gives a little squeeze. She looks so incredibly vulnerable right now. "Does Aidan know?"

"Yeah," I softly murmur, pulling out my phone and then tipping my head to the side. "Get in."

She crosses her arms, her lips trembling as she tries to be stubborn.

I roll my eyes with a sigh and lift the phone to my ear.

"Any luck?" Savannah's sounding tired and stressed. I'm glad I can do something about one of those things.

"I found her."

"Oh, thank God."

A smile flickers across my face as I glance at Harley. "But she's not getting in my truck."

"What?" Savannah huffs, then puts on one of the best 'mother' voices I've ever heard. "You tell her to get in or she'll have me to deal with! I'll meet you at my place." She gives me the address and I can't help a little snicker as I hang up the phone.

Harley gives me a confused frown.

"She says you have to get in or deal with her."

A sharp, barking laugh pops out of her. "That's not that scary."

"I didn't have the heart to tell her that." I wink, and Harley's expression softens, her lips starting to wobble again.

"Come on, Surfer Girl. You honestly saying that you'd rather hitch a ride to who knows where with some creeper?"

"You calling yourself a creeper?" she retorts.

"I'm not taking you out of town. And at this time of night, you could get picked up by a creeper. I don't get it. Aren't you trying to run from a sleaze bucket right now? Why risk getting picked up by another one when there are people in town who care about you and want to look after you?"

Her eyes glass over, and she dips her head with a little sniff.

I soften my voice. "Wouldn't you be better off taking Savannah's invite? You know she'll look after you."

Her nostrils flare and she swipes a finger over her face, catching the tears before they fall.

"Get in the truck, Harley. It's the right move."

After that, I don't say anything, just sit there listening to the engine and giving her a chance to make the decision. If she starts walking again, I'm following her. I know the terror of running from someone who wants to hurt you. She's probably pulsing with fear and unrest right now. All I can be is a calm presence that might help settle her nerves.

It takes her nearly five minutes. I know because I glanced at my watch about fifteen times. But eventually, after a quiet weep, she lets out a shuddering sigh and walks around to the passenger door. It lets out a loud creak as she wrenches it open and jumps in.

I open my mouth to congratulate her, then change my mind and give her a smile instead.

Her shoulder hitches and she sniffs again, resting her elbow against the window frame and gazing out into the darkness.

We drive to Savannah's place without saying a word.

## 28

# THE SAFE HOUSE

## SAVANNAH

I text Aidan and Jed as soon as I get off the phone with Griffin.

I can't believe the intensity of relief that's pulsing through me right now. I have been seriously worried about Harley. And not being able to find her has sucked.

Maybe it's the fact that Jed and Aidan have been stressing out as well. I've been feeding off their emotions. I'm not sure, but Harley's been found, and I just want to deflate on the couch and shake for a few minutes.

Parking my car in the drive, I notice that Dad's left the front light on for me, but the rest of the house is dark. I don't want to wake him, so I sneak around the side of the house and creep in through the den. This is where Aidan and I would secretly make out on the nights we weren't ready to say goodbye.

It's with a weird sense of nostalgia that a few minutes after I've arrived, he's tapping on the door. I sent Jed and Griffin the same instructions, so hopefully they'll all be showing up soon. But for now, it's just me and Aidan.

I let him in, suddenly feeling awkward as memories flood me. Glancing at the couch, I picture us snuggled up together, watching a late-night movie and kissing through most of it. We never got too hot or heavy in this room, just some petting, and all our clothes remained on. I wasn't ready for that next step, and thankfully Aidan never pushed the issue, even after that one time at his place where we nearly went all the way but I just couldn't go through with it.

I shudder to think how horrible Harley must have felt when Bryson tried to make a move. Aidan notices my expression and lightly touches my elbow.

"You okay?"

I nod. "You?"

He gives me a grim look and shakes his head, pacing into the room and fisting his hands.

"She's been found. She's okay."

He spins with an anguished frown, then plunks onto the sofa, scraping his fingers through his hair. "I want to kill that guy. What kind of sick f—" He pulls in a sharp breath, like if he lets go he might just lose his mind.

"Hey." I sit down beside him and run my hand across his shoulders.

"What do I say to her when she walks through that door?"

The tension in his shoulders is nearly unbearable. I rub at the taut muscles and try to relax him. "You can't be angry like this. She's probably feeling vulnerable and afraid. That's why she ran."

"But why didn't she run to me? Why'd she try to break up?"

I sigh and shrug, then try to think about it from her perspective. "What would you do if your mom had a boyfriend, and he tried...touching you when you didn't want him to?" It's a struggle to get out the words. The very idea makes me sick. I hate that it happens. And I'm proud of Harley for taking off. I just wish she'd run in a different direction.

"She could have told me," Aidan whispered. "I'd protect her."

"I know you would."

"I hate it that she doesn't let me in."

"She obviously struggles to trust people. And if her mom won't believe her, then I can understand why."

"But she can trust me." Aidan taps his chest. "She can trust me with anything."

"I know." I give him a gentle smile. "And she'll figure that out soon enough."

Aidan closes his eyes, his shoulders slumping

forward like he's just run a marathon he didn't train for.

I wish there was more I could say to make him feel better, but I'm kind of stumped. Harley's put him through the ringer tonight, and I see where she's coming from, but I feel sorry for Aidan too.

Thank God Griffin found her.

The door clicks open. Aidan and I both jump, then shoot to our feet as Griffin walks into the room, tugging Harley in behind him.

I give him a grateful smile and nearly want to cry when he looks at me. He's got such a sweet, kind face. I wish he were mine.

Aidan brushes past him, wrapping his arms around Harley before she has a chance to say anything. His tall body envelops her and her head is lost from view. "I'm so glad you're okay." Aidan chokes out the words.

Harley's arms appear and wrap around his middle. Her words are muffled against Aidan's T-shirt, but I think I hear a "sorry" in there.

"It's okay." He kisses the top of her head. "You're safe now. No one's going to hurt you."

She grips the back of his shirt and squeezes tight.

I blink at my tears and cross my arms, glancing at the floor when Aidan pulls back and kisses his girlfriend.

Griffin softly clears his throat and scratches the back of his neck. His awkward look away is kind of cute, and I end up smiling at him. He catches my expression and grins, giving me a swift wink before clearing his throat a little more loudly.

It's enough to break the kissing spell. Aidan and Harley return to us, her cheeks tinging pink as she rests her forehead against Aidan's chest. His large hand starts stroking her blonde locks and he looks at me.

I smile and step forward. "Harley, you're welcome to stay here for as long as you need to."

It takes her a minute to look up, but when she does, her eyes are glassy. "Are you sure? Will your dad mind?"

"I don't think so." I shake my head. "I have a trundle under my bed. You can take that."

Tears build on her lashes, a couple slipping free as she gives me a wobbly. "Thank you."

"It's still not good enough," Aidan mutters, wiping at her tears. "You shouldn't have to be kicked out of your home. You should report that asshole."

She sniffs and pulls away from him. Crossing her arms, she pinches her biceps and shakes her head. "He hasn't actually done anything to me yet. The first time he tried, I figured out the look on his face and managed to get away before he even got near me. This time, as soon as I walked in the door and saw him there, I just..." She runs her tongue over her top teeth. "I didn't even know he was coming back. He probably thinks he's being all romantic surprising my mom, but she wasn't there. And the look on his face..." She shudders. "He told me I'd grown prettier while he was away, then looked at his watch and asked what time my mom normally gets home." As she closes her eyes, a few tears slip free.

"What'd you do?" I whisper, not wanting to know but desperate at the same time.

She swallows. "I ducked past him and locked myself in my room. He pounded on my door while I grabbed my stuff and snuck out the window. I couldn't get my board or anything. I just had to run."

I rub my roiling stomach while Aidan turns a dark shade of repulsed and livid.

"Will your mom be worried?" Griffin softly asks.

Harley shrugs. "She knows I hate Bryson. Last time he was home, I stayed away. When I tried to tell her why, she accused me of sabotaging her relationship. You know, because I obviously don't want her to be happy." She sucks in a ragged breath and more tears build. She swipes them away with an angry huff.

"That sucks." It's a lame thing to murmur, but I just feel so incredibly sorry for her. I don't know what else to say.

Although Aidan seems to be vibrating with a cocktail of emotions, he manages to softly brush his lips across Harley's head and fiercely whisper, "I'll never let him touch you."

# 29

## CAN'T GET ENOUGH OF HER

### GRIFFIN

"Neither will I." Savannah nods, standing up straight and trying to look way tougher than she actually is.

Damn, she's adorable.

"I won't either." I share a silent promise with Aidan before smiling at Harley.

She gives me a quivery grin and leans into Aidan's shoulder. He's a solid guy and exactly what she needs right now. It's sad that she didn't feel like she could run to him in the first place, but I guess they have only just started dating.

I don't want to admit my ugly family features to anyone, and she probably doesn't want to either. Especially to these well-off, complete families who epitomize the American dream.

A knock on the door makes us all jump. Savannah gasps, then lets out a shaky laugh, touching her chest and giggling, "That'll be Jed."

"Jed." Harley spins and wrenches the door open, lurching into his arms before he's even made it through the door. He hugs her back, lifting her off her feet and walking into the room before dumping her down and pulling back to hold her shoulders. With a stern look, he shakes his head. "Girl, you gotta stop running. You're gonna give me heart failure!"

She lets out a shaky, watery kind of laughing cry, then hugs him again. "I'm sorry."

"At least we found you quicker this time," he mumbles, then continues to tell her off. "And breaking up with Aidan, are you crazy?"

She pulls away and throws her arms in the air. "I freaked out, okay?" She sniffs and swipes her finger under her nose. "How was I supposed to admit my twisted family life to someone so perfect?"

"I hate to break it to you, HQ, but he ain't perfect." Jed points over Harley's shoulder and grins at Aidan.

The tall guy shakes his head and pulls Harley against him, kissing the back of her head before wrapping his arms around her. She snuggles into him and glances up with a mouthed apology.

"You've already said that, and I won't make you say it again." He kisses her nose and I glance at Savannah's face. She's watching them with an affectionate smile.

Weird. I was kind of thinking she'd be jealous or something, but she actually looks happy for them.

I can't get enough of this girl. She's something else. I don't think I've ever met someone with such a big heart. Damn, I wish I could have her. Pain squeezes my chest and I'm about to say that I should go, but Jed talks first.

Glancing around the room, he bobs his big head and murmurs, "Nice digs."

"Oh, uh, thanks." Savannah grins, her cheeks turning rosy—making her even more beautiful.

I seriously should leave.

Again, I'm about to say it when the internal door pops open and a man who has to be Savannah's father appears. His hair is disheveled, his eyes are squinting against the light, and he looks a mixture of irritated and confused.

"Savannah? What's going on?"

Her eyes bulge for the briefest second before she puts on a sweet smile. "Oh, hey, Dad." Her voice is bright and warm, like she hasn't been busted with a bunch of strangers in her house. "Sorry, I didn't mean to wake you. I'm just hanging out with some friends and…"

Her dad glances at his watch, slightly incredulous as he scans the crowd, obviously not recognizing anyone but Aidan.

"Hey, Dr. Green." Aidan puts on his best smile.

The man rolls his eyes and mutters, "It's Kevin. Still Kevin."

Aidan clears his throat and scratches the back of his head, obviously embarrassed. "Sorry, sir. I mean Kevin." He winces, then tries to smile again.

Savannah steps into her father's line of sight, slightly saving Aidan's ass. "They're about to leave. Except Harley. She's staying the night."

He gives his daughter a withering look before pulling in a breath and then pasting on a smile. "Nice to meet everybody. I'm Kevin, Savannah's blurry-eyed father. Not to be rude, but I have work in the morning, and I'd like you all to get the hell out of my house. Please."

"Sorry, sir." Jed apologizes first, already opening the side door.

When Kevin's eyes land on me, I avoid the question of who I am and raise my hand in farewell. "Good night."

My eyes brush over Savannah, who turns in time to give me a brief look of longing before I slip out the door after Jed. It kind of kills me, knowing how she feels. Knowing I feel the same way and there's nothing I can do about it.

Seeing her dad is a really good reminder of why falling for her is a bad idea. But she's making it damn impossible not to.

## 30

# MAKEOVERS AND MANICURES

## SAVANNAH

Sleeping was hard.

By the time I got Harley set up and into bed, I was exhausted, but as soon as my head hit the pillow, my mind started churning. I relived every word from the evening, re-pictured all the little moments. Griffin popped into my head repeatedly, pushing to the front in spite of my efforts.

I drifted off eventually but woke early, so I decided to get up and make my father an apology smoothie.

Dumping strawberries into the blender, I then throw in a handful of blueberries before adding the milk and protein powder. Dad walks into the kitchen just as I'm pouring him a glass.

I hold it out with a smile, and his eyebrows rise in appreciation before he takes the glass.

"I see someone is feeling a little contrite this morning." He winks at me, then takes a sip.

"Maybe." I shrug and grin. "But the smoothie's working though, right?"

He licks his top lip. "It's delicious. But you'd be forgiven with or without it." Coming around the counter, he pecks my cheek, then gets busy preparing a lunch for himself.

I help him out, collecting fruit from the bowl and preparing some veggie sticks.

"So, do we need to go over the house rules?" Dad's voice is casual, but the question is pretty damn loaded.

I give him a sideways glance. "No, of course not. Come on, Dad, it's not like we were having an orgy down there. We were standing around talking."

"You invited a group of people I don't even know—"

"You know Aidan."

He silences my interruption with a narrow-eyed glare, and I bite my lips together.

"You invited a group of people I don't even know into the house without asking. That's not okay, Savannah Sue."

I wrinkle my nose but am still compelled to argue, "You were asleep, you know."

He grunts and slaps a piece of bread on top of his ham and lettuce.

"Mayo?" I ask.

He shakes his head and slips the sandwich into the square-shaped container. I think it's kind of cute that

Dad still takes a homemade lunch to work each day. He could just buy food from the hospital cafeteria; it's not that bad. But old habits die hard, I guess. Mom used to make his lunch every day. Maybe he hates the idea of not doing it. Like somehow it will diminish her memory a little more.

The thought makes me sad, and I swallow, wanting to end our conversation on a good note. "Dad, I am sorry, okay? Do you want me to wake you next time?"

"No, I want you to stop inviting people over when you should be asleep in your bed."

I wince and quickly explain. "We had a mild crisis. It's not like I planned it earlier in the day."

"What crisis?" Dad takes a seat to finish his smoothie.

I lean my hands on the counter and wonder how much to say. "Can Harley stay for a while?"

He narrows his eyes at me. "A while? I don't even know this girl."

"She's my surf instructor."

"And she doesn't have a house of her own?"

Okay, here it is. I pull in a breath and hope Harley won't mind, but I never lie to my dad and if she's going to be staying with us, he deserves to know. "Well, yeah, um…" I start drawing a pattern on the counter with my finger. "The thing is, her mom's boyfriend is back in town and he's a real creeper, and Harley doesn't feel comfortable being there with him."

Dad stops drinking, a look of disgust wrinkling his

face as he gets what I'm saying. "Has she spoken to her mother about it?"

"Her mother doesn't believe her. She thinks Harley is trying to break them up just to hurt her."

"Has he... does she need to report him to the police?"

I shake my head. "He's never gone that far, but he suggests it." I lean forward and rest my elbows on the counter. "It makes me sick and heartbroken all at the same time. The part that kills me the most is the fact that her mother doesn't seem to care."

Dad's expression changes again, his eyes glassing over as he reaches for his phone and stares at the screen for a moment. "Well, I'm...glad you do."

"Thanks, Dad." I smile and take his empty glass away to rinse and place in the dishwasher.

When I turn back, he's standing and gazing at me with a wonky smile. "You're just like her, you know? She took in every waif and stray she could." He swallows and sniffs, smoothing a hand down his shirt before leaving the kitchen to continue getting ready for work.

His words both warm and depress me.

I love that I'm like Mom, but that pining look on Dad's face, that shattered despair. Why'd she have to die?

Swiping a finger under my eye, I will the tears back. I can't let Dad's raspy voice and tumultuous expression affect my day.

I have to—

"Is it okay?" Harley creeps into the kitchen, nearly scaring the crap out of me.

I jump and gasp, then scramble to find my smile.

"Sorry," she murmurs, then points over her shoulder. "I heard your dad moving around upstairs. Is he cool with me being here?"

"Oh yeah. Totally." I brush my hand through the air like it's no big deal. "You can stay for as long as you like."

Harley looks pleasantly surprised, and I give her a triumphant smile. Her swallow is loud and kind of endearing. I don't think she's used to people looking out for her. My heart squeezes with affection and I quickly turn for the fridge.

"You hungry? I make pretty amazing smoothies if you want one."

"Uh...okay."

I glance over my shoulder. "Take a seat."

"Thanks." Harley perches on the edge of the stool and watches me prepare my second smoothie of the morning. I make it just the way Dad likes his. "Man, this is weird."

I pause before pushing the Blend button. "What is?"

She starts nibbling her thumbnail, then admits, "I haven't had a friend who's a girl in a really long time. I've almost forgotten what it's like. Sleepovers...and well, I've never had a smoothie breakfast."

"No way!" I giggle. "You've been seriously missing out. I'm like the sleepover queen. We can do makeovers, paint our nails, watch romantic movies."

The more I talk, the more Harley's nose scrunches. It's kind of funny. I blend up the smoothie, then pour it into two glasses. Sliding hers across the counter, I raise my glass and pronounce, "Welcome to my world, Harley."

She doesn't move to clink our glasses together, so I place mine down without taking a sip and grin at her. "What is it?"

"Makeovers and manicures?" She grimaces.

I throw my head back with a laugh. "The look on your face." I keep giggling and point at her. "You look like I said I'm from outer space and I'm about to probe you with some alien device."

She wraps her small fingers around the big glass and gives me a nervous smile. "That's exactly how I feel. Everything you just suggested is…terrifying."

"Even the romantic movies?"

"Especially those!"

I can tell she's only kidding, although I bet she hasn't watched a true girly movie in years. I'm so going to have to do something about that.

As Harley takes a tentative sip of her smoothie, I start scheduling the day in my head. This could seriously be so much fun. I picture Harley with curlers in her hair while I sit there painting her nails. The image makes me laugh.

"What?"

I tell her what I just imagined, and she grins and shakes her head. "I'm so not that kind of girl."

"I know! That's what makes it so funny."

She starts laughing with me and we're soon in hysterics as we paint more and more pictures, turning Harley into something she will never be.

And you know what?

I kind of love that about her.

I've never had a friend who just wants to be exactly who she is—no makeup, no screens, no illusions.

She may keep her home life locked up tight, but I love that there's nothing fake about her appearance. She's just a girl who loves to surf. There must be something kind of liberating about that, being 100 percent comfortable in your own skin.

# 31

## A LOSING BATTLE

### GRIFFIN

I t's slightly overcast today, but the waves are rolling in nice and steady.

These conditions are perfect for newbies, and Ryder Rentals' business has been steady as we rent out boards to families and the odd brave one who thinks they can surf without too many instructions.

Aidan's handed out so many business cards for Harley, she'll probably pick up a few clients after today.

I cringe as the guy with black spiky hair wipes out yet again.

"This is killing me," Aidan mutters, moving out of the shed and heading down to the water. He's no doubt going to give the guy some free tips. I understand why. Watching him try and fail is freaking painful.

I grin as Aidan calls the man out of the water and sets about trying to teach him on the sand first. The guy seems open to his suggestions, and ten minutes later, he's walking back into the surf with the longboard.

"Think he'll manage?" I ask as soon as Aidan's within hearing range.

He rolls his eyes. "Who knows? He seems to think he knows what he's doing."

I snicker and keep my eye on him before scanning the water to check out the other swimmers and boogie boarders.

Trinity's in the lifeguard chair today, but she'll have her work cut out for her. The beach is only getting busier. I'm guessing Marshall will be taking on extra shifts soon.

Aidan stands outside the shed, his feet planted in the sand as he scans the water the way I am. He'd make a good lifeguard. He'll get all his qualifications too, and by the time that rolls around, I'll be long gone with no chance of getting jealous.

I clench my jaw and try not to think about it.

When I picked up Harley last night, it took me right back to that night Phoenix nearly caught me and I decided to not only leave the Bay Area, but to actually split California altogether. I was lucky enough to get picked up by an old guy who didn't care what my story was. He just drove me south and didn't ask any questions. I can't even remember where he dropped me off. I've slept in so many different places now, they all just kind of blur into one long memory that I find hard to separate and put into an exact timeline.

Aidan lets out a sigh and I glance at him. "You okay, man?"

"Yeah." He nods, adjusting the shades on his face. "Just can't stop thinking about Harley and what might have happened if...things had gone differently."

"It's eating you up, huh?"

"I'm trying not to let it, but..." He shakes his head, his fingers curling into fists. "What if he had touched her? What if she hadn't slipped away? What if you hadn't found her?"

"You're gonna kill yourself with those questions."

"I know." He sighs. "I wish I could switch my damn brain off."

"I'm guessing you didn't sleep much last night."

"Struggled to get to sleep, yeah." He scratches the top of his head, making his hair stick up at funny angles.

I hide my grin and wonder if I should tell him, but then he starts patting it down and arranging it. The poor guy is obviously struggling to relax. Tension is radiating from him.

Lightly slapping his arm, I remind him, "She was found. She's safe, and she's staying with someone who actually cares about her."

"Yeah." Aidan blows out a breath. "Thank God for Savannah."

*You got that right. She's perfect.*

I bite my lips together so I'm not tempted to say that out loud.

"And thank God for you." Aidan glances my way, flashing me a grateful smile.

"It could have been any of us. I was just the one heading in the right direction."

"Man." Aidan shakes his head. "When Sav called to tell me you'd found her, I could barely contain my relief. The feelings were almost too big to deal with, you know? It kind of surprised me. Getting that breakup text was brutal. I just..." He shakes his head again. "I don't know what it is about Harley, but she's got me. All the way. I've never felt like this about anyone before. It's so intense and kind of mind-blowing."

I raise my eyebrows, surprised by how open he's being.

He's staring out at the water while he talks; maybe he's oblivious to the fact that I'm actually here and am listening to every word.

"I thought I loved Savannah, I honestly did, but what I feel for Harley is next level, man. Like, I love her. I seriously love her."

"Have you told her that?" I murmur.

"No way." Aidan snickers. "I don't want to scare her off."

I chuckle with him for a minute.

"It seems kind of fast to feel this way," Aidan mutters. "Sometimes I worry that I'm being overly romantic about this whole thing, but then I see her and I feel it all over again. Being with her makes me happy. Just seeing her makes me happy. And when I'm not with her, I'm thinking about her. That's love, right?" He spins to look at me, but all I can do is shrug.

I've never been in love before, so I'm not exactly the right person to ask.

But I get what he's saying. I understand what it's like to think about a person constantly, to feel better about life when they come into view.

My heart hitches as I spot something on my left and realize how much brighter the world just became.

Savannah and Harley are walking over to the shed. They're talking and laughing together, their hair floating on the breeze. They both look hot in their swimsuits, but all I can really see is Savannah's smile, the shape of her face, those two dimples that took hold of me the first time I saw them.

*I wish. I wish. I wish she was mine.*

Glancing away, I try to keep my eyes on the water, but I can't.

By the time the girls approach the shed, all I can see is Savannah.

She's all I want.

And I'm not sure how much longer I can deny myself the pleasure of her company.

The walls I'm so desperately trying to protect myself with are crumbling faster than I can build them. Am I just fighting a losing battle?

I must be, because all I want to do is spread my arms wide, fall to my knees and surrender.

# 32

# SCREW COMMON SENSE

## SAVANNAH

Well, I never got to give Harley a manicure or a makeover, but surprisingly, I wasn't disappointed.

Instead, we lounged around watching *To All the Boys I've Loved Before*, which I've adored since the first time I saw it. It's so relatable, even if the mom parts do make me cry. Harley was really quiet throughout the movie, and afterward she made us watch *Ready Player One*, just to "get the girly out of our systems."

I laughed but complied, then afterward made her admit that she loved my movie choice. It took a lot of effort to get those words out of her mouth, but she eventually caved. "Okay, fine, I adored it! I loved every moment of that sappy, sweet, romantic movie, and Peter is like..." She got this goofy smile on her face, her cheeks tinging pink as she hugged a pillow to her chest. "He makes me think of Aidan."

I didn't say anything, and her expression fell, like she felt guilty for loving my ex-boyfriend. It should suck a lot more than it does, but for some reason I'm okay with them together. I like Harley, and I didn't want to ruin our morning, so I just rolled my eyes and started singing the chorus for "She's in Love with a Boy." It was one of my mom's favorite songs. She was a total country music freak. It used to drive me nuts, but now those songs feel a little bit like home. I listen to them sometimes, when no one else is around, and pretend Mom's sitting next to me on my bed, belting out her favorite tunes.

I'm not sure if Harley knew the song or not, but I didn't even get through the chorus before she threw a pillow at my head, then laughed and said, "Shut up."

I nearly tossed the pillow back, but a pillow fight in our pajamas? I just couldn't bring myself to be that cliché. Instead we slowly got ourselves organized, ate lunch, and then came down to the beach for a surf.

It was so much fun.

Who knew a girl like me could find something like surfing so thrilling and addictive? The salt in my hair, the sand sticking to my skin—I thought I'd hate that, but I don't mind it at all.

I probably look like a mess getting out of the water, which I do struggle with a little, but the fact that Harley doesn't care makes it easier to let go.

Even so, as I'm drying off, I try to tame my hair and make it look mildly respectable. As soon as it's dry enough to manipulate properly, I'll braid it over my shoulder or go for one of those messy buns at the back. Just something I can do without a mirror that won't look completely terrible.

I'm hyperaware that Griffin has been in the Ryder Rentals shed all day. I wonder if he's been watching me. I think maybe he has. I've glanced up there so many times, and once or twice I've caught him staring at me.

I don't mind so much.

Even though he's not interested, it still gives me tingles to think he's noticed me. He's aware.

Maybe he does want me after all, but something is holding him back?

I kind of want to play with that idea, but then it might give me too much hope. Especially if the truth is that he just doesn't like me.

Maybe I suck at kissing?

The thought makes me frown.

"You okay?" Harley throws her towel over her shoulder.

"Huh?" I blink and look at her.

Her eyes narrow as she tries to figure out why I'm suddenly so flustered. Then she looks to Ryder Rentals and my cheeks start to heat like the sun.

"Stop it," I mutter.

She snickers. "Why don't you just go talk to him? He's right there."

"Because he doesn't want me to talk to him."

"Oh, okay, so he called you last night because he didn't want you to talk to him?"

I huff and look away from her.

"Come on, Sav. You know you want to." Harley glances at the shed, her face lighting with a grin as Aidan appears out the door and starts walking toward us. "If it were me, I'd just go up and ask him, 'Why the cold shoulder?' then see what he says."

I let out a scoffing laugh. "You so would not do that. When you thought you'd lost Aidan, you went into hiding and got drunk off your ass, so don't try and sell it that you're all amazing with talking about the big feels." I soften my argument with a wink and a smile, hoping I haven't offended her.

After a pause that's just starting to get uncomfortable, she snorts. "Okay, so I don't like talking about my feelings, but you're good at it. I mean, you were brave enough to look Aidan in the face and break up with him. I freaking texted the guy."

"Because you didn't mean it."

"Well, you kind of didn't, right? I mean, you wanted him back, right?"

I squeeze my eyes shut and sigh, wishing this conversation had never started.

"I'm sorry. I didn't mean to offend you, I just... I

know you like Griffin, and he's a nice guy, and it'd be cool if it worked out."

My eyes creep open just as Aidan gets within hearing range. This conversation is now officially over. I silently tell Harley that with a pointed look. She winks at me and smiles as Aidan's hand glides across her shoulders.

"Hey, babe," he whispers, kissing her softly.

He used to call me that, but he seems to say it differently with her.

I swallow and get busy packing up my bag.

"So, this is weird." Aidan points between us. "I haven't said anything, but I gotta say it now."

I stand up and hitch the bag onto my shoulder. "What's weird?"

"You two. Hanging out. My ex and my girlfriend becoming BFFs."

Harley snorts and pats his stomach. "Like I would ever use the term BFF."

I start to giggle as I suddenly picture her strutting through her school with blonde pigtails and a miniskirt, spouting off about her BFF.

It's a funny image, and I hope they won't ask me to explain why I'm laughing.

Thankfully Harley just grins at me.

I smile back, then check my watch. "We better split or you'll be late for work."

She groans.

Aidan squeezes her against his side. "I handed out a

bunch more cards today, babe. Hopefully you'll pick up a few more lessons."

"Thank you," she murmurs and kisses his T-shirt. She really is short next to the guy. It's kind of cute.

"I'm actually just getting off now. Griff has got it covered for the last couple hours. Why don't I take you to work, and then Sav can be a free agent?"

"A lucky agent," Harley grumbles.

I give her a sympathetic smile but want to remind her that she has a boyfriend who is willing to drive her to work, a guy who cares about her. He'll no doubt be there after her shift as well, willing to drive her back to my place, to be whatever she needs him to be.

If anyone is lucky, it's her.

I bite my lips together, not wanting to start a game of comparisons. When I think about what brought her to my place last night, then I'm the lucky one.

Aidan and I share a quick look and I put on a smile.

"Catch you guys later." I raise my hand in farewell, then point to Aidan. "You still remember where the spare key is? If you're picking up Harley after work, she can just let herself in." I then look at Harley. "I'll arrange to get a key cut for you this week."

Her eyes widen with surprise. "You don't...have to do that. I mean, will your dad be okay with that?"

"Harley, you're our indefinite guest. Of course I'm getting you a key." I smile. "I trust you."

Her smile disappears, and she suddenly looks like

she's about to cry. Blinking quickly, she sniffs and murmurs, "Wow, thanks."

Who knew that three little words could mean so much to her? I smile, liking her even more than I did this morning.

Aidan kisses her head and steers her toward the stairs that lead up to the parking lot.

I watch them go, then wonder what to do with my time.

Lettie is spending a second night with her friend, and Dad's probably still at work.

I should swing past the hospital, but, selfishly, the idea of hanging out in that cold, sterile place talking to an unresponsive Skylar is kind of depressing. I want to stay out here in the sunshine. My legs and arms are too jellylike to surf again just yet.

Glancing north, I think about wandering up that way. I'd no doubt bump into Craig and some of his buddies, but do I honestly feel like hanging out with those guys? Simon's not too bad, but Jonah and Craig—ugh.

I grip my bag strap and gaze at the ocean, trying to decide what to do. There are chores at home. Dad would probably appreciate me doing some grocery shopping.

Or I could—

"You look like you don't know what to do with yourself." Griffin appears on my right, his smile warm and friendly. He keeps walking until he's only an arm's length away, then stops in the sand, facing out to the water like I am.

My lips fight a grin, but I quickly lose the battle and admit with a smile, "Just wondering what to do with the rest of my day."

He shrugs, crossing his arms and lightly clearing his throat. "You could hang out here for another hour or so, then come have dinner with me."

What did he just say?

It takes my brain a minute to compute and I slowly angle my body toward his. "Dinner? With you?"

"Yeah…" He draws out the word, turning so we're face-to-face.

I tip my head and study his expression. He's a hard read, even without shades on. His brown eyes are looking right at mine, his mouth relaxed. His entire posture oozes calm, unhurried peace. How does he do that all the time? I feel like my insides are constantly wound tight—the churning cogs and wheels grinding together, on the verge of breaking apart.

Running my tongue over my bottom lip, I narrow my eyes and ask, "If I do that, will you stop talking to me for a couple of days afterward?"

He cringes, and I snatch a glimpse of unrest, the calm façade breaking at the edges.

For some reason that makes me feel better. He's normal, just like the rest of us.

Flicking a couple of dreads off his face, he sighs and

looks out to the ocean. "Yeah, maybe I shouldn't be asking you out."

I cross my arms and don't bother hiding my irritation.

I'd rather he just outright tell me that he's not interested rather than messing with me. This whole asking me out and then changing his mind is so much worse, and I need to tell him that.

"Look—"

"Thing is, I really want to ask you out." He rushes out the words, looking raw, honest and strikingly vulnerable for the briefest moment.

That flash of sincerity melts my heart, and all the feels I've been trying to fight come screaming to the surface—a hot, bubbling affection I can't deny.

My throat is suddenly thick, making it hard to talk, and I end up squeaking out my question. "So what's the problem, then?"

"I..." He huffs and looks pained, his face bunching. "I don't know if it's wise. I don't want to...hurt you."

"Why do you assume you'll hurt me?"

He winces, then lets out a hiss. "I'm a nomad. I'm not sticking around forever. I can't... I can't stay."

"Why not?"

He swallows and looks to the sand. "Savannah, there's things you don't know about me. Things I can't... I can't really tell you."

*Hmmm, well that's completely intriguing.*

Some would say that I should run the opposite direction while I still can.

But all I can hear is the voice in my head telling me that if I don't take this chance right now, I'll regret it forever. So what if I only get one date with him? Do I really want to pass that up?

Why should I always do the responsible, sensible thing?

For once, I don't want to think about the future or anybody else. I just want a date with Griffin.

Without another moment's hesitation, I nod. "Well, thanks for the warning."

His smile is sad and resigned. It's kind of adorable. He looks like a wounded puppy dog.

With a grin, I drop my bag in the sand and take a seat. "I'll just wait for you here, then."

I should really be going home to shower and pretty up, but I'm worried if I disappear, he might change his mind. At least if I stay within view, he'll be forced to follow through with his invitation.

He's still standing there gaping at me.

I glance up and give him my best smile, feeling pretty damn empowered right now.

Whatever comes of this date, I'm glad I said yes.

# 33

## A MELTING RESOLVE

### GRIFFIN

Okay, I did not expect her to say that.

And now she's sitting in the sand, smiling up at me like she's just won a trophy.

Damn, how can I resist her?

It's impossible to think of anything cool to say, so instead I give her what is most likely the goofiest smile ever and mumble something about heading back to the shed.

Concentrating on work quickly becomes a challenge. My eyes keep drifting to the sand where Savannah is lying on her towel. She doesn't seem bothered by the wait.

I'm still surprised she just sat down and stayed. Two hours is a really long time to just hang out. Why didn't she go home and shower up?

Why doesn't she come over and hang out with me?

*Because you didn't ask her to, you idiot. You told her to wait there!*

I suck in a breath and ignore the internal berating. I kind of need the space to figure out what I'm going to do tonight.

Temptation wars with common sense for the rest of the afternoon, but when she's still there after I lock the shed, I know I can't ditch her.

Truth is, I don't want to ditch her.

She sees me coming and jumps to her feet, shaking out her towel before rolling it around her arm.

"Thanks for waiting. I hope you weren't too bored."

"No." She grins. "I don't mind watching the world go by."

Her dimples are so sweet, I can't even explain what I love so much about them. And it's not just her dimples. Everything about her is sweet.

I've never had the chance to hang out with a girl like Savannah before. Those beach bunnies and resort flings I had were with flirty, brazen women who weren't afraid to tell me exactly what they wanted. All they were after was shallow fun.

Maybe that's why I'm so hesitant with Savannah.

She's not like that.

She's got depth. I don't have to spend much time with her to see that. She knows what it's like to burn, to suffer, to bleed. She knows heartache, and yet here she stands in the sand, smiling her sweet smile and melting my lightweight resolve.

I hold out my hand to her. "Come on. Let me drop this stuff up at the main office, and then I'll take you out to dinner."

Without hesitating, she slips her hand into mine. I lightly squeeze her fingers, my entire body ignited by her touch.

And then she asks me about my day. "Tell me the highlights, the lowlights, and everything in between."

I wonder if this is something her mother used to say after a school day, but I don't have the courage to ask. I don't want to do anything to wipe that smile off her face, so instead I comply and tell her all the insignificant details of my day.

We walk up the beach, probably looking like an established couple rather than a first date.

Talking is easy and when we reach the main office, we end up standing outside the door for several minutes before I realize that I'm standing there still holding the cash box.

Savannah waits for me outside and I rush to lock away the money and sign out. Devon sees her outside the windows and wiggles his eyebrows at me. "No wonder you're in a hurry."

I ignore his snicker and bolt back out the door, resuming our highlights/lowlights conversation.

It's Savannah's turn, and I soak in her voice as she tells me about her dad, the movie marathon, and how much she adores surfing. I offer to join her sometime, then start talking about other spots, acting like seeing her again will be no big deal.

My inner voice is warning me against future plans.

Future plans are dangerous and should be avoided at all cost.

*Just be in this moment, man. Nothing more!*

I clear my throat and stop talking, opening the door for Savannah to get into my truck. I'll drop her back at her car after our date.

"So, where are we going?" She buckles up and I smile at her.

"I know this place with an amazing view."

Her forehead wrinkles as she most likely scrambles to think of restaurants with amazing views. She's no doubt imagining a bunch that I can in no way afford.

With a soft chuckle, I fire up the engine, which grunts then starts chugging like the old, reliable truck she's always been. I tap the dash as a silent thank you, then reverse out of the parking lot.

"Seriously. Where are we going?"

"Trust me. I think you'll love it."

"O-kay." She leans her arm on the window's edge and rests her head on her knuckles, grinning at me.

I flick on the radio and we listen to a little MKTO while we drive to my favorite burger joint. They make these monster burgers that are so damn good.

"Oooo, I love burgers," Savannah chirps. "I've never been here before." She glances over her shoulder, looking out the back window of the truck. "Not exactly sure what you mean about the view though."

I laugh. "We're getting takeout."

"Oh! Why didn't you say that? I've been racking my brain trying to figure it out." She lightly slaps my shoulder as she jumps out of the truck.

I grin and take her hand like it's the most normal thing in the world. Her fingers fit pretty damn well between mine and I'm not sure I ever want to let go. Slipping into the burger bar, I stand back while she scans the menu and eventually settles on a burger with bacon and pineapple. I go for the BBQ Beast, which has two patties, bacon, special sauce and enough lettuce and tomato to make it a tower of deliciousness.

While we wait for our order, we talk about our favorite foods and I learn that Savannah is a fan of Thai, which I haven't eaten too much of.

"Next time, it's my turn to buy, and I'm taking you to this great place near my house. It's like the only Thai restaurant in Ryder Bay. Funny thing is, it's owned and run by this Latino chick who's spent most of her life traveling the globe. She calls it culinary research." Savannah giggles. "But I'm not complaining. Her trips to Thailand have taught her so much and I adore her... and her food."

I force a smile, trying to push aside the thought that there shouldn't be a next time. This is it. This is our date, and I have to focus on the here and the now.

"Order twenty-one!" the guy at the counter calls.

"That's us," I murmur, jumping up to take the bag, plus grab a stack of extra napkins.

Savannah takes our drinks, and then I drive us up to a lookout I discovered a couple of weeks ago. It's probably a make-out spot for couples or something, but if you come early enough, there aren't many people around. It blows my mind, because the sunset from this spot is so freaking amazing. Why don't more people come out to enjoy it?

Reversing the truck into the perfect spot, I then jump down and lower the tailgate, so Savannah and I can eat our food while watching the sun go down.

It's probably the best evening I've ever had.

Talking comes easy. I keep the conversation focused on the present or just recent history, and we manage to keep going for two hours straight. The sun sets while I tell her stories about working in Mexico. We finish off our food and drinks while she tells me about Walton Academy and Skylar.

I catch the juice dribbling down my chin, then laugh and hand her a napkin so she can do the same. It's funny listening about her posh school when she has a blob of ketchup on the corner of her mouth. She wipes it away and I'm sure she's blushing, but it's kind of hard to see in the dim light.

Scrunching up my burger wrapper, I tuck it back in the paper bag and then start hunting for the old lantern I keep in the box of the truck bed. It's an easy find, and I light it with one of the three matches left in the box.

Must grab some more soon. I never know when I'm going to need to light this thing.

Carefully placing it behind us, I smile at the soft glow on Savannah's face when she turns to glance at it.

"Wow, that reminds me of some old Western."

"I know." I chuckle. "I picked it up at a secondhand store at the beginning of the year. Isn't it cool?"

"I love it." She tucks a lock of hair back into her messy braid and swivels around to rest her back against the edge of the truck.

I copy her so we're face-to-face, the vast ocean on my left and the warm lantern on my right. My knee brushes hers and I feel the tingle down my leg. Clearing my throat, I ask her a question, hoping to learn even more about her.

"Other than surfing, what do you like doing with your spare time?"

And so I learn a little more about Skylar. I read between the lines and figure out how controlling her best friend can be, but also that Savannah's the kind of person who doesn't mind going with the flow. She seems to enjoy following, is content to be led.

It makes me wonder what she'd do if she had to really decide something for herself.

I guess she kind of did that this afternoon when I gave her an easy out and she plunked down in the sand and waited for me.

I can't help a grin as I shuffle to get a little more comfortable and focus on the sound of her voice. She has a beautiful voice—soft and melodic. I'm pretty sure I'd be happy to listen to it all night.

The conversation between us rides a wave from light laughter to serious undertones, but every time it dips, it picks up again. It's a pretty incredible ride and it makes me wish I could be 100 percent honest with her. When she opens up about her mom and the way it makes her feel, I want to tell her about my shitty childhood and how I can relate to some of what she's been through. Losing a mother at any age sucks.

I have no idea what time it is when the words between us seem to ebb and fall into a peaceful silence. The night sky is black, the stars above us twinkling bright. I should probably get her home. A couple of cars have arrived since we did, and they've parked a fair distance away. I can only imagine what's going on inside them.

With a thick swallow, I glance out at the black ocean and murmur, "It's probably time to wrap this up, I guess."

She lets out a heavy sigh and unearths her phone from her bag. She winces and nods, "Yeah, probably." Her fingers fly over the screen as she types a quick text. I'm assuming she's letting her dad know where she is.

That must be nice.

Having someone to check in with.

As liberating as my lifestyle is, it can get kind of lonely.

But that's my cross to bear, right? My choice.

"I don't want it to be over," Savannah whispers as she slips her phone away. She gives me a shy smile. "I don't want you to ignore me the next time I see you."

I squeeze my eyes shut and scratch my forehead, unsure what to say.

"I know. I mean, I think I know...why you did it. The whole not hurting me thing. Not wanting to get attached because you're not here long-term. And there are things you don't want to tell me."

My eyes are still closed when she reaches for me, curling her fingers around mine. I flinch but quickly capture her digits and open my eyes.

"But that's my risk to take." She looks down at our hands and rubs her thumb over my knuckles. "And when you do leave, I'll probably hate it, but even if it's tomorrow, I've still had the best night of my life."

"The best?" I blow out a breath. "That's high praise."

She blushes and slays me with her dimples.

"I like being with you." Her voice is feather soft and beautiful.

With my free hand, I brush my fingers down her cheek. "I like being with you too."

She bites the edge of her lip and pulls in a breath to say something, then stops.

I gently squeeze her fingers. "What?"

"No, it's embarrassing." She shakes her head and starts twirling the end of her braid with her index finger.

"Come on. You can tell me anything."

She snickers and holds her breath, then lets it out in a rush and blurts, "I really want to kiss you again."

She says the words so fast I nearly miss them, but as I drink in the look on her face, the words compute and I swear if I wasn't adoring her before, I am now.

She's basically taken out her heart and stuck it straight to her sleeve. And now it's my turn.

I can either lean back and mumble some bullshit about keeping this a friends only deal, or I can lean forward and put my heart on the chopping block.

It's not really a choice when there's only one option I'm gonna take.

I lean forward and press my lips to hers.

## 34

## SPECULATION IN THE DRINKS AISLE

## SAVANNAH

I went to sleep, hovering in a dreamlike state above my bed.

Not really, but I felt like I was floating as I replayed Griffin's delicate kisses over and over in my mind.

Although I'd texted Dad that I'd be home soon, I drew that soon way out. I think I snuck in the door around midnight, but how could I honestly do anything else?

Griffin's soft, warm tongue in my mouth, his strong hands gently grasping the back of my neck, the heat radiating from his body. All of those things are far too addicting. I couldn't just wrap that up and call it a night.

It was actually him who pulled away and forced us into the cab of his truck. It was him who drove me back to my car. But it was also him who pressed me against my driver's door and kissed me good night.

I thought my heart was going to burst right open. I can almost hear the bubble of emoji love hearts rising out of me.

The thought makes me giggle, and I start humming as I apply a fine layer of makeup and step back to examine myself in the mirror.

Harley left hours ago for an early surf with Aidan, and then she has two new surf lessons before her shift starts at Freshmart. Hopefully she'll be able to quit that job soon, if Aidan can keep bringing in those surf lessons. I think he's kind of proud of himself for looking after Harley that way.

With a grin, I swivel sideways to make sure my sundress is sitting right. I'm not heading to the beach today. As tempted as I am, I need to visit with Skylar, and there are a bunch of household chores to get through.

Scarlett wants me to drop her and her friend at the new mall near Walton Academy. It's going to eat into my day, but I'm in too good of a mood to complain.

"Lettie, time to go!" I call as I step out of my room and trot down the stairs.

Grabbing the shopping list off the refrigerator door, I scan it to make sure I haven't forgotten anything. I'll prepare dinner tonight so all Dad has to do is heat it. Griffin gets off work at six, and I want to be available to hang out with him.

We haven't officially arranged anything yet, but when I texted him this morning, he said he'd like to see me. I did a little spin and hugged the phone to my chest.

I'm planning on grabbing some Thai takeout and meeting him by his truck. I wouldn't mind a repeat of last night.

The smile on my face is actually starting to hurt, but I can't stop grinning. Happy bubbles are bursting in my chest, rising and popping in a constant stream. I forgot how tingly and warm a new crush can make you. Whatever I'm feeling for Griffin is super intense and I'm loving it.

"I'm ready." Lettie skips down the stairs. She appears to be in a good mood this morning, and I send up a silent thank you prayer.

Slinging her handbag over her shoulder, she actually smiles at me before heading to the door.

I breathe in a happy lungful of air and follow my sister out to the car.

The ride north is an easy one. Lettie and Johanna talk the entire way there, babbling on about everything Skylar and I would never talk about. We'd go to a mall for clothes, makeup and shoes. My sister is going to the mall to buy props for her Instagram account.

Bless her.

We couldn't be more different if we tried.

There's one lone bookstore at this new mall, and I

bet they'll spend the bulk of their time hanging out in it.

"So I'll come back and get you at three." I point to Lettie's watch. "Don't make me have to come and find you, okay? Set an alarm or something so you don't lose track of time."

She rolls her eyes. "I got it."

Johanna snickers at Lettie's surly tone, and I force a bright smile. I won't let my happy day be tainted. "Have fun!"

Lettie ignores me, grabbing Johanna's arm and pulling her into the mall without so much as a good-bye. I sigh and suddenly wish I hadn't pointed at her watch or told her to set an alarm. It's weird how one teeny tiny thing can turn my smiling sister into a grumpy cow.

Clenching my jaw, I check traffic and pull away from the curb, determined to keep my mood upbeat and positive. I'm heading to Aviemore Hospital, which is hardly a hotbed of joy, but I'm determined to tell Skylar all about my date and make it sound just as fantastic as it actually was.

---

I spent two hours at the hospital.

Marlo wasn't there when I arrived, so it gave me a chance to tell Skylar everything. She had no choice but to listen. In a weird way, I missed all of her interruptions. I used to tell her every detail of my time with Aidan and she'd always ask me to expand, get to the juicy parts. She'd smile over our kisses and squeal at the sweet things he used to say to me.

I'm pretty sure she'd smile and squeal about Griffin, probably even more so because he's potentially a better match.

Aidan and I got together because there was no one else around. I did enjoy being with him, but that intensity, the rising bubbles that I'm feeling with Griffin, I never really had that with Aidan. Or at least not so strong.

I shouldn't compare. They are two completely different people, and therefore it's two completely different relationships, but Aidan's been my only serious boyfriend and it's hard not to.

Pulling out my shopping list, I enter the grocery store just around the corner from my house and grab a shopping cart. It's a big one this week, because Dad has let the cupboards run dry. Usually between me, Dad and Rosalie, we manage to keep the house functioning, but Rosalie has dropped her hours during the summer break, which means I need to pick up the slack.

Dumping my purse in the top part of the cart, I start my rounds and am halfway through when I bump into Craig. He's in the drink aisle, holding a can of Monster Energy and a can of Red Bull. He obviously can't decide which one to pick.

"Hey, Craig." I get his attention and he glances up, giving me a half smile.

"How's it?"

"Yeah, good." I don't really want to talk to this douchebag, but we are in the same friends group. Politeness made me say hello and politeness will keep me here for a few minutes.

Lifting up the grocery list, I stupidly state the obvious. "Just doing my shopping."

"Yeah, I can see that." His eyebrows wrinkle.

"So, uh...what are you up to this afternoon?" I suddenly hope he doesn't think I'm fishing to hang out. I should have worded the question differently.

He studies me for a second, then shrugs. "Not much. Catching up with Si and Jonah for a game of basketball. Would have invited Aidan, but that dickwad's gone and got himself a job. What the hell was he thinking?"

I spread my hands wide. "He's getting paid to hang out on the beach. It's not a bad gig."

"Yeah, I s'ppose." Craig frowns and I wonder if he's annoyed with Aidan for pulling away from their circle. He's kind of created a new life for himself with Harley, and his old friends are no doubt feeling dissed.

Maybe I should say something to him. Skylar sure would.

"You seen her lately?" Craig glances at me, then to the ground. "Skylar?"

"Yeah." I nod, aware that I haven't seen him once at

the hospital. "You should go visit her. Dad says she needs to hear familiar voices."

"Yeah." Craig's head starts bobbing. "Yeah, I should. I'm not a big fan of, you know…hospitals."

"I don't think anyone really is." I raise my eyebrows. "She's your girlfriend though. I mean, isn't she?"

He clears his throat. "Yeah, I don't know. I mean, I hope so, but she… well, it happened before we had a chance to…" His words trail off, a dark look crossing his face.

"What is it?" I grip the cart handle.

Craig glances over his shoulder then leans toward me. "I overheard Dad talking on the phone this morning. I only caught his side of the conversation, but he thinks Skylar was pushed."

"What?" I can barely breathe the word.

"Yeah, he didn't want to think that at first. I mean, he went and saw Wyatt, questioned the guy for ages, but he swears black and blue that he never touched Skylar."

"He told me the same thing."

"Yeah, but is he telling the truth?" Craig frowns. "The guy's a—"

"What does your dad think?" I interrupt, not really wanting to hear Craig's opinion of Wyatt Mattley.

Craig shakes his head with an irritated frown. "The guy who owns the Fish Shack told Dad that he saw Wyatt storming past his window about twenty minutes before Skylar fell, so it can't have been him. The timeline doesn't work."

"I can't imagine Wyatt doing that to her anyway." Even as I say the words, my blood runs a little cold.

Do I really know that quiet, awkward guy well enough to assume he wouldn't hurt her?

What if the timeline is slightly different? It's not like Aidan would have checked his watch before diving in the water after Skylar.

I chew my lip, trying to process it all.

"Thing is, this morning, Dad got confirmation that some man with dreads was loitering down at the pier that night. Dad was going in to interview the witness today, but from what I picked up, this dreadlocks guy was the one who pushed her."

The air in my lungs turns frigid. "Dreads?"

"Yeah." Craig shrugs. "I was wondering if it's that Ryder Rentals guy. Do you know him?"

I can't say anything as the thrumming in my heart works its way into my head.

Griffin.

No, that doesn't work.

I can't make that work.

But he said there were things he couldn't tell me. He didn't want to get involved because he might have to split soon.

That can't be the reason why.

He's a nomad, not some creeper!

"I gotta go." I choke out the words and push my

cart away from Craig, refusing to stop even when he calls my name.

Thank God he doesn't follow me.

Trying to finish the grocery shopping is a joke. All I want to do is run to the beach and make sure Griffin didn't do it.

There has to be some mistake.

Griffin isn't like that.

He put himself in the line of danger to protect me a couple of times. He wouldn't push someone off a pier!

# 35

## TOO CLOSE FOR COMFORT

### GRIFFIN

As soon as Marshall radios me up to the main office, I know something is wrong.

The second I spot the squad car in the lot, my gut twists and I nearly bolt right then, but that'll make me look bad, so I force my quivering limbs to walk into Marshall's office. I order my stiff lips to form a smile, and I force my croaky voice to say, "Afternoon."

"Hello, son. Take a seat." Officer Malloy points to the chair beside his, and I share a quick glance with Marshall before sitting down. He's standing behind his desk, looking grim, and my twisted gut starts to ache.

Shit.

They know.

How'd they find out?

What'd I do wrong?

Is it the social security number? I've been using it for a while now. I thought that was solid. Maybe another part of my ID has slipped up.

I'm scrambling to work it out when Office Malloy tells me, "I need to talk to you about the night Skylar De Beer fell."

My mind has been so busy freaking out over my ID that it takes me a minute to register what he's said.

"I'm sorry?" I shuffle in my chair, not sure if I should be relieved or wary.

"We've had a report come in that you were seen on the pier that night. I'd just like to go over your where-abouts again."

Shit. Shit!

I wasn't on the pier that night.

I was at home. Well, not my home. I was squatting in someone else's house!

"Uh..." I lick my bottom lip and try to remember what I said last time we spoke. "I finished work at six, then headed home to watch some TV."

I'm pretty sure that's right.

Looking up, I watch the officer's face, hoping he believes me. His mustache twitches as he stares down at his notes.

"Last time I spoke, you said you lived alone."

"I do." I nod.

"So, no one can verify your story?"

I frown and lean back in my chair.

"Come on, Dayton." Marshall throws his hand up.

"Griffin's a good guy. If he says he was home watching TV, then he was. If I'm going to believe anyone, it's him. He's honest, responsible, and he wouldn't hurt a fly."

I swallow as Marshall sings my praises. The word "honest" pulses in my head like a drumbeat. If only he knew. Shit, I wish I'd never had to lie to him.

I wish there was a way out of this mess!

I'm gonna have to split soon, but if I leave too quickly, will that just make me look guilty?

Officer Malloy sighs. "Did you do anything on the way home? Get takeout? Stop for groceries? Anything I can follow up with."

"Probably." I squeeze my eyes shut. "There's a great burger joint I eat at a lot, but I'm just trying to remember if I went there that night." My eyes pop open and I look at him. "But what difference does it make? Didn't Skylar fall later that night? If I stopped for food on the way home, the timeline for me being on the pier when she was could still fit. I wish I could tell you that I was with a girlfriend or some buddies, but I was alone, and I have no alibi."

The officer gives me a hard look, and I shift in my chair again.

"Look, who reported this lie?" Marshall snaps, crossing his arms and frowning down at Officer Malloy.

"I'm not really at liberty to say," he mumbles.

"Dayton, gimme a break. You're accusing my best guy here."

With a little tut, the officer frowns down at his notepad and mutters, "One of the surfers. He said he saw a guy with shoulder-length dreads on the pier that night. He described you perfectly."

What?

I scramble to think who'd want to make up some bullshit lie about me. Scanning faces in my mind, I wander through the beach and suddenly it hits me like a freaking missile.

"Ripper." I grit out the guy's name, then share a look with Marshall.

His pale eyebrows dip together.

"Uh…" Officer Malloy flicks back through his notes. "Not Ripper."

"What did he look like?" I lean forward in my seat, resting my hands on my knees.

"I can't really tell you that."

I let out a sharp huff. "Look, if it was a tall, muscly guy with a crew cut and a tattoo of a naked chick running from his shoulder to his elbow, then I know him as Ripper. He's got it in for me because I saw him hassling a girl down on the beach the other day. I told him to shove it. He's pissed with me and making up stories so I'll get in trouble."

My heart is pounding right now.

I'm telling the truth, but it still feels like some kind of lie, because I can't tell the whole truth. I'm trying to defend myself, when I'm actually guilty. Not of pushing or hurting Skylar, but still... I'm not as innocent as I'm trying to appear and it's doing me in.

This is too close.

If Malloy runs an intensive check on me, he could find a hole. Even a pinhole can become a massive tear. Things could come to light.

"I know Ripper," Marshall backs me up. "The guy's a sleaze and I hate having him on my beach. I've spoken to Axel a couple of times about keeping him in line."

"From what I've heard, he hassles girls a lot." I glance between the two men, then mumble, "It wouldn't shock me if *he* was the one down on the pier that night, demanding something from Skylar that maybe she wasn't willing to give."

My comment hangs in the air and I watch the two men share a silent look.

Flipping his notebook shut, Officer Malloy slips it back into his breast pocket and starts fidgeting with his pen. "I know the guy you're referring to. I won't tell you if he's my witness or not, but I can tell you that I'll have a chat with him. I'm trying to follow every lead I can on this one." He looks slightly abashed, and a little pained. This case is obviously getting to him.

I sit back with a sad frown. "You honestly think she was pushed?"

He rubs a hand over his mouth. "I don't want to think that, but..." He shakes his head. "Until she wakes up, we're never really going to know. Every lead I think I get never pans out."

He can't tell us about the case and what he's managed to find yet, so I don't bother asking.

"Well, let's just hope she wakes up soon," Marshall murmurs.

I glance at my boss and add, "And let's hope she remembers."

Officer Malloy swallows and bobs his head, then gives me a forced smile. "It'd sure make my job a lot easier." Bracing his hands on his knees, he looks between his feet and shakes his head. "Every day that goes by, I worry she's not coming back to us."

"She will." Marshall nods. "Jeff and Marlo need her to. We can't believe anything else right now."

Scratching the edge of his mustache, Officer Malloy agrees with a nod, then rises to his feet. Holding out his hand, I'm obliged to take it and accept it.

"Sorry for putting you through a second round of questions. I'm just trying to be thorough."

"No problem." It's a struggle to get the words out and then form a smile.

He doesn't seem to notice and takes his leave.

As soon as he's gone, I want to fold in half, but Marshall is standing there watching me.

I give him a pained grimace.

He snickers and shakes his head. "Don't worry about it. I believe you, and I won't let Dayton hassle you again." He points at me. "I was telling him the truth when I said you're my best guy."

The kind words rattle me.

Part of me wants to cling to them and promise to never leave Ryder Bay. Like Savannah, Marshall is just another reason to stick around.

And that's the part that scares me.

I can't stay.

I'll need to hold out for a little while longer so I don't make myself look suspicious, but I can't stay. Today was too close. In the next few weeks, I'm gonna need to move myself along.

The thought kind of kills me, and I can't even fake a smile as I take my leave and head back to the shed.

## 36

### TOO YOUNG FOR THIS CRAP

### SAVANNAH

This afternoon has been shit.

All I've wanted to do is find Griffin, but responsibilities—ones that shouldn't be mine—have stopped me.

Lettie and Johanna called for an early pickup, so after unpacking the groceries at home, I headed back up to collect them, then played taxi service after they begged me to stop at one other place on the way home.

I sat stewing in the car, wondering what I was going to say to Griffin when I saw him.

Of course, I don't believe the lies. He wouldn't hurt Skylar. But still, the idea of someone spotting him down on the pier that night has completely thrown me.

Griffin is kind of secretive. I'm worried he won't tell

me the truth if I ask. Why am I falling for this guy? I should be running the other direction, but every time I think that, I feel so incredibly sad and gutted that I have to concede how strong my feelings are.

I've only had two dates with him, and the intensity of my feelings should be freaking me out, but still I want more. I want Griffin to be innocent. I want him to stay so we can be together.

What if this accusation runs him out of town?

Lettie told me off for speeding on the way home. We ended up getting into a bickering match about it. Poor Johanna. She sat in the back, super quiet and no doubt uncomfortable. When I pulled into the driveway, Lettie stormed out of the car, slamming the door and then yelling at me, "I'm staying with Johanna tonight!"

I jumped out of the car and bit back, "Have you checked with her mother? You can't just invite yourself to someone's house, Scarlett. It's rude."

She let out a little scream and stamped her foot. "I can stay there whenever I damn well want. She said I could. She knows how difficult living in this place is for me."

And with that, she turned on her heel and ran inside.

Difficult?

That spoiled little brat thinks living in our house is difficult?

She has no freaking idea. I wanted to grab her and

tell her, shake her shoulders and make her listen, but what was the freaking point?

Johanna scrambled up the stairs after my sister and I got busy preparing dinner. Thank God Louis is still with Grandma and Grandpa. He doesn't need to see Lettie and me fighting.

I was halfway through dicing up the chicken when Lettie returned with her bag and thumped it down on the kitchen counter. "Just so you know, Johanna called and checked with her mother. I'm welcome to sleep over again. She's coming to pick us up now, so you don't have to drop me off."

I gave her a tight smile and managed to grit out, "Have fun."

She glared at me. "I've texted Dad already so you don't have to tell him. I'm capable of making my own plans."

My jaw worked to the side as I continued focusing on the chicken, and not slicing the tip of my thumb off. It's kind of hard to do when your eyes are glassing with tears. I kept my head down so she couldn't see them.

I never know how to respond in those situations. Do I apologize because she thinks I mother her too much? Is that what she's trying to oh-so-subtly say?

Thankfully Johanna's mother showed up a few minutes later and the girls rushed out the door with a hurried goodbye.

I was left alone with my sniffles and the chicken.

By the time Dad got home, dinner was prepared. I felt bad just leaving him to eat alone, so I sat with him, forcing the food down and waiting for a reply text from Griffin that was not coming. I couldn't send him a fourth one. I'd just have to go find him.

"Well..." Dad pushes the plate away and smiles at me. "That was delicious."

"Thanks," I murmur, placing my fork down and giving up. Hopefully Dad won't notice my serious lack of appetite. "What are you doing tonight?"

He gives me a tired smile and runs a hand over his head. "A big part of me wants to plop down in front of a movie and fall asleep, but I've been invited out for drinks."

"With who?"

"Donna and her boyfriend." He winces.

"You worried you're gonna feel like a third wheel?"

He shakes his head then shrugs. "I don't know. I think other people will be there too, I just... It's weird going without her."

I swallow, feeling way out of my depth on this one. What would Mom say if she were here? I scramble for the right words and eventually settle on, "You can't spend the rest of your life working and falling asleep in front of the TV. Mom would call you boring." I give him a weak smile. "You should go, Dad. You should." I nod as if to assure myself I'm saying the right thing.

He mirrors my expression, looking so vulnerable and uncertain it hurts my heart.

"Go." I nod again, then point to the stairs. "It'll be good for you."

Wiping the edge of his mouth with the napkin, he bunches it on the table beside his plate. "Maybe I should, but not until I've cleaned up. You cooked, so I'll deal with the dishes."

"Thanks." I carry my plate into the kitchen for him and scrape the leftovers into the trash.

"What are you up to now?"

"I'm gonna head out to see a... some friends," I hedge, not wanting to go into the details. If he asks me, I'll give him specifics, but I don't really want to spill until I hear Griffin's side of the story.

Dad grunts. "The ones from the other night? They're not going to be crowding out my house again, are they?"

I grin and shake my head. "No."

He winks at me and kisses my cheek. "You get going, then, sweetie. Have fun."

I move to leave the room, then stop and point at him. "You promise you'll go out tonight? I'm not going to come home and find you asleep in front of the TV?"

He raises his right hand and gives me a scout's honor. "I promise."

"Good." I grin, then spin to grab my stuff and leave.

I don't even know where to start looking for Griffin. I should have skipped dinner and made sure I met him on the beach, but Dad needed me.

With a heavy sigh, I reverse out of my driveway and suddenly feel way older than my seventeen years.

---

I don't find him.

Ryder Rentals was locked up for the night and no one was around. I texted Aidan to ask if he knew where Griffin was, but he had no idea. He doesn't even know where the guy lives…and neither do I.

After aimlessly cruising the streets for an hour, I eventually give up and return home.

If I thought my afternoon was shit, I didn't know squat. My evening has been the worst, and I'm fighting tears when I pull into my street.

I sure hope Dad is having a better time than I am.

Easing on the brakes, I turn into my driveway and jerk to a stop.

Griffin is perched on the rock beside the mailbox.

Emotions roar through me like a tidal wave and I can't decide what to feel as I slam out of my car and walk over to him.

"How long have you been here?" I pull out my phone to see if I missed a message from him. "I've been driving the streets looking for you." Nope, my phone screen is blank. "Did you not get my texts?"

He stands up with a heavy sigh. "I got your texts."

"And you suddenly forgot how to reply?" I snap, my emotions roiling.

His eyebrows flicker with confusion. "How do you know?"

"Because you wouldn't hurt someone like that."

He's touched by my belief, I can see it in his eyes. The edges of his mouth curl up with a sad smile as he reaches forward and cups my cheek with his hand. "You're too good for me."

The words make my heart sink.

What is he saying?

Taking a step back, I put some distance between us. Is he trying to tell me this isn't going to work? Like he doesn't deserve me, so he's just going to leave?

That's it.

He's leaving.

That's why he couldn't text me today, because he wants to take off, but didn't know how to tell me. And now he's standing on my doorstep saying goodbye, probably out of guilt or some kind of honor because he's such a freaking nice guy.

This isn't fair!

I don't want to hear goodbye!

I shake my head, my lips wobbling as I warn the tears back. "You wish you hadn't taken me out last night, right? You had a great time, but it's not going to work." I let out a ragged breath and scrape my fingers through my hair. "I guess you did warn me."

"Sav, it's not like that."

He reaches out, but I retreat a little farther away. "It *is* like that."

I need to get a handle on myself.

He's here. He hasn't snuck away into the night. I could reach out and touch him. This is exactly what I've been wanting to do all day, and yet I'm standing here telling him off like some irate mother.

I close my eyes and fight the swell of tears. I'm too young to be a mother! I don't even want that stupid role and now I'm standing here treating the guy I'm crushing on like a child!

Covering my eyes with my hand, I sniff and silently beg the tears not to fall.

"I'm sorry," Griffin whispers. "I should have texted back, but I didn't know what to say, and then I just couldn't stop thinking about you, so I decided just to show up. It was stupid, I should have texted you back. I should have called or...or something."

His fingers skim down my arm, so I lower my hand and blink, then force myself to look at his face.

He's beautiful. The porch light illuminating his freckles and that apologetic, sweet look on his face. He's beautiful.

And I like him too much to stay mad at him.

"You're here now." I sniff and try to force a smile. "Is everything okay though? I mean, did it all work out with the police and everything? I've been worried sick about you."

"I wasn't on the pier that night."

"I know." I nod.

"It's not because of you."

"I hate that line. Just tell me the truth!"

I'm not much of a shouter, unless I'm arguing with Lettie. It feels weird yelling at Griffin. I hate that I'm doing that. Biting my lips together, I look to the ground between us, that big gap that suddenly feels a mile wide.

"I'm a nomad," Griffin whispers. Part of me wants to block my ears and start singing "la-la-la" obnoxiously loudly, but instead I quietly shuffle my feet and listen. "I shift around. I don't like to get attached, you know?" He stops talking, so I glance up and see him grimace, fisting his dreads into a ponytail and looking out across my front yard as he mutters to himself, "And now I'm falling for a girl who'll keep me grounded. And I shouldn't stay grounded."

My quivering lips twitch with a tentative smile. "I don't know how to feel about that statement." He looks at me and I swear my heart feels his gaze. It beats with yearning, making my voice tremble. "Part of me is like 'Yay, he's falling for me.'" My forehead wrinkles as I pull in a ragged breath. "And the other part is bummed out because you don't want to be grounded. You don't want to stay with me."

He sighs and steps forward, turning the mile into an inch. His touch is featherlight, but I feel it throughout my entire body as the pads of his fingers press against my cheek, tracing the line from the corner of my eye to the tip of my chin.

I look at him, catching his eye and holding his gaze. "Which part will win? The wings that want to leave me or the heartbeat that wants to stay?"

He can't answer me.

All we can do is stare at each other with the big question hanging between us. The tip of his tongue runs across his lower lip, and I fight the urge to kiss him.

I want to pretend like this conversation isn't happening.

I want to go back to last night where even though I knew the risk, it felt like a really safe bet. It's weird how I was so 'live in the moment' yesterday and now I'm standing here demanding some kind of future from him. Is that unfair of me to expect that?

I sniff and look to the ground, conceding in my head that he did warn me.

"I'll never leave you without saying goodbye." His husky voice sends a warm shiver through my torso. His fingers tip my chin up so we're looking at each other again.

I drink in his sweet expression and want to smile, but all I can manage is a sad, halfhearted effort. "But you will leave me."

"Not tonight." He shakes his head. "Not in the next heartbeat." I catch the beginnings of his smile as he leans forward and presses his lips to mine.

His soft touch and warm mouth are impossible to resist, and I wrap my hand around the back of his neck, pulling him close and holding on while I can. His strong arms secure me to him, and I close my eyes against the unknown, the dreaded goodbye. I need to be in this moment. Even if it makes the inevitable goodbye hurt even more, I need to kiss Griffin right now. I need to soak in every second of him while I have the chance.

## 37

## CONTENTMENT

## GRIFFIN

I can't decide if tonight has been a success or a failure.

I'm kissing Savannah right now, so that's a big win.

But I couldn't leave her, which is an uber fail on my part.

I mean, I do want to stick around for a few weeks until this whole Skylar mess blows over, but I shouldn't be making out with this girl when I'm inevitably going to leave her.

I feel bad.

But kissing her feels so damn good.

I can't just walk away.

Not tonight.

At least I didn't lie. I told her I'm leaving, and I promised to never do that without saying goodbye.

How the hell I'm supposed to walk away from her is a problem for another day.

Her tongue slides into my mouth, distracting me. I grip the back of her cotton dress and hone my senses into feeling every part of her soft body pressed against mine. Her fresh, flowery scent, the wisps of hair tickling the top of my arm as she tips her head to deepen the kiss even more. I hungrily kiss back, desire pulsing through me in a set of dangerous waves. Waves that could knock us right off our feet.

A soft throat clearing registers in the back of my brain, and it takes me a second to acknowledge it.

I'm still kissing Savannah, lost in her touch.

Another throat clear and I finally get it.

Pulling back, I snap out of my daze and notice Harley smirking at me.

"Sorry to interrupt, I just..." She points at the door behind us. "Do you mind if I just...and then you can keep going, for as long as you like." She grins at Savannah, wiggling her eyebrows as the two of us pull apart with an embarrassed snicker.

I glance up to the road and spot Aidan, his car engine idling as he raises his hand and waves at me.

"Have a good night, you two!" He laughs and drives off as Harley slips inside.

Savannah tucks a lock of hair behind her ear, her cheeks tinging red.

"I guess I should..." I point over my shoulder and take a step back.

Her head jerks up, her eyes filled with such alarming sorrow that I have to stop moving.

With a thick swallow, she points over her own shoulder and whispers, "Do you want to come in? Just for a little bit. I'm not ready to say good night."

Her pleading expression does my heart in and I nod before I can think better of it.

Slipping into the house after her, I follow her to the den where I was last time. Her house is lush. I admire the sweeping staircase up to the second floor, trying to walk softly on the gleaming tiles. I only spare a quick glance into the kitchen as we walk past, but this house must only be five or six years old. Ten at the most.

"How long have you lived here?" I whisper, wondering where her Dad's room is and if he minds me sneaking into the house.

She holds the den door open for me and closes it once I walk through. "Dad's out, by the way. You don't need to whisper."

"Oh." I smile and click my fingers as I scan the room.

"Take a seat." She points at the couch against the wall and I plunk down on the blue cushions.

Savannah tucks her legs beneath her and curls up beside me. "We moved here when I started middle school, so that's like six years?"

"Cool." I nod and glance at the paintings on the wall. There are three of them and they look to be done by five-year-olds. I bet they were. I bet her mom adored each one and framed them just to make a point. I don't know the woman, but from what Savannah's told me, she seems the type to do that. "This place is nice." I nestle farther into the couch. "A real home."

"Yeah," Savannah whispers. "I like it. Although it's not the same without her. She made it more homey than I can."

"She was the mom." Savannah doesn't say anything, and I can't help wondering if she feels like she can't fill her mother's shoes. "It's not your job, you know? You're the daughter. The big sister."

Her swallow is audible, and I glance at her to make sure she's not crying. Her eyes are glassy, but no tears have fallen. With a grateful smile, she leans her head against my shoulder. I lift my arm so she can snuggle against my chest.

It takes a little shuffling to get comfortable, but I soon find myself lying full length along the couch with her tucked in beside me. It feels so damn good I don't think I ever want to move.

Her arm drapes over my waist, and as I stroke the top of her head, I feel her starting to relax.

It's a peaceful sensation and my own body begins to fall as our quiet conversation turns to whispered mumbles and then sweet nothings as we drift off to sleep together.

I don't think I've ever felt more content in my entire life. Sleeping soundly is never easy for me, because I'm always on edge that someone might show up or catch me in their home. It's different when I'm actually invited into one, which is why when I hear a door click open, then a forceful smack of wood on wall, I jump like I've been shot.

"What the hell is this?" A deep voice makes my eyes snap open, and any peace I may have been feeling is long gone, and potentially lost forever.

Savannah's dad is standing in the doorway looking ready to kill me.

# 38

# A FRACTURED TEAM

## SAVANNAH

Being jerked out of sleep is kind of harrowing.

I didn't even realize I'd drifted off until my dad started yelling.

I've gone from perfect bliss to a waking nightmare in a matter of seconds, and my brain is scrambling to align everything.

"Get out!" Dad points to the door, leaning over Griffin like he's some kind of imposter.

"Dad!" I blink and struggle to untangle my legs from Griffin's.

He helps me out, lifting my knee and sliding off the couch. Inching away from my irate father, he snatches his keys off the coffee table and mumbles, "Goodbye."

I hate that word coming out of his mouth, so quickly jump to my feet. "Wait! You don't need to be kicked out of my house." I spin to Dad. "You can't talk to him that way. We weren't doing anything wrong."

Dad's nostrils flare, his cheeks puffing out as he gets ready to open his mouth and spew more lava. I turn my back on him, facing Griffin with a pained frown.

"I'm sorry," I whisper.

His smile is kind. "I'll talk to you later, okay?"

"Promise?" My voice hitches and he pauses before walking out the side door.

He must know what I'm really asking, understands my fear. Was that mumbled goodbye the last one I'll ever hear from him?

His eyes gleam with sadness, but he doesn't break my heart just yet. "I promise," he mouths, then glances over my shoulder, his eyes bulging before making a quick retreat.

I have to admit, I'm kind of shaking as I turn to face my dad. I'm not used to seeing him angry, and I'll never get used to seeing him angry with me. It's happened maybe twice in my entire life. Compared to some dads, it's probably not that bad, but this is *my* dad. My sweet, uber-calm father whose ability to cope with stress is off-the-charts amazing.

But not tonight.

Tonight, he looks ready to explode. I can picture the top of his head coming off and steam spurting from his ears. The image is kind of comical, and I'm almost fighting a smile until Dad's shaking finger points at the door.

"That's your crush?" He's incredulous. "How old is he?"

"Uh… twenty-one? I think."

"You think? You mean you don't actually know?"

"I…" Squeezing my eyes shut, I try to capture that conversation. I'm pretty sure he said twenty-one, but Dad's making me flustered and I can't quite remember. In the end I huff and throw my hands up. "What does his age matter anyway?"

"Savannah, you are seventeen years old, and while you live under my roof you don't have guys sleeping over!"

"We weren't doing anything." I point to the couch and wish I was still on it, tucked against Griffin's side— safe and warm. "We just fell asleep."

"Wrapped in each other's arms! What was going on before that?"

I wince, hating Dad's assumptions. I never slept with Aidan, and I'm not sure I'm ready for that with Griffin either. We're still new.

But man, if he stuck around…

My cheeks grow warm as I capture a quick snapshot of hot and heavy with Griffin.

A little growl rises in Dad's throat and it snaps me back to the moment, where I blink and can honestly tell him, "Nothing. We just talked, that's all."

He shakes his head.

"That's the truth!" I counter. "Yes, I have kissed Griffin, but I didn't lie here on this couch making out with him. I invited him in, we got talking, lay down together and fell asleep. What other details do you want?"

Dad's simmering, his face mottled with patchy red splotches.

I sigh. "What do you want me to say, Dad?"

"You promised me that you'd ask before inviting people into this house." He points at me. "I expect more from you, Savannah Green!"

He never calls me Savannah Green unless he's really pissed off, and it sparks something inside of me—some kind of low-lying irritation that tramples right over my remorse and unearths a shit-ton of angst that I've obviously been harboring for too long.

Throwing up my arms, I shout, "I know! The expectations are pretty damn high around here!"

This stumps Dad. "What?"

He was no doubt expecting an apology from his usually mild-mannered daughter.

But not tonight.

I'm steamed too.

Maybe it's the fact that the best nap I've ever taken has been ripped away from me. Or maybe that my time with Griffin has an expiration date and Dad just ruined what little time we do have. But tonight, I don't just want to apologize, bow my head and shuffle off to my room.

Tonight, I'm obviously hungry for a showdown.

"How can you stand there yelling at me, acting all righteous and expecting an apology, when you treat me like your equal most of the time? But as soon as I fall asleep next to a guy I really like, you freak out and accuse me of only being seventeen and not old enough to date a man who isn't in high school anymore. Well screw that, Dad! I am old enough! I have to play mom to my siblings, I have to do the grocery shopping, manage this house when you're at work, cook meals, do a bunch of stuff that none of my friends ever have to do!"

"Savannah—" Dad tries to stop me, but I plow right over his interruption.

"You apologize for putting too much on my plate, tell me to get a hobby, but you don't really want me to do those things! You need me to be the good daughter who waits on everybody in this house, because you can't manage on your own! I'm sorry if this is letting you down, but maybe I can't manage this role either!"

My voice starts to wobble and crack at the end, and I'm super annoyed by the fact that I'm starting to cry. I'm trying to be strong here and the tears aren't helping.

Before they can actually fall, I push past my speechless father and am relieved he doesn't follow me. I don't want to be forced into an immediate reconciliation. I just want to go to bed and pretend like none of this has happened.

I hate yelling.

And with Dad too.

We're the allies in this house. A team.

But tonight, the team's been broken, and I don't even want to fix it right now.

Thumping into my room, I forget that Harley's in there and flick on the light.

"Oh, shit, sorry," I quickly mutter and switch it off as she sits up blurry-eyed.

"Are you okay?" Her voice is sleepy, but I wonder if she's faking it. Surely she heard me shouting.

Clenching my teeth, I mutter a soft, "I'm fine. Good night."

It's a blatant lie, but she doesn't push it. "Night, Sav."

I creep past her and get ready for bed, sniffing at my tears the entire time. Once I'm finally under the covers, I curl into a ball and set the tears free. They softly trail down my face, and I can't seem to stop them no matter how hard I try.

# 39

## A STREET RAT WITHOUT A HOME

### GRIFFIN

I haven't seen Savannah today.

The only update I've gotten was from Harley, who walked past the shed about half an hour ago to give me a message.

"Savannah's not feeling great. She's going to catch you tomorrow."

I frowned at Harley's vague explanation.

When she noticed my expression, she rolled her eyes and elaborated. "I didn't hear all the details, but there was yelling for about fifteen minutes, and then she stormed up to bed, told me she was fine and cried herself to sleep. I tried to convince her to come out for a surf today, but she refused to leave her room."

"What's going on?" Aidan butted into the conversation.

I gave him a sharp look that warned him not to get involved.

His confused frown was almost comical as he backed away. Harley will no doubt tell him once I'm out of earshot anyway.

"Was she grounded?"

"I don't know." Harley shrugged. "I didn't see her dad when I left this morning. I'm guessing he's at work already. Look, she's probably going to mope in her room for the day, then be fine tomorrow. Just give her some space."

It makes me glad that I didn't text her this morning like I wanted to. I tried about five times to write the perfect message and, in the end, deleted everything and gave up.

I've been worried about her, wondering what her father said after I left. Wondering if she's grounded.

Shit. I want to make this right.

I hate the idea of Savannah crawling into bed and crying herself to sleep. And I just left her, thinking it was the best move. Maybe I should have stayed, stood my ground and defended her.

Would that have made things worse?

With a sharp huff, I slump back in my seat and absentmindedly re-twist one of my locs. It's a habit I got into about a month after getting the dreads. I re-twist about two or three a day. By the time I do my whole head, I'm ready to start over. With over a year's worth of practice, it's kind of automatic, and I'm usually unaware that I'm even doing it.

But today I'm aware of everything.

The sound of the waves hitting the shore, the smell in this dank rental shed, the way my insides are simmering with unrest, the fact that time is ticking in slow motion. People's laughter on the beach is grating; even Aidan's friendly chatter is getting on my nerves.

His shift finishes in a couple of hours, and then I'll be on my own for the rest of the afternoon. I'm kind of pleased. It's hard making friendly conversation when all I can think about is Savannah and what I'm going to say the next time I see her.

It should be goodbye.

I can't stay. I can't get wrapped up in a relationship. I'll be doing everyone a favor if I pack my bags and slip out of town. I won't come between her family. With her mom not around, they need each other, and I won't cause any kind of rift between them.

"You okay, man?" Aidan's voice makes me glance up.

I force a smile and lean forward. Has Harley had a chance to tell him yet? It doesn't seem like it. Maybe she's waiting for me to go on my lunch break and then she'll spill.

I peer out at the beach. For a Friday, things are moving kind of slowly. We've rented out a bunch of boards, but it's not the steady stream from earlier in the week. I'm surprised. Tomorrow will probably be stupidly busy, just to make up for it. I'm down to work the entire weekend—if I'm here.

I grimace. The idea of ditching Marshall is a killer as well. At least Savannah's the only person I've promised to say goodbye to.

Damn, that's going to suck on every level.

"Uh… Griff?" Aidan's still staring at me. Waiting for an answer.

"Yeah." I bob my head. "Yeah, I'm good. Just, uh…" I shrug. "Hungry. I'm gonna take an early lunch. Is that okay with you?"

Aidan looks like he doesn't believe me, and he shouldn't. I'm talking total bullshit right now. Thankfully he's kind enough to smile and agree. "Happy eating."

I force out a laugh, grab my phone and wallet, then take off before he can try to figure out what my problem is. He'll no doubt be clued in by the time I get back.

I need to get a handle on this whole thing. Will seeing Savannah do it?

Should I ignore her request and just show up at her place?

Nah. I think seeing her will just tear me up some more. I need to save that up for my final goodbye.

The thought is a rock in my gut.

*But it's right, man! It's not just about you.*

I'm leaving to protect her. To get out of the way of

her awesome life. Me and my lies will only hinder it. If I care about her, then I should go.

*But not until you fix it.*

The thought stops me in my tracks.

Fix it.

I need to fix it.

With a heavy sigh, I have an idea that could work to mend a bridge. I don't love it, but it's all I've got right now. Picking up my pace, I find a quiet spot around the back of the main lifeguard office where no one can hear me. I then spend the next minute searching Google for the number of Aviemore Hospital.

It takes three transfers, but eventually I get through to Dr. Kevin Green's office.

My heart is pounding as I listen to the rings, and I don't know whether to sigh with relief or disappointment when it switches to voice mail.

"This is Kevin Green. I'm unavailable to take your call right now. Please leave your name and number after the tone, and I'll get back to you as soon as I can."

The tone is a prod on the back, and I stand up straight, fumbling with my words. "Uh, hello, Dr. Green. Uh...this is Griffin."

*Shit, hang up, man. Hang up now!*

But it's too late for that, I've already started talking.

"I just wanted to call and reassure you that nothing happened last night between Savannah and me. I'm sorry if you felt like I disrespected her, or you, in any way. It wasn't my intention to fall asleep on that couch, I just was so relaxed and...happy." I whisper the last word, feeling how true it is. "Your daughter is an amazing person. She's a credit to you and...and your wife. I'm so sorry about that, by the way. Um...I just... I won't... I don't want to do anything to disrupt your family life, and if you don't want me around, I'll respect that. Savannah loves you so much, and I may not know her half as well as you do, a quarter even, but I do know she'll be hurting over upsetting you. She's such a kind, sweet person. Her heart is... well, it's huge. I don't deserve even the smallest portion of it and won't... I won't take it. I—"

A second tone beeps, letting me know I've spoken for too long.

I hang up, tapping the phone against my short beard and wondering if I should call back and leave a second message, but I'll probably just end up waffling.

How do you tell the father of the most amazing girl you know that you're falling hard, but are actually getting ready to leave? The contradiction is too confusing to put into words.

Scratching at my aching temples, I slowly step out of the shadows and shuffle off to find a little food. I'm not hungry, but force down an egg salad sandwich. It'll have to tide me over until the end of my shift...which doesn't come in a hurry.

After what feels like the longest day of the century, I head to my truck and drive to the house I've been staying at. I park a couple blocks away and go get some dinner before walking to the deserted home. It's quiet and empty, just the way I need it to be.

Dumping my bag on the end of the bed, I pull out my cash box and unlock it. I carefully count my savings and figure that I've easily got enough for a quick getaway. I could probably also manage a different ID if I need one. Although Griffin Ayala has served me pretty well so far, seems bulletproof. I should just stick with it.

Unfolding my fake birth certificate, I stare at the incorrect information and try to own it the way I should. I mean, most of the time I can. I'm Griffin Ayala, born and raised in San Diego.

But I'll never be able to ignore the real truth.

With a shaky sigh, I unearth one of the two pictures I've kept from my past.

Gazing down at the photo, my heart burns as I stare at my mother. Her smile is dazzling as she holds her two sons on either side of her. I must have only been about three in this photo. I don't know if we were homeless at that point, I can't remember. We were all laughing for whoever was taking the picture though.

Brushing my thumb over the image, I try to remember myself as Griffin Bram Jones, son of Michelle and the asshole who left her pregnant, cashless and looking after a two-year-old, Phoenix.

How did she do it?

How did she smile like that when life was such a damn struggle?

She always knew how to find something good in every moment. No matter what we were facing, she'd look at me and Phoenix, point her finger at us and say, "Come on, boys, let's find a drop of sunshine."

It'd be anything from the fact that we got to eat two meals instead of one, or the shelter had room for us that night...or if the day had been especially bad, it'd be the fact that she loved us more than anything in the world.

With a heavy sigh, I run my hand across my short beard and think about how much I've changed.

I'm not Griffin Jones anymore. I can never be him again.

And I never want to be.

I'm not the kid who roamed the streets of Vallejo anymore. I've become the nomadic surfer, and in some ways, I feel more myself as this person than I did as Phoenix's kid brother—the street rat without a home.

"You're still homeless," I mutter, dropping the photo and slumping onto the edge of the bed with a heavy sigh.

I don't know how long I sit there with my head in my hands, staring at the floor until the world starts to buzz. My vision is blurry, my mind running a movie reel of me and Savannah, me at the beach, me on a surfboard, me talking to Marshall, hanging out with Aidan.

Me being Griffin, the guy from Ryder Bay, and loving every minute of it.

Do I really want to leave that?

But how can I stay?

Pulling myself out of that funk is damn hard, but I force my body straight and pack all my things away. It's dark by the time I zip up my bag and tuck it into hiding under the bed. Rolling out my sleeping bag, I fluff the pillow, then check my watch.

It's still too early for sleep, but what else am I supposed to do?

I could call Savannah. Even though she said tomorrow, it's been a full day since I saw her.

With a cringe, I lie down and gaze up at the ceiling, my mind consumed with missing her. The picture in my head is crystal clear. I can almost feel her beside me, smell her sweet hair, and feel every contour of her body as she lies against me, our legs intertwined.

It hurts to think I'll never have that again.

Reaching for my phone, I decide I can't wait any longer. I need to call her, hear her voice...and then make a time to meet up so I can get one final kiss before slipping out of Ryder Bay.

It's going to freaking hurt, but a promise is a promise.

My thumb is poised over her name when I hear the lock on the front door click open.

# 40

## RECONCILIATION ON THE BEACH

### SAVANNAH

A soft knock on the door makes me jerk and look over my shoulder.

I'm still on my bed. I've been there most of the day, hiding out. I have no idea what's been happening outside of my room, and I still don't care.

Waking up was torture. My head was pounding from too much crying; I felt like someone was playing it like a drum, but using a hammer instead of a stick. When I got up to use the bathroom and caught a glimpse of myself in the mirror, I knew the outside world was not an option for me today. My eyes were puffy and swollen, red blotches covered my cheeks.

Yeah, it was an indoor day for me.

When Harley tried to invite me out, I refused and

then asked her to pass a message on to Griffin. I didn't even want to text or talk to him.

Part of me is humiliated that he was forced out of my house, and another part of me doesn't want to face what's coming—the inevitable goodbye. If anything is going to run Griffin out of town, it'll be my dad. I don't want to hear his goodbye. If I just make myself unavailable to see him, I'm protecting myself, right?

My logic actually sucks and is completely contradictory.

I don't want Griffin to leave me, so I avoid him at all costs, meaning I'm not actually seeing him so he might as well not be around anyway.

Argh!

It's so incredibly stupid, and it's taken me most of the day to realize how dumb I am.

Whoever's outside my door knocks again. I wish they'd identify themselves, although the only real options are Lettie or Dad, and I'm not in the mood for either of them.

"Savannah." Dad stretches out my name, warning me that I need to answer him or he's going to barge on in.

I press my lips together and roll onto my side so when he opens the door, he can't see my face. My back's actually starting to hurt from spending so much time in bed, but I'm not going to admit that if he asks.

I just want to wallow.

Why won't he let me?

My door handle clicks and I squeeze my eyes shut, gripping the edge of my pillow.

"Honey, we need to talk."

"I don't wanna talk," I mumble.

"That may be the case, but we need to no matter how you're feeling right now."

I keep my back to him and don't say anything. With a heavy sigh, he approaches me and perches on the edge of my bed. I can feel his hip against my spine.

"Savvy, I love you. But I'm human, and all I saw last night was my baby girl wrapped in a stranger's arms. You gotta let me be shocked."

His soft confession is so sweet and endearing. I roll over before I can even think about it and look at his torn expression. He obviously feels kind of bad about how everything went down, and it makes my eyes fill with tears.

He mirrors my expression and swallows before casting his gaze around the room. "You been in here all day?"

"Yes," I whisper.

Picking up the empty Pringles can and the chocolate bar wrapper off the floor, he gives me a sideways look.

I shrug. "There's an empty tub of Ben & Jerry's in the trash too."

This makes him smile just a little, then shake his head. "Come on, sweet girl. Let's go for a walk."

A walk. Dad's classic reconciliation tactic.

For as long as I can remember, whenever one of us

got into serious trouble, after our timeout or "consequence"—as my parents liked to call it—was over, Dad would always take us for a walk. It'd just be an amble through the streets or along the sand. A chance to clear the air and talk about our feelings. We'd always return to the house happy and smiling.

Not sure the happy and smiling will happen tonight, but he's probably right, a walk would do us good.

"Is Lettie around?" I sit up, taming my hair into a ponytail, before going to my closet for footwear.

"I spoke to her before I left work. She's doing another night at Johanna's."

I roll my eyes, in spite of the fact that I feel grateful. "I'm pretty sure she hates me."

"She doesn't hate you," Dad counters.

Poking my head out of the closet, I give him a withering look that tells him I don't believe it.

Dad sighs and runs a hand down his tie. "She's just going through a challenging phase."

"And taking it out on me," I harrumph, then shut up, plunking down to slip my shoes on. I don't really want to talk about Lettie right now.

"She'll get there, Savvy. We just have to be patient with her." Dad's voice shakes, and even though I can't see his face, I know he's thinking about Mom and how much we've all lost.

I wonder how things would have gone down last night if Mom had walked in on me and Griffin. Dad must have felt so out of his depth. Even though I've had a boyfriend before, it was someone Dad knew well. A fellow classmate. In Dad's eyes, a safe bet.

Griffin's a complete unknown to him, not to mention the fact that he's older.

I wish I could explain how awesome he is, but I doubt Dad wants to hear that there's lots I don't know about Griffin, because there are things he can't tell me.

Yeah, that'd go down just great.

Finally ready, I come out of the closet and pull my shirt straight.

Dad stands with a smile and tips his head toward the door. "Let's go."

Snatching my phone off the stand, I quickly text Harley to let her know I'm out with Dad.

We're just walking out the door when she replies.

*Good luck! I'm at Aidan's place. We're just starting a movie marathon so won't be back until late.*

I send her a couple of emojis to let her know I got the message, then slip the phone into my back pocket.

"Everything all right?" Dad double-checks the door is locked, then catches up to walk beside me.

"Yeah, I was just checking in with Harley."

His smile is sweet as he wraps his arm around my shoulders and gives me a gentle squeeze. "The mother to all."

I sigh and shake my head. "I don't want to be, but who else is going to do it?"

Dad drops his arm, sliding his hands into his pockets while we stroll down the street. I'm assuming we'll head for the stairs leading down to the beach. The moon is out tonight, and the beach will be beautiful... peaceful. I think we both could use some peaceful tonight.

"I'm sorry about all the pressure you feel I'm putting on you." Dad's voice is soft and husky. "I don't mean to do it, and please don't take what I'm about to say the wrong way, but you're such a natural, Savannah. Just like Mom. You don't have to be told or directed, you just instinctively know what needs doing and you get on with it. Scarlett and Louis have no idea, whereas you just silently seem to know everything about how to keep the house functioning."

I don't know how to respond, so I just don't say anything.

Dad glances at me, obviously hoping for something, but all I can do is stare straight ahead. My throat is swelling with emotion.

I guess Dad just gave me a big compliment. I'm a natural.

But do I really want to be a natural mother at seventeen?

No!

I want to be cool like Harley.

I miss Skylar. When she's around, she forces me to act my age when I'm out of the house.

Shit, and now I'm falling for an adult as well. A man, according to my dad.

What the hell is wrong with me?

Irritation simmers in my stomach. "I'm feeling old before my time, yet you treated me like a kid last night. It was humiliating."

"I'm sorry," Dad murmurs. "Truly, I am. I just saw you two and freaked out."

I huff. "You can trust me!"

"I know. I know. But it's not just you I have to trust. It's him as well." His expression is pained. The streetlight is bright enough to show me his struggle. "I don't even know the guy. All I saw was his big arm around you and I...I..." He shakes his head and sighs. "I probably could have handled it better." We reach the end of the street and meander down the pathway. Dad stops at the top of the stairs, letting me go first.

We don't say anything until we reach the bottom and walk around the big boulders.

The beach is quiet and empty. This end by the cliffs often is, unless there's a teenage party happening. I think of Skylar and the last time we were down here. A shudder runs through me before I can stop it. Crossing my arms, I squeeze tight and resume walking once Dad's beside me.

"Tell me about him." Dad nudges me with his elbow. "What's his name again?"

"Griffin," I murmur and can't help a little smile. "He's a really sweet guy, Dad. He works at Ryder Rentals. He's a surfer, and one of the nicest people I've ever met. He saved Louis's life."

"So that was the guy. I've been meaning to thank him for that. I kind of feel bad that I never got around to it."

"Yeah, well you should. He deserves it." I nudge Dad back with my shoulder and he snickers.

"He called me today."

"What?" I blink.

"Left a message on my phone at the hospital, apologizing for how things went down last night. Telling me how great you are."

My chest restricts, buzzing with a mixture of warmth and sadness.

I don't want him to go!

"He does sound like a nice guy. I guess I'm just worried about the age gap, but maybe I can get over it, as long as you don't sleep with him." He gives me a sideways glance and my cheeks catch fire.

"Dad! I didn't sleep with Aidan."

"So? This is someone completely different. Love can make us break our own rules. It happens."

With an embarrassed swallow, I clear my throat and try to reassure him, "I'm not ready for that yet. Besides, Mom told me it'd be a good idea to wait until after I graduated high school. I don't want to let her down.

And Griffin would never force me to do something I don't want to."

"How do you really know that?"

I stop in the sand and glare at my father. "I know it, Dad." Tapping the center of my chest, I give him a pointed look. "I *know* it."

After a long beat, Dad bobs his head. "I understand." With a shrug and a sigh, he continues walking. "Why don't you invite him over for dinner, so I can get to know him better?"

My eyes start to mist with gratitude. Dad notices and wraps his arm around my shoulders.

"I'll try, Savvy. I honestly will. Last night just made me so aware that you're not a little girl anymore and you won't be around forever. One more year and you'll be heading off to college. I know I'm gonna be lost without you...and not just because of what you do for everyone in the house, but because I'm going to miss you."

I'm gonna miss him too, but if I say that, I might just break down and blubber, and I'm seriously over the whole crying thing.

"I guess I just..." Dad's voice trails off as his pace slows. He squeezes my shoulder, forcing me to stop beside him.

I glance up at his face, noticing his shocked confusion before following his gaze and gasping.

A shadowy lump is out of place along the water's

edge. It's hard to make out what it is, but it's long and unmoving. Not a rock. More like a body.

My blood runs cold as I gape at the lifeless lump. Ocean water is running up the sand and breaking over this person's feet and legs.

"Is that...?" I breathe. "Are they dead?"

Dad doesn't give me an answer. Instead he starts running, his feet splashing through the water as he races to check it out. Dropping to his knees beside the body, he feels around the neck, obviously looking for a pulse.

My heart is in my throat as I follow him. Part of me wants to keep my distance, but Dad might need my help, so I force myself to keep moving until I'm right behind my father.

The person is rolled away from us, so it's hard to tell what happened. Maybe he or she is injured, drunk, drowned, high. I won't know until I see the person's face.

Peering over Dad's shoulder, I initially think it's a woman. Long hair is splayed across the sand.

But then I realize those long strands are more like clumps of rope.

Like dreads.

I suck in a sharp breath and rasp, "Griffin!"

## 41

## SPIKING PAIN AND SAD CONFESSIONS

## GRIFFIN

Someone just said my name, but my head hurts too much to respond.

My lips are swollen and aching, my mouth full of blood. I can feel it still coating my teeth. I'm pretty sure my left eye is so bruised and puffy, I couldn't open it if I wanted to.

Someone is poking my neck.

"He's got a pulse."

It's a man. His voice is calm and easy, but still I resist when he tries to roll me over.

I'm not strong enough to fight him and the world spins as my body tips sideways. Now I'm lying on my back. Cold water is tickling my feet, but everything hurts too much to move them.

"He's a mess." A girl is crying beside me. I can feel soft hands on my arm, gently gripping.

I don't know who it is, but I like the sound of her voice. I want to hang onto it. Maybe if I hold tight enough, it'll drag me away from the flashes of pain that keep spiking in my head.

Memories are like firebolts that hurt and sting.

A fist to the face.

A knee to the stomach.

Knuckles and shoes crunching my body as three guys hold me down and pound the living shit out of me.

I tried to fight them off, to run, but they were too big. Too enraged.

Something sharp prods my ribs and it feels like a hot poker. I groan and try to move away from it.

"You're hurting him," she cries.

"It's okay." The man keeps feeling around my torso. "I'm just assessing him before we move him. I think he might have a couple of cracked ribs, and that eyebrow will need stitching, but…" He pushes my stomach and I clench my jaw. "I don't think he has any internal bleeding. Help me move him up the beach."

They shuffle around and I'm helpless as they each grab under my arms and haul me out of the water. I can't help the pained moans until they stop jostling my wasted body.

"We need to get him to the hospital for X-rays and a full checkup."

"No." The word leaves my mouth in a whisper.

"Griffin?" The girl leans in close. "He just said something."

I lick my lips, slow like a tortoise, and manage to rasp, "No hospital."

"But..." The girl moves away. "Dad, he said no hospital."

"What?" the man snaps. "It's not an option. We're taking him to Aviemore, and then we're calling the police. This guy has had the crap kicked out of him, and we need answers."

"No," I groan, managing a little more volume.

I wrestle to open my eyes and manage to crack my right one enough to make out blurry images. They're on either side of me. I stare at the fuzzy man then tip my head to look at the girl.

"It's okay." She trails her fingers through my whiskers. "We're going to look after you."

And that's when I see her.

"Savannah." I whisper her name like it's some kind of healing drug.

"Yes." She smiles a blurry smile and my body wants to roll right into her, wrap my arms around her waist and just hold on.

She can help.

She knows me.

She...

Doesn't really know me at all.

But I have to tell her. I need her help.

Grasping her hand with what little strength I have, I weakly beg, "No hospitals. No police. Please. I can explain, but just…promise."

She goes still and I can sense her looking over my body, staring at her father.

Shit. Her father.

"Savannah." The way he says her name, I can tell he's shaking his head.

"Please. Let's just get him home. We can reassess from there."

"We should be calling an ambulance."

"But he said no hospitals!"

"Why?" the man snaps, then leans over me. "Why? Why no hospitals? Why no police?"

His stern bark makes me flinch then swallow. I have to give him something, so I murmur a soft "Broken the law."

"What?" the man barks.

"Please." I lick my lips. "I can explain."

"Dad, come on. Let's just get him home. He can explain everything once you've fixed him up."

"Savannah, he just admitted to being a criminal!"

"I know that!" she screeches. "But he's also a very injured man, and I want to hear his story before anybody else does. So please, I'm begging you, let's take him home and we can deal with it from there."

Savannah's dad lets out a sharp sigh and starts muttering under his breath. Grabbing my shirt, he leans in close, his voice shaking as he whispers, "The people who did this to you, they still around?"

"I don't think so," I rasp.

"Did you see who they were? Do you know why they pummeled you?"

I close my eyes, exhaustion and pain radiating through me. "I don't know them. Tried to run, but they caught me. It was dark. Couldn't see faces."

"Will they be looking for you now?"

"No. I think they were done with me."

"Please, Dad," Savannah whispers.

Her father is still hesitating. I sense him moving beside me, maybe scanning the area to make sure the thugs aren't around.

I wish I could tell him with complete assurance that we're safe, but I don't really know.

When I first heard the front door click open, I slipped off the bed and hid along the edge. I wasn't small enough to fit under it, but I was hoping the owners would linger in the kitchen so I could gather my stuff and split. I was just reaching for my bag under the bed when one of them barreled into the room. For some weird reason, he didn't turn on the light, but he jerked to a stop when he sensed me. No doubt saw my shadowy form, lurking on the floor. I raised my hands and opened my mouth to explain, but he just let out this roar and charged me.

There was no way I could fight him. I was already squatting in his house, and if the police got involved, I couldn't be accused of assault as well. So I did my best to shove him away and run. My hand was just pushing the window open when he grabbed me from behind and two more guys raced into the room. They pinned me to the floor and went to town.

I didn't have a chance to see faces. No one bothered turning on a light. All I could do was brace myself for each blow. Once my body was radiating with every pain imaginable, they dragged my aching carcass to the edge of the deck and flung me over the side.

I was in too much pain to move at first. They could have easily assumed I *was* dead. I'm not sure if that was what they wanted, or whether teaching me a lesson was their main goal. I didn't want to stick around to find out, so I forced my agonized body off the ground and stumbled into the darkness, walking for as long as I could stand it, then finally giving in and passing out on the sand.

"Dad! Come on! We have to help him."

"Okay, fine," Dr. Green huffs. "Run home and get the car. Run fast. Don't stop. Don't talk to anybody. We'll wait for you here."

"Thank you," she whispers before disappearing from my side.

I lie still, trying to control the waves of pain and nausea riding through me.

"Fists and shoes?" Dr. Green quietly asks me. "Any other weapons?"

"No," I murmur. "Just wrath."

"Why were they so angry?"

I don't want to tell him, but what choice do I have? Licking my lips, I fight the burn of humiliation and softly admit, "I was squatting in their house."

Silence.

Then gentle fingers lightly probe my face, inspecting the wounds.

I wince but stay still.

"That's the law you broke?"

"Yeah." I choke out my answer.

"So you're homeless, then?"

Letting out a heavy sigh, I tiredly slur, "I've been homeless most of my life."

# 42

## A SALE OF THE HEART

### SAVANNAH

By the time I reach the house, I'm barely breathing. My fingers shake as I wrestle to unlock the front door and hunt down Dad's keys. Thankfully they're on the hook where they should be.

Popping the trunk of his Volvo station wagon, I lower the back seats and spread out the blanket so Griffin will be able to lie in the back.

Griffin.

Poor, bloodied, beat-up Griffin.

I'm fighting tears as I wrench open the driver's door and head back to the beach.

I want to know what happened to him.

I want to kill the guys who hurt him.

I want to find out what he meant about breaking the law.

As much as the idea makes me quiver, I also don't believe that he'd intentionally be a criminal. I just can't make that work.

I mean, he's Griffin! The sweet guy who saved my brother, the man with the gentle kisses and perfect words for every occasion. The person who is stealing my heart.

He can't be a criminal!

Screeching to a stop next to the curb, I race out the door, leaving it open as I tear down the beach.

Dad is helping Griffin to his feet, and I quickly slip under Griffin's other side to support him. He hisses and clenches his jaw while we steady him.

"We'll take it slow, all right?" Dad inches forward.

Griffin nods and we work our way to the car. It's painfully slow, and Griffin is waning by the time we get to the roadside. He leans against the car and I stay by his side, keeping him up while Dad sees what I've done in the back.

"Good move," he mutters while helping Griffin shuffle around the car, then easing him into the back.

I climb in after him, kneeling near his head while Dad drives us home.

Brushing my hand gently over his messy dreads, I try not to cry as I gaze down at his misshapen face. Whoever did this was pissed. They really went to town on the guy. I can only imagine the kind of pain he's in.

Anger roils through me, but I keep it down deep,

not wanting to do anything that will cause Griffin more stress.

Questions continue to barge through my brain, demanding answers I can't give.

Griffin's lips part and I lean closer, thinking he's about to speak to me. My hair tumbles off my shoulder, puddling on his chest, and his face is so close I can feel his breath tickling my chin.

"It's okay," I whisper.

"I'm sorry," he slurs.

I don't know what he's apologizing for, but I let it slide. He's too beat up and in pain to have to dish out an explanation right now. All I can focus on is getting him patched up.

As soon as Dad pulls into our driveway, he runs around to help me ease Griffin out of the back. It takes a few groans and one stifled cry of pain before he's standing again. It tears me up, but I press my lips together and refuse to cry. He needs me to be strong right now.

Dad's amazing. His calm, easy manner is like a balm. He's so unflustered by sickness and pain. Unless it was Mom. Watching her die was the hardest thing Dad's ever had to do, I'm sure of it. He would have known better than anyone what her body went through. The pain. The suffering. The deterioration.

I blink, forcing the ugly memories from my mind and focusing back on Griffin, who is now swaying on a dining room chair.

"Should he lie down?" I ask Dad as he walks away to get the first aid kit.

"I'll grab a sheet and we can lay him on the table," he calls over his shoulder.

That sounds kind of uncomfortable to me, so I make sure Griffin is resting safely before dashing into the lounge and grabbing a cushion for his head.

Screw the blood. We can buy another cushion anytime.

Dad's clearing off the dining table and laying a sheet down as I run back in. I glance at the medical kit beside him. We don't just have one of those Band-Aids and antiseptic cream first aid kits; ours is an industrial-strength, mini emergency room kit.

And I'm incredibly grateful for that.

Griffin hisses as he lies down.

"It's okay. Easy now," Dad murmurs, pulling on his gloves and getting prepped.

"What do you want me to do?" I ask.

"Go wash your hands, then put some gloves on. You can be my assistant."

I do as he says, my hands trembling the entire time. Getting the gloves on is a mission, but I manage in the end. I glance at my father and raise my eyebrows. He then starts quietly instructing me where to wipe and what to pass him.

Dad starts with Griffin's face, stitching up the gash on his eyebrow before washing the rest of the blood away. I'm still kind of surprised that Dad didn't insist on the hospital and the police...until Dad finishes with Griffin's face and then starts talking.

"So, how long have you been squatting in that house?"

I jerk still at the question, my eyes rounding as I glance at Griffin and then back to my dad. Neither of them will look me in the eye, so I eventually have to ask, "Squatting? What do you mean?"

Griffin sighs, then winces. "I told you I was a nomad, but I guess I should have told you I was a homeless one."

I reach for his hand without thinking about it, my heart aching for him as I slip my fingers between his. He squeezes back and keeps talking, his voice trembling while Dad sits him up to examine his battered torso.

"My mother was homeless when I was born. We grew up in shelters, and when she died, my brother and I got shifted from one foster home to the next. Eventually we gave up and just ran away. We've been looking after ourselves ever since." His sad face is pale, making his freckles seem that much darker.

I run my free hand down his back, trying to soothe him.

"So where's your brother now?" Dad asks.

Griffin goes statue still, blinking like he only just realized what he said.

"My brother?" he hedges, then glances at me, and something in his expression shifts. Like a sheet falling off a window, whatever veil he's been hiding behind flutters to the ground and there he is—raw and exposed.

Sucking in a ragged breath, he murmurs, "I don't know."

I want to glance at Dad, but Griffin's staring at me, silently begging me to forgive him. "What is it?"

"I'm not who you think I am," he chokes out the words. "I'm... My name's not... I'm... I'm a fake."

Dad stops poking at his ribs, standing tall to study the guy. "What?"

"I..." Griffin shakes his head, then groans, lightly holding his side and muttering, "I screwed up. When I was fourteen, I did... we did something bad and I... spent time in juvie. When I got out, he wanted the money, but I didn't have it."

"Okay, just back up a little. What money?"

"We stole," he rasps. "And I took the fall. Phoenix wants the money back, but I don't have it anymore."

"What did you do with it?" I ask, my brain scrambling to keep up with this motherload of a confession.

"After I got out of juvie, I went back to my hiding place. By some miracle, the money was still there, so I took it and gave it to a homeless shelter in town. No one saw me, I just left the box on the desk and wrote 'anonymous donation.'"

Dad and I were not expecting that. We glance at each other in surprise, our confusion a mirror image of the other.

"It's the truth. I didn't want to steal it in the first place, but..." He sighs. "I just wanted to clear my conscience. But I can't tell Phoenix that. He'd kill me."

"Who's Phoenix? Is he your brother?" I ask.

Griffin nods. "He wants that money, so I ran. I skipped out on my probation and I've been moving around ever since. I can't do hospitals because I have no insurance, and I can't do police because I just can't risk getting found out. I can't afford for anyone to see through my fake ID."

"How have you managed to get work?"

"My ID is passable for that. I paid for a professional forgery." He winces. "I've been working resorts in Mexico and trying to stay under the radar."

Dad lets out a heavy sigh and crosses his arms, staring at Griffin with a look of concern and sadness. "What am I supposed to do with you now?"

Griffin looks at him, like he's too exhausted for a fight, like he can't run anymore.

Tears line my lashes, my heart hurting over his rasped-out story and the aching sadness on his face.

"The guys who hurt you tonight...do they know who you really are?"

Griffin shakes his head, then obviously regrets it, his grimace giving away the pain he's still in. "They were pissed that I was in their house. They caught me before I could sneak out. I didn't even get a chance to apologize or explain. They didn't even ask any questions."

"Which house was it?" I ask.

"There's a row of houses down near the base of the cliffs. Pale blue."

"I know the ones," Dad murmurs.

"Yeah, I chose the end one. Big mistake." He clenches his jaw. "My stuff's still there, hidden under the bed. Shit," he mutters, bowing his head. "I shouldn't have... A house is nicer than sleeping in the back of my truck, you know? But I shouldn't have..." His face crumples with pain and I think remorse.

I run my hand down his back. "Shhhh. It's okay. We can get your stuff back."

Dad gives me a slightly incredulous look, and I hitch my shoulder with a silent "What?" I'm trying to make Griffin feel better here.

Dad looks to the ceiling, then focuses back on our fugitive. "You can't afford rent somewhere?"

It's a lame question. Of course he can't; otherwise, he wouldn't be squatting in people's vacation homes. I'm assuming that's what he's been doing. Ryder Bay is a good choice for that.

"I have to keep spare cash in case I need a quick exit. And now that cash is in their house, with all my stuff. I hid it under the bed, but if they find it... Shit."

"What a way to live," Dad mutters, then looks at me, his expression grim.

I silently plead with him to go easy and he huffs out a heavy sigh.

"Are you going to call the cops?" Griffin asks, his voice weak and defeated.

Dad scrubs a hand down his face and groans. "I'm probably an idiot, but...for tonight, no. If the house owners find your stuff, that's just a consequence you'll have to deal with in the morning. I won't lie to the police if they ask me anything, but I won't go knocking on the station door either."

My chest deflates with relief, and I don't think I've ever loved my dad more.

"Look, Griffin, I..." He sighs. "I believe you're a good person. I don't want to be the one who lands you in hot water, so for tonight, you can take the couch in the den. Once you're fully recovered, we'll have a chat about your future and what you want to do with it. Living a life on the run is not a long-term solution." Dad's expression is sweet as he rests his hand on Griffin's shoulder. "How long have you been at this?"

"About two and a half years now."

"And how old are you really?"

Griffin frowns, then confesses, "Eighteen."

My lips part with surprise. He's only a year older than me, yet he's been homeless and living on the run. What kind of life is that?

No education.

No family.

He's turned out pretty damn amazing considering his upbringing. I think Dad can see that, because a sad smile pushes at the edges of his mouth. "Okay. Well, you've got a roof over your head until… well, until you're better."

Griffin opens his mouth, but obviously doesn't know what to say. His swallow is thick and audible as a tear slips from the corner of his eye.

I think I'm in love with him.

In spite of everything he's just told me, as I dash that tear off his cheek, I feel like I know exactly who he is, and my heart is sold.

# 43

# A FULL-BODY BEATING

## GRIFFIN

I'm in shock.

Aside from Pedro, I've never told anyone the truth before, and they're taking it with such grace and ease, it's actually made me cry. When Savannah wiped that tear off my cheek, I nearly broke down like a baby, but I held it together, clenching my aching jaw and trying to be stoic as they helped me off the table and guided me to the den.

Easing onto the couch hurts, and I can't help a groan when Dr. Green supports my head and gets me settled.

"Try not to move around too much. Those meds should kick in soon, but they won't ease the pain completely." He gently touches my puffy eye. "You're young and strong. I'm confident you'll make a quick recovery."

"Thank you," I rasp, still on the verge of breaking down.

I've met plenty of good people in my time, but this level of kindness is off the charts. This guy should be dumping me at the police station, but he's giving me a place to heal.

Savannah perches on the edge of the couch, careful not to touch my aching body.

"You're not staying down here," her father softly tells her.

"I know." She glances at him, then back down at me. "I'll just say good night then come straight up."

Her father nods and takes his leave.

Savannah slips her hand into mine, her thumb rubbing circles over my knuckles. "Can I get you anything before I go?"

I gaze at her. Even through my tired, blurry vision, she's beautiful.

My tongue skims over my swollen lips. They're sore from all the confessing. I feel like I've taken a full-body beating from my outsides all the way to my soul.

"I'm sorry," I slur, fighting a wave of tears.

"For what?" she whispers.

"Not being honest with you."

Her mouth lifts on the edge, a dimple appearing in her right cheek. "I don't think you've ever lied to me, have you? I mean, other than your age and name, but…

everything else was true? All the resort stuff, the people you've met on your travels? Every time you've shared a little piece of your heart with me...that's all true, right?"

"Yeah, that's all true."

Her smile widens. "So, I do know you, and I like who you are, no matter what your name is."

My eyebrows bunch and I squeeze her hand. "I don't deserve that."

She sighs and looks away from me, biting her lips together as she looks across the room. "I know you've made some mistakes in your past, but you're not a bad person. I want the rest of the story, in every little detail you can give me. But I'm pretty sure that no matter what you say, I won't change my mind about you." She gazes back down at me, her smile warm and sweet. "I see you. I know the person you are now. You're not a fraud."

It hurts, but my lips curl at the edges, mirroring her smile. I meant what I said about not deserving her. I'm not sure I ever will, but damn if I don't want to try.

As she leans down and brushes her lips across my cheek, I'm pretty sure I've never loved anyone until now.

## 44
## NIGHTTIME SUSPICIONS CAN BE RECKLESS

## SAVANNAH

W hen I get to my room, I notice that Harley's not back yet.

I'm kind of pleased she didn't show up when Griffin was lying on the table. Dad had already cleaned everything away by the time I left Griffin's side. I think he was lingering to make sure I did, in fact, leave the den.

He gave me a relieved smile when I walked out, then hugged me good night before I went upstairs.

I can't believe how cool he's being with all of this. He must see the same things in Griffin that I do—a good soul who's been thrown a bunch of bad breaks.

The stealing money thing has my mind reeling. He was just a little older than Lettie when he did it and then got sent to juvie. I seriously have no idea with my pampered life. I mean, I lost my mother, but so did he, and at least I was left with a loving family around me. Griffin had no one but an older brother, who I'm guessing led him astray. He sounds like a total asshole, demanding stolen money off him. Griffin said he took the fall, which I'm guessing means he protected his brother and took the punishment for them both.

Why are people like that?

My mind churns as I think about the people who beat up Griffin. Their behavior is kind of extreme if you ask me. Why didn't they just call the police?

The bedroom door clicks open and I bolt upright, switching on my bedside lamp and catching Harley's pale, bug-eyed expression.

"Are you okay?"

"Your dad just caught me sneaking in and I thought he was going to give me the third degree. He barked at me to get up to your room." Her eyes bulge and I give her an apologetic smile.

"Sorry. It's been a rough night."

She plunks down on the end of my bed, tucking her foot under her butt. "What's up?"

I sit up fully, crossing my legs and snatching my pillow so I can hug it while I talk. This is huge, and although I haven't asked Griffin's permission to confess all, I trust Harley and tell her everything except for the part about Griffin's fake ID and his juvie history. But I do tell her about the fact that he's spent most of his life homeless and has been squatting in vacation homes while living in Ryder Bay.

She's silent, her mouth agape for most of it, but at the end I reach forward and touch her arm.

"You can't tell anyone."

"I wouldn't. Ever. This... We have to protect Griffin."

"I know, right? That's how I feel. It's weird, the logical part of me should want to go to the police, but..." I shake my head. "I don't want him to get in trouble for squatting."

"I want those guys to get in trouble for beating him up though." Harley frowns. "What assholes!"

"It's so extreme." I agree with her. "The thing that's bugging me is why didn't they just call the cops? Why beat the crap out of him?"

"You said he got away. Maybe they were going to call the cops after teaching him a lesson."

"But then they'd get in trouble for assaulting him." I flick my hand up. "They should have just held him down and called the police."

"They must have been so super pissed that he was in their home." Harley leans back on her arm, shaking her head and looking mildly confused.

I'm confused too. "It seems like a really violent way to deal with it. He said he tried to run, so it's not like he was attacking *them*. But they pummeled him. It's like they wanted him punished."

"Or silenced," Harley murmurs, her frown deepening.

I sit up a little straighter. "Do you... Do you think

they were trying to cover something up?"

Harley purses her lips in thought. "Did Griffin mention finding anything in the house?"

"No." I follow her train of thought, quickly jumping on with her. "You think they're hiding something there. That's why they didn't want to call the police. Maybe they wanted to deal with Griffin on their own?"

"Man, we should be calling the police about them!" Harley mutters.

"We can't. Griffin has too much to hide."

"You think they'd nail him for the squatting thing? I think the assault is worse."

I swallow and don't elaborate. Griffin's checkered past is not my story to tell. Resting my chin on the top of my pillow, I mumble, "I just don't want him to get in trouble."

"Yeah, good point." Harley nods and sits up straight. "Man, this is huge. Not sure how I'll sleep tonight. My mind is whirring."

"Mine too." I gaze past her at my bathroom door. "I want to go check out that house tomorrow."

"What?" Harley squeaks.

"Griffin's stuff is there. All his money, everything. I want to get it back for him."

"Are you just planning on waltzing up and knocking on the door? I highly doubt people like that will hand over his stuff with a smile."

I grimace. "I know, but I want to check out the place anyway. What if we can find out what they're hiding and then call the police ourselves? That way, they get busted and Griffin can stay out of it."

Harley's eyebrows rise, her lips fighting a smile.

"What?"

She breaks into a grin. "You've got balls, girl."

I snicker, my cheeks heating with embarrassment. "You want to come with me."

"Hell yeah." Harley grins.

## 45

## A PERSON'S CHARACTER

## GRIFFIN

Sleeping is pretty damn hard when every inch of your body is hurting.

My legs. They're about the only thing to have survived the attack, although I do have a decent-sized bruise on my thigh.

Shuffling on the couch, I stifle a groan and take in a sharp breath through my nose. I could use another dose of painkillers, but the idea of getting up and moving is too much.

I'll just lie here in silent hope that the pain will ease on its own.

My mind drifts in and out of sleep, but I'm aware of movements in the house, noises upstairs, a toilet flushing, a blender in the kitchen, sunlight making the curtains pale.

When the den door cracks open, I lift my head and spot Savannah's dad easing through the gap with a tall glass of liquid and something clutched in his other hand.

"Morning." His voice is deep and husky, like that's the first word he's said since getting up.

"Hi." I swallow and try to open my left eye, but it's still too puffy.

"Let me help you sit up." He crouches down, tucking one hand beneath my knees and the other under my shoulders.

I hiss as he moves me into a sitting position. It takes a moment for my head to stop spinning, but eventually the world comes back into alignment and I swallow the pills and water he gives me.

"How you feeling?" Kevin takes a seat beside me, examining my face and lifting the edge of the T-shirt he loaned me last night.

I clench my jaw until his gentle prodding is done, then manage a short "Felt better in my life."

"You ever been beat like this before?"

"Just once."

He gives me a look that demands an answer, so I softly sigh and tell him the truth. "When I wouldn't tell my brother where the money was."

Dr. Green studies me for a moment, then nods and shuffles on the couch like he's getting comfy. "I know you feel like crap, but I need you to do something for me, son." I'm afraid to ask, so I don't say anything. "I need you to tell all. I want your history in every gory detail, and I'm not leaving this spot until you tell it to me."

Since the day I split Vallejo, I've never breathed a word of my past to anyone except Pedro, who I trusted with my life.

Last night was huge for me, and it looks like this morning is going to be even bigger. My tongue skims over my swollen lips. Telling this is going to hurt in more ways than one, but I force my mind and body to do both.

I start talking, croaking out my pathetic life story until I end up in Ryder Bay, meeting the most beautiful person I've ever seen. I can't look at Savannah's father the whole time I'm talking, and when I'm done, I rest my head back against the couch and close my eyes. I'm spent.

Silence falls between us like gentle rain and I don't have the energy to break it. Waiting for some kind of response is torturous. I don't think he'll kick me out on my beat-up ass, but will he change his mind about the police thing?

Fear trickles through me, building into a steady stream of anxiety, until I crack my good eye open and turn my head.

Dr. Green is looking at me with a sad smile, his voice rough with emotion as he says, "I'm sorry. Sounds like you've had a tough time of it."

I swallow my heart back into my chest and sit there

quietly, waiting for his next move. It's a simple one. He passes me the smoothie, encouraging me to get some food into my body.

Sucking on the straw, I relish the cool sweetness easing down my throat. It's the best damn smoothie I've tasted.

"This is great," I croak. "Thank you."

"You're welcome." He rests back on the couch beside me and I have to ask...

"Why are you doing this for me?"

"I'm a doctor. It's my job to take care of people."

"No." I snicker. "I don't deserve it. You've heard my story. You have every right to kick me out of your house. Out of Savannah's life. Why aren't you?"

He takes a minute to answer, biting the tip of his tongue and squeezing the bridge of his nose. "I love my daughter. Very much. My kids are...so incredibly precious to me, and they've lost big already. I just know that kicking you out will hurt Savannah. I'm not willing to do that."

"But I'm a... I'm a fake. I lied."

"You're not a fake," he counters. "You've just sat there and told me the truth. I don't know how I know it, but you're not lying." He lets out a soft, breathy laugh. "Call me a fool, but..." He shrugs. "It all started when I got your message yesterday. It took a lot of courage for you to call me, and as I was listening to you, I could sense that there's something inherently good about you."

I swallow, not knowing what to say.

"You may have done things in your past, but you seem like an honorable person. You saved my son's life."

I go still and whisper, "You don't owe me for that."

He turns to smile at me. "And there you go. Being honorable again."

I don't know what to say, so I just rest my aching head back against the couch.

"You care a lot about Savannah. I could hear it in your voice. You know you should run, but you don't want to leave her. You think you don't deserve her, but she makes you happy."

"She does," I croak and close my eyes, picturing her sweet smile and wishing I didn't have to leave.

"She cares about you too. She'll fight for you. I can see it in her, and it worries me that if I try and force you guys apart, then I'll lose her." He sighs. "Maybe I'm the world's worst dad, I don't know. But I figure if you're as nice and honorable as you seem, then there's no danger in my daughter hanging out with you." He scrubs a hand over his mouth. "Unless you're planning on breaking her heart by leaving." I go still, my fuzzy brain trying to catch up with what he's saying. "From everything you've just told me, it sounds like you keep moving because you're scared of getting caught. But what if you stop running? What if you stay and make Savannah as happy as she makes you?"

My eyes pop open and I jerk my head off the couch,

too surprised to think the action through. Pain shoots down my spine. I blink to center myself and try to get a handle on my shock. "Did you just ask me to stick around?"

"I did." He nods.

"How? How do I even make that work?"

Dr. Green raises his hands with a shrug. "I'm not going to be telling your secret to anyone. Seems to me like that's part of your past. You might want to face it at some point. Start using your real name. Make everything in your life official. Real." His pointed look has a touch of humor to it. "But I get it if you don't want to. You've turned yourself into a new man. The only thing left to do is find yourself a legitimate place to live. Then this gig you have going doesn't need to be disrupted."

"But..." I can't quite get my head around this conversation. It's surreal. "You'd be cool with a guy like that dating your daughter?"

"Son, I don't care about the color of people's skin, I don't care what they wear, and I don't care if they're the CEO of a company or a homeless beggar. What I do care about is people's character. I care about how they treat others." He raises his eyebrows. "The fact that you're willing to walk away, hurt yourself in order to save my daughter, says a lot about you as a person. So I'm going to choose to trust you." His gaze sharpens and he gives me a pointed look. "Don't make me regret that."

"I won't, sir."

He nods, believing me. "Now you can stay here until you get better, but then you need to find a place to live. Marshall's a friend of mine, and I suggest you trust him with the truth. He might be able to help you out."

"I'll lose my job." I shake my head.

Dr. Green gives me a grin that I don't understand. "I wouldn't count on that."

## 46

### CRAZY INSANE

### SAVANNAH

So we're doing what we've never done and are hanging at the north end of the beach. We've got our surfboards and towels, but it's all a ploy to check out the house and try to get Griffin's stuff back.

I didn't mention this at all when I checked on him this morning. Dad had left for work already, and Harley was getting a late breakfast for us while I snuck into the den.

Griffin was asleep, his beat-up body actually looking relaxed. As desperately as I wanted to wake him and ask how he was doing, I sat there watching him for a few minutes before being sensible and walking out the door.

While I nibbled on Harley's scrambled eggs that she

made me, I couldn't stop thinking about the house and his stuff and eventually I just said, "Let's go now."

"To the house?" Harley whispered.

"Yeah." I nodded. "We'll take the boards and pretend we're going surfing. If anyone is at the house, then we can just walk right past and actually surf. We won't look suspicious."

Harley chewed on her thumbnail, her eyes darting around the kitchen before she finally nodded. "Okay. We'll do it."

"Are you gonna tell Aidan?"

"Not yet." She shook her head. "I mean, I will, but I'm gonna wait until after. We're not due to meet up until after lunch anyway. His mom's making him spend some time at the hospital this morning."

I winced, knowing I should probably be doing the same thing. It was a weird jolt to realize I hadn't thought about Skylar once since finding Griffin on the beach.

But getting his stuff back is important, so she'll just have to wait, and I can tell her everything once I know he's safe.

Gulping down the last of my orange juice, I hurried Harley to finish up and before long we were down on the sand, walking past the row of blue houses.

"He said it was the one at the end," I murmur as I lay the longboard down and glance over my shoulder.

The houses have been there ever since I moved to Ryder Bay. They used to be white but were repainted a couple of years ago. They look like old but nice holiday homes, probably built in the late eighties or early nineties. They have that kind of style about them. Stucco homes right on the beach. Perfect for vacationing.

Harley crouches down by her board and looks past my knees, checking out the house.

"It looks empty. No car in the port."

"We're gonna need to get a little closer to see if anyone's inside." My voice trembles just a little.

If the people who caught Griffin last night beat the crap out of him, what will they do to us?

This is crazy insane, but I've never felt more motivated in my life.

Skylar's usually the one convincing me to jump out of my comfort zone, but this time it's all on me. I'm terrified, but I have to take this step. Griffin needs me to get his stuff back and I don't want to let him down.

"Okay, so how are we supposed to do this?" I ask.

Harley shrugs and purses her lips in thought. "Let's just casually walk up the beach like we know exactly what we're doing. Once we get close to the house, we'll walk up those stairs and stand in the carport for a few minutes, see if we can hear anything above us. Voices and stuff."

"Sounds good." I swallow, pulling the towel off my shoulder and dropping it on the board. "These will be okay here, right?"

Harley stands and glances at our stuff. "We'll be

able to see them from the house. If it's empty, one of us can sneak in and get Griffin's stuff while the other keeps watch."

"Right." I bob my head, trying to hide the fact that my insides are going nuts.

I don't do this kind of thing.

Sneak around.

Break into people's homes.

But it's for a good cause.

I care about Griffin, and I'm willing to take this risk for him. All I can hope is that his bag hasn't been found already.

Biting the edge of my lip, I follow Harley up the beach.

"Stop doing that. It's making you look nervous," Harley mutters out the side of her mouth.

I replace my teeth with a quick swipe of my tongue and concentrate on looking casual. That's really hard to do when you're actually thinking about it, but I force a smile when an older guy jogs past us.

As soon as we reach the stairs, we pause, and I glance around us before gripping the rail and ascending. Harley's right behind me, not saying anything. The silence between us is kind of nerve-racking, but I can't think of anything to say either.

All I can hear is my heartbeat in my head.

I'm trying to shout over it, remind myself what we're doing here. It's potentially the stupidest thing

I've ever done. And Harley is right behind me, backing me up.

As we reach the top of the stairs, I spin around to face her.

"Thank you." The words come out quick, with just a little wobble.

She smiles and then winks at me. "Don't get all emotional on me now. Let's just get this done. Then I might even let you hug me."

I snicker, grateful for her spunky attitude.

We rush across the carport and rest our backs against the wooden lining, staring out at the beach while listening for noises inside.

"Can you hear anything?" Harley softly whispers.

I shake my head, but strain to listen for something other than the ocean in front of us. I'm struggling to hear anything other than the waves.

"Okay." Harley licks her lips. "You want to go in, or do you want me to do it?"

Of course I want her to do it, but I feel like this is my responsibility, so I force myself to say, "You keep watch."

"Got it." Harley squeezes my wrist, probably trying to encourage me, but her touch is unexpected and I flinch, banging into the wall behind me.

We both gasp and go still.

"Sorry," Harley mouths, but I wave off the apology, too busy listening for noises inside, waiting for big guys to run down and beat the hell out of us.

Why are we doing this again?

With our breath on hold, we scan the carport, looking above us, around us, waiting for someone to come out of the house and check it out.

After what feels like a painful eternity, we realize we're not being busted.

"Let's just go together," Harley whispers against my ear.

I nearly tell her that this is crazy and we should walk away.

But I can't do that to Griffin.

If there's even a chance his stuff is still hidden under the bed, then we have to take it.

I nod and reach for her hand. We squeeze each other's fingers before letting go and sneaking around the side of the house.

The narrow strip of grass on the cliffside hasn't been attended to in a long time. It's long and tickles my legs as we wrestle along the strip and rest at the corner, again, listening for anything that might catch us.

Nothing.

We're good.

I run my hand along the edge of the house and ease my body up the final step. We're now visible from the road and I hold my breath, scanning the street and not breathing until I sense that no one is watching us.

At least I hope they're not.

"Sav, here," Harley whispers behind me.

I spin to see her easing a bedroom window open. It's wide enough for us to fit through.

Shit, this is insane.

I'm about to break into someone's house!

Gripping the edge of the frame, I struggle to hoist myself up, but Harley gives me a little boost. For a chick her size, she's surprisingly strong. I end up kind of tumbling through the window and cracking my elbow on the wooden floor.

Crap, that hurts! I bite my lip against making any sound and scramble back so Harley can get through. I wait against the wall, cradling my elbow and looking around the room. There are bunk beds tucked into the corner. Big ones with a double on the base and wooden stairs leading up to a single. White shelves with books and toys are lining the other wall, and there's a big square mat in the middle with roads printed on it so the kids can run their cars and trucks around it like a mini town.

It seems weird that people with kids would behave so badly toward a squatter. Did they lash out in fear for their children's safety? Feels kind of extreme to me.

I frown and glance at the floor, my eyes rounding when I notice something odd. The floorboard where my elbow hit is tilting on the edge. I kneel down to investigate as Harley's feet appear beside me. "What are you doing?"

"Check this out." I wedge my finger into the gap

and lift the board, wincing when it knocks against the others.

Harley crouches down beside me, her eyes on the door as I peer into the gap and feel my blood run cold.

Two little bags of white powder and three stacks of money are hidden in the gap. This is not what I expected to find in a child's bedroom. This is what I expect to see in some hitman's briefcase—the kind I read about in books or watch on TV.

I frantically tap Harley's arm, pointing at my discovery.

Her eyes bulge.

Something bizarre is going on here. And it's freaking me out.

"Let's get Griff's stuff and then get the hell out of here," I whisper, so quietly I can barely hear myself.

Harley nods, but pulls the phone from her back pocket and starts taking photos.

I wince, wanting to tell her she's crazy, but knowing it's probably a smart move. No wonder these guys didn't want to call the cops. No wonder they beat the crap out of Griffin. Maybe they thought he'd discovered their stash or was trying to steal it.

Maybe they don't own this house either and have been using it to store their shit until the real owners show up.

Easing away from Harley, I crawl to the bunk bed and feel around underneath it. Nothing. No bag.

Griffin must have been sleeping in a different room.

I gently clear my throat to get Harley's attention and point to the hallway. She nods and tucks her phone away, replacing the floorboard while I ease further into the house.

From what I can tell, it's empty, which relaxes me enough to hurry to the next doorway.

The door is shut, and I don't know if I have the guts to open it, but this could be the room with Griffin's stuff inside.

Grimacing, I curl my fingers around the knob and nearly jump right out of my skin when I sense a flash of movement on my left.

I whip my head to check it out and can't help a small scream when I spot a tall guy looming at the end of the hallway. He's staring right at me. I can't see his face because the sunlight behind him is making him a silhouette. A scary-ass silhouette.

With a soft yelp, I turn and start racing back to Harley, but he grabs the back of my hair before I can reach her.

I scream, hoping to warn her, then start thrashing against his painful grip.

An arm comes around my waist, locking me against his solid body.

"Oh, you're not going anywhere, sweetie." He laughs into my ear and an ugly chill races down my body as I recognize the voice.

Ripper.

# 47

## PANIC AND PAIN

### GRIFFIN

I don't know how long I slept for, but when I wake, the house is quiet.

"Savannah?" I call out weakly as I struggle to sit up.

No one replies, and I force myself off the couch and painfully shuffle through the house. I use the bathroom first, my head spinning as I try to aim straight.

My body feels worse now than it did when I first got beat.

Flashes of shoes and fists attack me again and I lean against the bathroom counter to steady myself. Staring at my reflection is an ugly business. My eyebrow is patched up and the mottled bruising on my face makes me look like a beast.

I slowly swivel away and wobble into the kitchen where I find a glass and gulp down some water, spilling it on my shirt as it dribbles out from my swollen, useless lips.

I've never felt this pathetic before. Even Phoenix didn't get me this bad. But it was just me and him. Last night it was me and three, and that's why I came out half-dead.

Thank God they didn't chase me down the sand and finish me off.

I place my glass in the sink and wobble back to my room. I want to call for Savannah again, but don't really want to disturb her if she's sleeping.

She probably doesn't want to see my ugly face today anyway. After everything I told her last night... Shit, she'd have every right to avoid me.

I know she said she liked me and everything, but a good night's sleep might have changed her mind. With a pained wince, I ease back onto the couch, and that's when I see a note on the coffee table.

*Morning,*
*Hope you're feeling a little better when you wake up.*
*Gone surfing with Harley.*
*I'll see you later.*
*Take care of yourself today. Be kind to you, until I get back and can take care of you myself.*
*xx*
*Savvy*

I smile at her sweet words and press the note to my lips.

Leaning back on the couch, I close my eyes, happy that she went surfing and didn't stick around here all day until I woke up. She needed to get out and burn off some energy. Surfing is always good for the soul.

Man, I can't wait to see her though.

My mind drifts with images of her on the waves, that triumphant, sweet smile as she rides the longboard to shore. It's a beautiful image and makes me wonder if Dr. Green is right.

Should I stay?

A tap on the door jolts me away from the question and I jerk, then groan as pain rockets through my chest.

The door eases open and Aidan walks in to find me, cradling my side.

"Shit, are you okay, man?" His eyes bulge as he walks toward me. "Marshall said you were sick, not beat. What happened?"

I lick my lips, then croak, "Had a run-in with a few guys last night. I'll be all right."

"Do the police know?" Aidan eases down beside me, anger flashing in his eyes as he checks out my wasted face.

"Don't really want them involved," I murmur.

"Why not?"

I sigh and rub a hand across my aching head. "It's a long story."

Aidan hesitates before answering, obviously wanting more.

He's not going to get it.

Not today.

"Okay," he finally mutters. "Marshall's worried about you. Kevin called him this morning, saying you were sick and staying here. I found that kind of weird, so figured I'd use my lunch break to check it out."

I can't help a soft snicker. "It is weird. I can't believe he's letting me stay."

Aidan shrugs. "He's a good guy."

"Yeah, he is." I glance at Aidan. "What did Marshall say?"

"Not much else. He's covering your shift at the shed today."

I grimace, hating that I've put him in that position.

"Don't worry about it, man. He's not mad or anything, but he'll probably want to know what happened to you."

"Yeah," I croak, knowing I need to tell him at some point. Savannah's dad seems to think it's a safe enough bet. I don't quite understand why, but maybe I should. Marshall's the one who gave me the job. He's been nothing but good to me. Maybe the truth won't get me fired.

Aidan shuffles on the couch while I'm thinking,

glancing at the door behind him. "You seen Harley around?"

I point to the note on the table. "She's gone surfing with Sav. They left before I woke up."

"Really?" Aidan looks confused, reaching for the note and reading it. "I didn't see them at the beach."

This makes me pause. "You didn't see them?"

"No." He shakes his head, looking disappointed. "Maybe they decided to surf near the pier or something."

"Since you guys hooked up, I haven't seen her surf one time without saying hi to you first."

"I know, right?" Aidan tugs out his phone. "Not that she'll get this." He starts tapping on the screen.

I watch him, worry niggling me as I try to think why the girls would say they're going surfing but then not show up at the beach.

"Axel's down there today. Maybe they saw him and split someplace else."

I grunt, thinking about the dark, imposing force and figuring Aidan's probably right.

"They wouldn't go for the cove." Aidan's talking to himself, tapping his finger on the edge of his phone. "I guess there's the north end." He glances at me, then shakes his head with a grin. "Nah, I don't think Harley would touch the north end, even if she was with Sav."

I can't smile with him.

Even if it didn't hurt like hell to move my mouth, I still couldn't do it.

Something is wrong. I don't know why I'm feeling it, but...

Aidan's phone starts ringing. He glances at the screen, pleasantly surprised, and answers it with a grin.

"You're actually calling me? Babe, this has got to be a first, since—" He sits forward, suddenly worried.

My guts twist uncomfortably.

"Hey, hey, slow down. What happened?"

I shuffle in my seat, my ribs protesting as I try to get closer and eavesdrop on the conversation.

"You what?" Aidan frowns. "Axel? Harley, what are you do— Harley! Harley!" He shoots to his feet and yells one more time. "Harley!"

With a raging grunt, he grips the phone and glares at me. "She hung up."

"What's going on?" I've moved to the edge of the couch, my body radiating pain, but I can't give a shit about that right now.

Something's wrong.

Something's very wrong.

Aidan's face is pale as he calls his girlfriend back and listens to it ring.

"What's going on!" I grab his attention.

Aidan's expression buckles with annoyance. "She said something about going to the north end to get some stuff and they ran into trouble. She was running. Out of breath." Aidan growls and tries calling again.

"Did she say anything about Savannah? Did she say where they were?"

"She said something about needing to help Savannah, but she didn't say where or anything, and then she started yelling 'Axel' and hung up."

North end.

Get stuff?

No. I gently shake my head. She wouldn't.

Shit!

I lurch to my feet, nearly passing out at the sudden movement. Aidan steps forward to steady me, gripping my arms so I don't topple over.

"I think I know where they might be," I manage as I cling to his arms and force myself to stay upright.

Fear is pulsing through me in sick waves.

"We need to move," I rasp, stumbling forward.

"Dude, should you be going anywhere?" Aidan's grip on my arms tightens.

"We've got to get to her," I grit out. "Let's go."

Aidan doesn't question me further, helping me out the door and to his car. His face is bunched into a scowl, his jaw clenching and unclenching as worry no doubts eats him the same way it's eating me.

As soon as I'm in the passenger seat, he turns to me with an anxious frown. "Should I be calling the police?"

My mouth goes dry. I hate that word. That question.

But if Savannah's in trouble…

I can't put my shit above her safety. If she's in danger, we need all the help we can get.

This could be the end for me, but screw it…what choice do I have?

"Yeah," I finally croak. "We better call the police."

Closing my eyes against the nauseating dread, I lean my head back against the seat and listen as Aidan calls the cops.

"Where do we think they are?" he asks me.

I grip the edge of the seat and murmur, "You know that row of pale blue houses by the cliffs?"

"Yep." Aidan starts the car before he's even finished the call.

His tires squeal on the road as he relays my words to the cops. "The one at the end."

Damn, I hope I'm right.

Or wrong.

I want to be wrong, because the idea of those guys even looking at Savannah makes me want to tear their eyes out, but if they've hurt her...

Shit, why'd she do it?

I already know the answer to that question, and it hurts to think about it.

She snuck back into that house to save my ass.

It was a crazy insane thing to do, but she did it for me.

I don't think anyone has ever risked themselves for me before, and I don't know what to do with the emotion pounding through me.

She better be all right.

I don't know what I'm gonna do if they've hurt her.

## 48

## THE DUCT TAPE DEMON

## SAVANNAH

"Y ou smell good." Ripper sniffs my hair and bile surges in my stomach. Fear is closing up my windpipe, but I manage to struggle against his grip, writhing my body to get away from him.

He just snickers and pulls me tighter against him, nipping my neck through my hair and making me whimper.

"I'm gonna enjoy you," he singsongs.

I shudder, closing my eyes and starting to pray harder than I ever have before.

Harley hasn't appeared, and all I can hope is that she got out and is getting help.

*Be quick, Harley! Be quick!*

Panic skirts the edges of my mind, making me want

to blubber. When Ripper starts shunting me toward the closest bedroom, my vision blurs.

This can't be happening to me.

I grunt and push back, digging in my heels and resisting him with what little power I have. The guy is big, strong, and I'm no match. Lifting me off my feet, he carries me into the room and dumps me on the bed.

I scramble to get away from him, but he pushes me back, then snatches my wrist when I try again. Lunging forward, I sink my teeth into his hand.

I don't know what possessed me to do it. I'm not a natural fighter, but I'm scared, and instinct is driving me on this one.

He howls and lets me go, gripping his fist while I crawl to the end of the bed and make a break for the door.

I don't get far. Another person appears in front of me, a guy I've never seen before. He's big and imposing too, pushing me back into the room and glaring over my shoulder at Ripper.

Rough hands catch me and pull me back, fisting my hair. "Try that again and you'll regret it." His voice is trembling with anger, but then lightens up when he speaks to his friend. "She's a feisty one. Help me tie her to the bed?"

"No." I start thrashing against him, but I don't have a chance.

"Do you honestly have time for this, man?" the

other guy grumbles, grabbing my ankles and hoisting me onto the bed.

"No!" I cry out again, screaming when Ripper yanks my arms over my head. My hands smack against the metal headboard and there's no point even fighting the tears now. They bubble over my lashes when I hear the duct tape rip. "No, please, don't!"

Ripper's pincer grip on my wrists is painful, his smile revolting as he wraps the tape around my wrists. I try to make it as difficult for him as possible. Desperation is fueling my fight.

"Stop it," he snaps, then glances over his shoulder. "Are you gonna help or what?"

The guy at the end of the bed rolls his eyes and comes around to hold my arms still.

"I'll let you have a turn after me." Ripper grins, and I swear I'm gonna puke all over this bed. My entire body is trembling.

The guy stares down at me while Ripper finishes securing my hands. The tape is cutting into my flesh, but he doesn't seem to care. He's on a mission to finally get what isn't his, and I feel helpless to stop it.

Tears shudder in my chest while his friend lightly taps my face. "Why you here?"

I sniff and jerk away from his touch.

"You looking for something?" he asks.

I turn my head away from him, so he grabs my chin and yanks me back. Tears are blurring my view of him, but I can sense he's about the same age as Ripper. His unshaven face is rough around the edges, with slightly puffy cheeks and an ugly look in his blue eyes.

"What were you looking for?" He slaps my face, irritated by my silence.

I gasp, the sharp sting radiating across my cheek.

"Stop it." Ripper bats his hand away from me, then peers down at my face, wiping my tears with his thumb.

I flinch and try to lean away from his touch. He grins and my stomach convulses.

"Shit, man, just hurry it up. We were supposed to be in and out last night."

Ripper looks up. "That wasn't my fault. I didn't know he was going to be here."

"We could have just let him walk out the door. He obviously thought we owned this place and was making a quick escape."

"If he'd seen my face, he would have known." Ripper spits out the words. "Besides, the guy was due a beating, and if you'd followed him like I told you to, he wouldn't be a problem anymore."

"I'm not killing someone for your satisfaction! He didn't see our faces. He doesn't know shit." His dark gaze shifts from Ripper down to me. "But she does."

A cold hard lump forms in my belly.

Ripper huffs and points to the door. "Just get the stuff we forgot. I'll meet you in the truck and we can split town for good."

The guy crosses his arms and points at me. "Do you

honestly have to do this now? We could pick up some chicks once we're out of town."

Ripper's hot gaze travels down my body. "No, this is something I've been wanting for a while." His feather light touch on my arm makes me squirm. "These hot-ass Walton girls are just too good to pass up, you know?"

His friend snickers. "Whatever, you sick bastard. Just don't take too long."

As much as I hate the guy who slapped me, seeing him walk out the door is terrifying. I nearly shout for him to come back, but my voice dried up the second Ripper caught me.

Shit.

Shit!

Perching on the bed beside me, Ripper trails his fingers down my face. I whimper and squirm away from his touch.

"Shhhh. Stop fighting it," he whispers. "Just let go like your little friend did."

His words freeze me, and I slowly turn to look at him.

My little friend?

Is he talking about Skylar?

"What did you do to her?" I manage to rasp, anger pulsing through me.

"I just gave her what she wanted." He smiles. "And deep down, I think you want it too."

"No," I grit out. "You pig. I don't want it!"

I thrash my legs, but he captures them with a laugh, pinning them against the bed when he straddles my thighs and reaches for my shirt.

"No," I whimper. "Stop. Please."

Fear is pulsing through me in nauseating waves. His hands will be on me, all over me, and I don't want his touch on my skin.

*Help me! Somebody help me!*

I'm screaming the words in my mind, but I can't get them out of my mouth. Shakes have taken over my body again, and all I can do is lie there and tremble. He's too strong. Too big. I can't fight this.

"Ripper!" A roar of salvation comes from the front door.

I don't recognize the voice, but I can hear the rage within it.

Ripper flinches and jerks to look over his shoulder. "Shit," he mutters, jumping off me and walking to the door.

"Ripper!" someone shouts again.

"Hey, Axel." Ripper puts on a friendly tone, shutting the door behind him.

As soon as I'm out of sight, I start yanking against my tether. It hurts and burns my skin, but I don't care. I have to get the hell out of here.

"What are you doing?" Axel demands.

"I could ask you the same thing. I thought you were surfing this morning."

I pause my thrashing when I hear a hint of nervousness in Ripper's voice.

Axel is a pretty big, intimidating guy. I'd bet on him in a fight.

A thump against the door makes me jump, and I quickly get back into my tussle with the duct tape.

"This is wrong, man. Whatever you're doing. Stop. Now." Axel's accent is getting thicker as anger rises to the surface.

"You're not my boss!" Ripper argues and I hear another crash.

"You're part of the crew. Does Shane know about this?"

"He's not my boss either. And I'm not part of your precious crew! I was only ever here for a short-term gig."

"What?" The question is a sharp bullet, cutting through the air. I can just picture Axel's black face darkening with rage. "We let you in, man!"

"You were just my cover. I had some stuff that needed a little cooling off period. This was a safe bet. Who gives a shit about Ryder Bay? But my boys are in town and we're ready to move on, so step back."

I hold my breath as I wait out the reply.

"You're not doing this." Axel's voice is deep with warning.

"You can't stop me."

"Where's the girl?"

Ripper snickers. "What girl?"

Another crash and a thump are followed by an indignant grunt and then a loud roar that makes me whimper. I get back to my useless attempt at escape, actually crying out in fear when the door shunts open.

"No, please!" I frantically work at the bindings again, panic coursing through me.

"Savannah. Stop." Small hands land on top of mine, but I keep thrashing anyway. "You're hurting yourself. Stop!"

The shout grabs my attention and I jerk to see Harley beside me. The second I register her, I let out a shaking sob.

"It's okay." Her voice is so strong and sure, her nimble fingers working at the tape. "I'll get you out."

I close my eyes, tears streaming down my cheeks as she calmly frees me. The tape hurts my skin, pulling off tiny hairs around my wrist, but I don't cry out at the pain. I'm too numb with relief to do anything but lie there and whimper.

"It's okay." Harley whispers the words over and over again until it starts to sink in.

Another crash from somewhere in the house makes us both jump.

Harley gasps and looks over her shoulder. "It's okay," she squeaks, but suddenly I don't believe her.

Picking up her pace, she rips the last of the tape off, freeing me with one painful yank.

I capture my wrist and hold it, scrambling off the

bed and peering over her shoulder when she leans against the door to check the hallway.

Glancing behind me, I scan the room, looking for a window to escape through when my eyes land back on the bed.

The bed.

Griffin's bag.

Dropping to my knees, I crawl forward and do a quick sweep under the bed. My hand hits a canvas bag and I wrap my fingers around it, yanking it free and hoping to the heavens that it's Griffin's stuff.

"Let's go." Harley snatches my shirt, pulling me to my feet and hauling me out of the room.

I can't see Ripper's friend as we run to the exit, but as we flash past the living room, I see Axel and Ripper locked in a bloody battle. Fists are flying while they grunt and hammer at each other, rolling across the floor and knocking into furniture.

Harley pauses at the door, staring in shock at Axel and obviously wondering whether or not to stay and help him.

"We've gotta go." I suck in a breath and capture Harley's hand, pulling her toward the exit.

She stumbles after me and we tumble through the open door just as a car screeches to a stop outside the house, and the faint sound of police sirens grows closer.

# 49

# GUILTY AND GRATEFUL

## GRIFFIN

Seeing Savannah stumble out the door, her face white with fear, nearly kills me.

I don't know what she's been through inside that house, but I throw my door open and jerk out of the car. Every step is painful, every movement wants to wipe me out, but I have to get to her.

A ragged sob leaves her mouth when she spots me.

I limp around the car, cradling my rib cage as she breaks into a run. She trips just before reaching me, and I lurch forward to catch her.

It freaking hurts but I hold on anyway, hauling her against me and wrapping my arms around her trembling body. She clings to my shoulder, resting her face in the crook of my neck. Her tears coat my skin and the amount she's shaking scares me.

"What happened?" I whisper, but she won't answer the question. She just holds tight, clutching a bag in her other hand and pressing herself against me, like she can't get close enough.

I shoot a worried look across the car and catch Aidan's eye. He has his arm securely around Harley and is asking her the same question, quietly demanding answers as he fights whatever rage is coursing through him. I get it, I'm fighting a blackness too.

Someone scared the shit out of Savannah, and if they hurt her as well...

"Axel's in there," Harley starts to explain.

"Axel." Aidan grits out the word.

"I saw him on the beach and got him to help me. Ripper grabbed Sav and I just ran."

"Ripper?" I snap.

"He was at the house." She turns to look at us, obviously trying to catch Savannah's eye, but she's still hiding against me. "I'm sorry I left you." Harley pulls in a shaky breath. "I just figured we needed help."

"You did the right thing," I answer for Savannah, then press my lips against her head. "Did he hurt you?"

She shakes her head, but her fingers curl into my shirt and I'm struggling to believe her.

"He had her tied to the bed," Harley murmurs, then looks to the ground.

The blackness tries to surge to the surface, choking off all common sense. I almost forget I'm beat. I almost run into that house with my fists clenched, ready to pound Ripper to dust.

"What?" Aidan's voice is incredulous. "Did he just grab you off the beach or something? What were you doing down this end anyway?" Aidan's questions make us all tense.

A police car pulls onto the street, Officer Malloy jumping out and following Harley's pointed finger. "They're trying to kill each other in the living room. Ripper is the guilty party. Axel was just trying to help."

With a grim nod, Officer Malloy unclips his weapon and heads toward the front door.

We wait on the street and I look to Harley, silently asking for more information.

She sighs and opens her mouth to explain, but Savannah beats her to it.

"I know you never asked me to, and you never would," she murmurs against my neck. "But I wanted to get your stuff back." Slowly leaning away from me, she holds out the bag clutched against her body. "Is this yours?"

I gaze at the canvas bag and nod before giving her a pained expression and lightly cupping her cheek. She did that for me. She risked so much to keep me safe and anonymous. I don't know whether to feel guilty or grateful. It's probably a mixture of both, slathered with a huge amount of overwhelmed.

Sucking in a shaky breath, she attempts and fails to

give me a smile. Instead more tears slip from her eyes. "I just want you to be safe."

Gently wiping the tears off her cheeks, I fight the urge to cry myself and study her face. I so desperately wish I could look at her with both my eyes, show her how much her risk means to me. How much I wish she hadn't gone through that. I don't deserve it, but her actions say so much. I've never had someone do something like that for me before.

I want to tell her I love her. That I'm grateful. But emotion is clogging my throat. Speech is impossible. All I can do is pull her against my side and hold her.

## 50

# PATCHED UP BY DR. GREEN

## SAVANNAH

I hiss as Dad rubs antiseptic cream on my wrists. His expression is grim, his skin pale. He's super pissed about what I did.

When he showed up at the police station and heard the full story, I thought he was going to pass out. Between his and Griffin's silent looks of shock and disapproval, I felt thoroughly reprimanded. Even Officer Malloy told me I was an idiot, in a polite way.

Both Ripper and Axel have been booked, although I'm hoping Axel will get out soon. Ripper can rot in jail forever. I made sure I told Officer Malloy what Ripper said about Skylar. He promised me he'll follow it up. The guy could be looking at numerous charges, including statutory rape, since Skylar is still a minor.

Officer Malloy actually looked relieved. Maybe this

Skylar case will be solved before she even wakes up. Ripper made it sound like Skylar wanted it, and maybe she did, but I wouldn't be shocked at all if Ripper went back for more and my bestie had changed her mind. I bet he pushed her right off that pier when she wouldn't give it to him again.

Asshole.

The guy who helped secure me to the bed has disappeared. I'm guessing he took that money and snuck out the window when Ripper and Axel started fighting.

So much for friendship.

I'm so exhausted.

Harley and I were interviewed for over an hour before we were allowed to come home. Dad, Griffin and Aidan insisted on staying with us. I'm kind of grateful, even if it was slightly humiliating admitting that we snuck into the house.

"Why'd you feel the need to go back?" Officer Malloy couldn't understand, probably because I couldn't give him the entire truth.

"Like we told you, Officer. We thought Griffin getting beat up was really suspicious. We wanted to check out the house," Harley explained, her voice so sure and confident.

I don't know how she did that.

My voice was leafy and brittle, like I couldn't find the volume switch. All I could do was rasp out my answers.

"That is police work," Officer Malloy scolded us.

"You can't search a house without good reason, and we didn't want to report Griffin because he was squatting there. We just wanted to get you a little evidence." Harley pointed at her phone on the desk. "Which we did."

With a heavy sigh, Officer Malloy tapped the phone with his finger and shook his head. I could almost hear him thinking, "What is wrong with the insane children in our bay?"

His sharp gaze hit Dad after that, and my poor father had to squirm while Officer Malloy told him off for not reporting Griffin's incident. I held my breath in fear that it would all come out. Worry for Griffin ate at me when he leaned forward and was so obviously getting ready to confess all.

My lips parted, my eyes rounding with a silent plea. I didn't want him to get in trouble. I don't want him to leave!

But Dad rested his hand lightly on Griffin's wrist and did the talking for us.

"He didn't want to press charges, and I couldn't force him to the police station, Dayton. He made a mistake. He shouldn't have been squatting in that house, but I wasn't about to bring his poor beaten butt up here to complain."

The police officer grumbled something in response before jerking out of his seat and going to talk to his superior.

About twenty minutes later, we were released and told to keep our phones on.

I hope they never call.

I just want this over with.

At least Griffin's identity and past is still safe.

Thanks to Dad.

I glance at his face while he quietly checks me over. "Any other injuries?"

"No," I whisper.

He gently probes my cheek, his expression buckling just like it did when I told him I'd been slapped there. "What you did was so stupid."

"I know." My eyes start to burn at the agonized look on my father's face. "I'm sorry."

He swallows and plunks down in the chair opposite me. After a long, heavy sigh, he reaches for my hand and gently runs his thumb over my knuckles. "I know why you did it."

"Are you still going to let me see him?"

He doesn't say anything, and the waiting is torture. "You understand that today could have gone so differently. I could be treating you for very different injuries right now." He chokes out the words, then starts to cry.

His tears set off my own and I lean forward, gripping his shoulder and resting my head against his.

I still haven't fully acknowledged the fact that I could have been raped today. At one point it seemed inevitable. I owe Axel so much, and I'm going to have to find the courage to thank him at some point.

"Dad." I sniffle. "It didn't happen. I'm okay."

He nods, quietly sniffing.

We stay that way for a little while, crying together until the tears are spent and we can sit back and wipe our eyes.

Dad snatches a couple of tissues out of the box and hands them to me. I dab my face and swallow, asking once again the question I desperately need an answer to. "Are you still going to let me see him?"

He scrubs a hand down his face before finally looking at me. "If I'd wanted him out of your life, I could have told Dayton everything. As much as I'd love to blame Griffin for today's events, I can't. He never asked you to sneak into that house. He never would have let you do something so reckless. He dragged himself out to find you, to help you. He's a good kid." Dad sighs. "And if he decides to stay, he's welcome here anytime."

I smile for the first time in what seems like forever.

Today has been long and harrowing, but as I wrap my arms around my father's neck and whisper my gratitude, I'm only left with one small question to disrupt the peace floating through me.

Will Griffin stay?

## 51

# A SLEEP OUT IN RYDER BAY

## GRIFFIN

D r. Green let me stay for a few more nights. I still look a mess, but my ribs are mending, and I can move around with only mild pain. He hasn't outright said it yet, but it's time for me to find a place to live. Squatting is no longer an option, and it's with a weird sense of relief and trepidation that I face down my other choices.

Instinct wants me to leave. It's all I've been doing for the last couple of years, and I can't just dismiss that option. I'd probably be doing everyone a favor if I just snuck out of town, but I promised Savannah I'd never leave without saying goodbye, and I honestly don't know if I can do that.

Scratching my whiskers, I pause outside Marshall's door.

I'm nervously taking Dr. Green's advice and opening up to my boss. It'll be a huge burden off my shoulders whether he fires me or not. Telling Savannah and her dad the truth hasn't been so painful. If anything, it's been kind of liberating. Marshall deserves the truth too. It's a risk, yes. If he fires me, I'm not sure I'll get another job in Ryder Bay and I'll be forced to move on, but it's the right thing to do. Savannah and I will survive, we just won't be very happy about it.

If I'm honest, I'll be freaking devastated, but she deserves a boyfriend she can be proud of. I want to be that guy for her. I want to be that guy for myself.

Fisting my knuckles, I rap on the door and wait it out, shuffling my feet until the ranch slider moves, and I see Denee's cheerful smile.

"Hey, bud." She winces. "Marshall gave me a heads-up that you were looking pretty bad."

"Better than I looked when he came to see me."

She smiles. "Come on in."

I follow her into the house, nerves pounding me as I scan their modest home. They live on the lower north side, close to the beach and the lifeguard offices. This house must be several decades old, but it's been well maintained and looks great. Denee is a graphic designer, but you can tell she has a flair for all things aesthetic. The house has this funky beach and surfing feel, with cool artwork from the fifties and beach shells as ornaments.

"Marsh, baby, Griffin's here," Denee calls from the kitchen. "Want a drink, sweetie?" she asks me.

I nod and take the fresh pineapple juice she pours. "Thanks."

"Do you need a straw?" She grimaces.

I test out a sip and tell her I'll be fine. My lips have mended first. Thankfully they're only a little swollen on one side.

"Griff!" Marshall appears, a broad smile on his face as he shakes my hand, then offers me a seat. "How you feelin'?"

"Yeah, I'm on the mend."

He frowns and shakes his head. "I sure hope they catch those guys."

"They got Ripper." I shrug. "He's the one who tried to hurt Savannah, so as long as he can't touch her again, I'm okay with it."

"You're a forgiving man." Marshall leans back in his seat, studying me with a smile.

I shuffle on the couch, placing my drink down on a coaster before rubbing my hands together and hoping that Marshall is as forgiving as he thinks I am.

He must sense my discomfort, because he leans forward in his seat and rest his elbows on his knees. "You okay?"

With a thick swallow, I reach into my back pocket and pull out the only two photos I haven't been able to throw away. Holding them out, I wait until Marshall takes them before pointing at the images.

"That's me and my mom before she died, and uh…" I tap my finger on the top of the other one. "That's my brother, Phoenix."

He nods with a grin. "You guys look close. How old were you in this photo?"

I shrug. "I don't know. Uh…twelve maybe?"

He snickers and hands them back. "You looked like trouble."

"We were." I wince. "Big trouble."

The look in my eyes must warn him that more is coming, because his smile drops away and he quietly murmurs, "Tell me."

So I do.

I tell him everything, from my birth name to my juvie record to the fact that I've been running ever since.

He takes it all with a calm expression, and when I'm done, I lean back on the couch, completely spent.

"Wow," Denee whispers from the doorway.

I didn't even know she'd been listening in and I jerk to look at her, an agonized grimace crossing my face.

"Oh, honey. You don't have to look like that." She perches on the arm of the chair next to her husband, running her hand across his shoulders. "Marshall's dad spent ten years in prison for armed robbery. He understands."

My eyes bulge, my lips parting when I spot the remorse on Marshall's face. "He was thirty-one when he got busted. He knew better. You…" His head shakes as he looks at the coffee table. "You were a kid."

"I still did wrong."

"But you made it right."

"Sort of. I mean, I should probably head back to Vallejo. I just—"

Denee cuts me off. "Or you could move in here."

Marshall doesn't even flinch, unlike me; I'm struggling to keep up with the unexpected invitation.

Denee grins. "We have a small guest house out back. It's got a toilet and shower. There's no kitchen or anything, but you can—"

"I can't. I can't just—"

"Yeah, you can." Marshall slaps his hand down on my knee and gives it a little squeeze. "I don't want my best employee squatting anymore."

"You're not firing me?"

"Of course not." He chuckles.

"But...what about my fake ID? My—"

"Yeah." Marshall grimaces. "That part's not cool, and we're going to have to fix it. I can't employ you under a false social security number."

My heart sinks, but I knew it was coming.

"You think you'd have the courage to work for me as Griffin Jones?"

And then my heart stops.

"I can still call you Griffin Ayala, and introduce you to people that way, but I think you should consider getting your name cleared."

"But what about Phoenix?"

"If he steps one foot in Ryder Bay, I've got your back, kid. But you need to stop letting him control your life. You can't hide from who you are."

"But I ran out on my community service. My counseling requirements."

"I'm sure if a judge heard your side of the story, they'd go easy on you. Especially if I testify about how great you are."

I work my jaw to the side, gripping my hands together. "But that'll put Phoenix in hot water. It feels like betrayal."

Denee clicks her tongue and gives me a sad smile. "He betrayed you, honey. You're paying the price for his bad decisions, and that's just not fair." Sliding off the arm of the chair, she crouches down beside me and rests her hand over mine. "You deserve to get a real driver's license. You deserve a high school diploma. Don't rob yourself of a fulfilled life."

"We'll help you every step of the way." Marshall pats my knee. "And you can keep working for me while we sort through this thing. I know it's going to take time. For now, let's just make your job volunteer work. We'll give you free food and board, plus a weekly allowance from our own pockets. That way I won't get in trouble with the IRS, and you can still get paid." He winks at me.

"I can't ask you to do that. I—"

He waves my protests away with a flick of his hand

and keeps talking. "Let me do some research and find out what steps we need to take to get you back on track, so I can employ you properly. As soon as that's done, we'll make the paperwork official."

I can't find the words to speak, so I just gape at them until they start laughing at me.

"I don't understand you people," I finally murmur, thinking about Dr. Green's swift forgiveness and acceptance of me.

My comment only makes them laugh harder, but I'm still too shocked to say anything.

I thought staying in Ryder Bay would bring me nothing but trouble, but this beachside town must feel like home for a reason.

The thought of becoming myself again kind of scares me, but there's a sense of freedom attached to the idea that's kind of appealing. Getting a high school diploma? That'd be freaking awesome.

After a beat that's probably way too long, I finally find my smile and hold out my hand. "Thank you so much."

Marshall wraps his fingers around mine and gives them a firm shake. "It's our pleasure, son."

"You're home now." Denee wraps her arm around my shoulders, and I figure she's probably right.

# 52

# FOUND

## SAVANNAH

G riffin left this morning without a word.

His stuff is still in the den, but I don't know where he's gone. No note, and he's not replying to my texts. So I've spent my time pacing the kitchen, then cleaning it. I figured since I had all the stuff out that I'd do the bathrooms as well. Rosalie is on a summer break. Dad figured he'd give her some time off while Griffin was staying with us. One less person we have to explain him to.

After a little persuasion, she took the vacation time, but I don't want her returning to a complete disaster of a house.

Lettie is tucked away in her room reading, and Harley's at the beach with Aidan. I should go join them, or head to the hospital. Lettie will be fine at home on her own. She's old enough to take care of herself.

But...

"Where's Griffin?" I mutter, storing the cleaning products in the laundry and stomping up to the shower.

I take my time getting ready, putting on a little makeup and choosing a nice pair of shorts and a black tank top. Slipping my earrings in, I turn and study my appearance in the mirror, only to be reminded that Skylar won't be seeing me anyway.

The idea of going to the hospital kind of depresses me, but it's the right thing to do.

Maybe after that, Griffin will be home and I can find out what's going on.

Tapping on Lettie's door, I peek my head into her bedroom.

"What?" She glances up from her book, obviously irritated by the interruption.

I fight against the urge to roll my eyes and force a smile instead. "I'm heading to the hospital for a while. If Griffin gets back, can you tell him where I am?"

"Okay." She shrugs and goes back to her book.

"Thanks, Lettie. I appreciate your help."

She glances back up, her lips curling just a little at the corners. I want to tell her that if she decides to go out, she needs to let me know. I want to remind her to clean up after herself if she makes her own lunch, but I hold my tongue and fight every instinct in my brain.

My sister is smiling at me, and I want to keep it that way.

"See ya."

"Bye." She rolls onto her back, holding the book above her head and jumping straight back into her story.

I close the door behind her and rest my head against the wood. Building bridges with her is going to be hard, but at least I didn't put my foot in it today. Maybe if I work on not mothering her, she'll start being a little nicer to me.

With a soft sigh, I push away from the door and head downstairs.

I hear movement in the den and veer away from the front door, rushing to see if Griffin's back.

He is.

And he's packing up his stuff.

I swallow, my throat aching already.

He hasn't seen me yet. He's busy folding his clothes and putting them into his bag.

He's busy getting ready to leave me.

To move on.

I'm never going to see him again, and it breaks my heart.

Fighting tears, I push the door open with a soft whisper, "I've run out of them, haven't I?"

With a surprised flinch, he turns toward the door, a smile rising on his lips until he sees my expression.

Confusion pulls his eyebrows together. "Run out of what?"

"Excuses for you to stick around." I sniff and look to the ground. "It's okay. I mean, I understand. Staying is scary and you…you should go. I know that's what you want to do. I just… you know, selfishly, I—"

His snicker cuts me off and I glance up, slightly offended that he's laughing at my heartache.

With a gentle smile, he drops his T-shirt onto the top of the bag and moves around the coffee table. Taking my face in his hands, he rubs his thumb across my cheeks before kissing the tip of my nose.

"I found a place to stay. Marshall and Denee are letting me move in with them for a while."

"You told Marshall?"

"That's where I've been all morning. I was too nervous to tell you about it before I left, just in case it went really badly, but he—*they* were amazing."

A nervous smile flashes across his face and I want to know what it means, but all I can do is squeak, "You're staying?"

The constant dread I've been living with is taking a while to dissipate and I can't quite get my head around his news.

He's staying.

He's staying!

His smile is sweet, his gaze tender as he caresses my cheekbones. "You're the only excuse I need to stay here. Yes, it's a little scary, but leaving would be so much worse."

My eyes glisten as I smile at him. I have no words right now. I'm too overcome with emotion. Griffin is staying. He's staying for me.

I want to tell him I love him, but my courage fails me, so I just show him instead, sliding my hands around his neck and closing the space between us.

He meets my kiss with his usual tenderness and then quickly deepens it. I relish the feel of his tongue sliding into my mouth—a warm, intimate promise that he's mine and I am his.

For now.

Maybe even forever.

Hope soars through me. My chest feels like it's filled with fairy lights, twinkling and sparkling with a giddy kind of joy that I've never felt before.

The phone in my back pocket starts to ring.

I ignore it, curling my fingers around Griffin's dreads when he tries to pull away from me.

"You going to answer that?" he mumbles against my mouth.

"I'm kind of busy right now."

Laughter rumbles in his chest and throat as he buries his fingers in my hair and we ignore the phone together.

But then it starts ringing again.

I moan my displeasure but refuse to acknowledge it.

Griffin pulls away, skimming his lips over my cheek. "Sav, it's gotta be important."

"More important than you?" I argue, pressing my mouth against his neck and enjoying his soft sound of approval.

He turns to nip my earlobe, his hand gliding down my back and plucking the phone out of my pocket.

"It's your dad," he murmurs against my skin. "You should probably answer it."

I've got ideas for where he can shove that thought, and I would quite happily throw my phone out the window right now, but then Griffin goes and swipes his thumb across my screen before handing me the phone.

I scowl at him.

He grins and leans forward to whisper in my ear. "I'll make it up to you. I promise."

"You better," I grumble, then wink as I press the phone to my ear. "Hey, Dad."

"Are you okay? What took you so long to answer the phone?"

"Uh... it was buried in my bag. Couldn't find it."

"Right, well I've got big news." His voice is kind of edgy and I'm immediately alert.

"What's up?"

"Skylar's awake."

I go still, not even breathing as I hear the news I've been so desperately waiting for.

My best friend's awake.

She's back.

"She's a little confused and quiet, but she's asking for you. You need to get down here ASAP."

Griffin's hand slides around my lower back, his beat-up face creasing with concern. "Everything okay?" he mouths.

I nod and swallow. "Uh. Yeah, sure. I'll…I'll be right there."

Skylar's awake.

I should be jumping in circles, doing a happy dance, but as I slip the phone back in my pocket, I can't help feeling this weird sense of foreboding.

She's asking for me, and all I can think is *What kind of demands is she going to make of me now? What will her expectations be?*

So much has changed while Skylar has been sleeping. Will she be able to accept it all?

I feel like I've reinvented myself without her, and now she's back.

She's back, and things are not going to be the same.

TO BE CONTINUED…

**Keep reading to find out what Skylar remembers about her fall…and how it's going to change everything in Ryder Bay.**

## DEAR READER...

Thank you so much for reading Savannah and Griffin's story. I love these two together, and I'm so stoked that Griffin decided to stay. I can't wait to see more of them in the next Ryder Bay novel.

The new group of friends that started forming in *The Impact Zone* is going to need to band together even more as they face the big question that's hovering over them...

Now that Skylar's awake, they can finally find out if this resident troublemaker jumped or was pushed.

But can she remember?
And how much has this accident changed her?

As Skylar wakes to a world of confusion, she must

decide who to trust and who to cling to as the long road to recovery begins. Her world is not the same anymore, and as memories return in flashing nightmares, she must face the harrowing truth of what happened.

Taking on her demons could break her, but if she can turn into the most unlikely set of arms, she may just survive.

*Face of the Wave* is releasing April 12th, 2019.

You won't want to miss this next Ryder Bay novel.

xx
Jordan

## ALSO BY JORDAN FORD

### BIG PLAY NOVELS

The Playmaker

The Red Zone

The Handoff

Shoot The Gap

### THE BROTHERHOOD TRILOGY

See No Evil

Speak No Evil

Hear No Evil

### THE BARLOW SISTERS TRILOGY

Curveball

Strike Out

Foul Play

### RYDER BAY NOVELS

Over the Falls

The Impact Zone

Face of the Wave (releasing April 2019)

# ABOUT THE AUTHOR

Jordan Ford is a New Zealand author who has spent her life traveling with her family, attending international schools, and growing up in a variety of cultures. Although it was sometimes hard shifting between schools and lifestyles, she doesn't regret it for a moment. Her experiences have enriched her life and given her amazing insights into the human race.

She believes that everyone has a back story...and that story is fundamental in how people cope and react to life around them. Telling stories that are filled with heart-felt emotion and realistic characters is an absolute passion of Jordan's. Since her earliest memories, she has been making up tales to entertain herself. It wasn't until she reached her teen years that she first considered writing one. A computer failure and lost files put a major glitch in her journey, and it took until she graduated university with a teaching degree before she took up the dream once more. Since then, she hasn't been able to stop.

"Writing high school romances brings me the greatest joy. My heart bubbles, my insides zing, and I am at my happiest when immersed in a great scene with characters who have become real to me."

# CONNECT ONLINE

Jordan loves to hear from her readers. Please feel free to contact her through any of the following means:

### WEBSITE:
www.jordanfordbooks.com

### FACEBOOK:
www.facebook.com/jordanfordbooks/

### INSTAGRAM:
www.instagram.com/jordanfordbooks/

### NEWSLETTER:
This is the best way to stay in touch with Jordan's work and have access to special giveaways and sales.
www.subscribepage.com/JF_RyderBay_signup

CPSIA information can be obtained
at www.ICGtesting.com
Printed in the USA
LVHW031101010420
651871LV00001B/148

9 780473 468477